HIDDEN MIRRORS

THE LOOKING GLASS OF THE SOUL

DonnaMarie

DonnaMarie

Published by Five Gem Press

Visit our Web site: www.HiddenMirrorsBook.com

Printed in the United States of America

First Edition: August 2012

10 9 8 7 6 5 4 3 2 1

ISBN: 978-0-985891-60-2

All illustrations created by Kimberly Payne

Cover design by PCI Publishing Group

I dedicate this book to the memory of

MR. CHARLES B. LEVEY

For giving me the greatest gift of all, my education,
without which, I would not be the person I am today
and this novel would remain unwritten...

ACKNOWLEDGMENTS

The talent for the original cover artwork belongs to an aspiring graphics designer, KIMBERLY PAYNE. The creativity and originality of the designs she submitted to me reach a depth of talent that is truly inspirational. There is no doubt; she has a successful career in her near future.

PROFESSOR DEAN ZIRWAS, Indian River State College, filled the void of my technical inabilities and I hope I don't owe him an apology for any bruises during panic moments, such as, the time the keys on my laptop popped off! Was I really typing that fast? Thank you for being there when I needed you time and again.

One of the most difficult moments in a writer's life is the first time you reach out to someone for the criticism you know must come for improvement. It's a pivotal point when you decide to stay in the game, or fold. For me, this trust went to TERRI LEONE, and there is no doubt, I made the right decision. She gave me the confidence, support and energy to move forward.

Thank you to my peer group of readers whom I asked to read and review the manuscript and offer candid opinions. Their constructive criticisms led to many positive changes along the way. They were JOE GHIOTTI, JOYCE CHMURA, JOHN MACALUSO, JACKIE MACALUSO, JOHANNA DONOVAN, DONALD SNYDER, and ANGELA ROBINSON. Also, thank you to DEIDRE CLAYTON, BARBARA FENNER, MARYROSE CUOCO, and my wonderful father-in-law, ROBERT D. GREENE, for their positive comments.

To a man I hold in the highest regard and with the utmost respect, MR. DONALD J. TRUMP, I offer my sincere appreciation for your supportive comments and encouragement to go forward with this. I didn't know where to go, but you opened the door and pointed the way. I am eternally grateful to you and will never forget that a man of your success and stature still takes the time to help a beginner, such as myself. This is why you are the man you are and the world is a better place because you are in it.

The woman I now refer to as the beacon that lit the path for me, RHONA GRAFF, I don't have enough words in my vocabulary to express my thanks. You cannot imagine how nervous I was to know that you might actually read it! You did, and your words of confidence lifted me to a whole new height. Your comments brought tears of joy to my eyes. Your advice was priceless.

My greatest cheerleader, MARY SHELLEY, my dear mother, never doubted for a minute that I could do this and I will never forget her faith in me. She's a special woman and I'm blessed to have her as my mother. My son, CHRISTOPHER GREENE, his wonderful wife, CHRISTINE, and my son-in-law, LEE GREEN (not a typo in the spelling!) were invaluable in their support.

To MONA GAMBETTA, I owe a great education for this and gratitude for taking so much stress from my shoulders. You truly have the patience of a saint. Thank you!

The real pillars of strength for me, however, go to the two people who stood on each side of me from the first stroke of the pen, so to speak. My daughter, KIMBERLY GREEN, and my husband, BOBBY GREENE, never once allowed me to give up, or lose my direction. They believed in me, took a chance on me, and were there for me at every turn. How does one thank the very foundation that holds you? I will simply say, "I could not do this without you!"

PROLOGUE

Opportunity seldom knocks loudly. Sometimes it's a mere whisper in the wind, or the slight touching of two strangers as they pass in a crowd. Therefore, it was when by complete chance, the manila envelope passed accidently into the hands of the unintended recipient.

Human nature, being what it is, made it impossible to stifle the urge to open it and reveal its contents. The information exposed left the reader with a choice that would determine the fate of many, the gain for one.

A plan in motion, a path determined; the beneficiary set forth as a trailblazer with the target set. Moral ethics lost to the power of greed. Principles lost in deceit, the devil himself holding hidden mirrors to deflect the truth, all the while mocking the soul now cast into the abyss of hell joining the others already lost.

Meanwhile, on the other side of the globe, a woman grasping to the pain of her past reluctantly forges forward and uncovers the secrets of her private hell. She cannot heal without the hurt and she cannot hurt without the truth, but to find it, she must enter the belly of the beast. She must look behind the hidden mirrors.

Profit is sweet, even if it comes from deception.

— Sophocles

CHAPTER

1

S lowly the helicopter lifted away from the ground, carrying its precious cargo. I sat there, not knowing for how long, when I saw the airborne paramedics place two people on board the helicopter, but it was a three-car pile-up. There were three ambulances at the scene, but I only saw one leave with its lights flashing and siren screeching. Finally, at a snail's pace, the traffic wormed past the wrecked cars with their drivers craning their necks for a look at the gruesome scene. A young policewoman with a bright orange vest waved her arms and pointed to the detour around the two tarps covering lifeless bodies who earlier this morning probably ate their breakfast without the slightest inclination that it would be their last.

I was only five cars behind the collision. The fog was so dense and everything happened so quickly that I was unaware until hearing the squealing brakes and unforgettable sound of metal against metal. If I hadn't dropped my keys getting into the car this morning, it could have been me. Just a second, or so and your destiny is changed. Nevertheless, it wasn't and I should have been so thankful, but instead I just felt numb. I had enough going on in my real world without thinking about what might have been.

The cars gradually increased speed after driving away from the collision. Five minutes down the road, the accident nothing more than a sad, unfortunate memory and life went on for the rest of the world.

Small patches of crisp, blue sky fought to emerge through the steel gray overcast and the fog dissolved away. I took a deep breath and exhaled slowly, telling myself that the next few days would soon be a memory and I would be on my way back home. Where was home though? I wasn't sure anymore. How long do you live somewhere before it becomes home? The sign ahead said, "Westbrook – 20 miles." Everything looked more and more familiar, but definitely not my home. Early yesterday morning, I left Georgia. Was that my home? I just didn't know anymore.

I thought of all the places I've lived the last twenty years, Dallas, Chicago, Orlando, Denver, Detroit, not to mention the small suburbs. My Georgia driver's license now places me just outside Atlanta. Three husbands will do that to you, especially when the first was military, the second one a commercial pilot and the third and perhaps the least one was a corporate executive who spent most of his time traveling between cities and affairs.

The northbound traffic on I95 thinned as I left Old Saybrook and crossed the bridge into Old Lyme. My destination was approaching quickly and I wasn't sure if I was prepared. I was thankful that I decided against driving straight through and at least had a good night's sleep before the final stretch this morning. Being exhausted and dealing with Karyn would be suicide.

Karyn, ever the bitch, Karyn, was more than overbearing and since childhood, I avoided her presence as much as I could. Receiving her phone call four days ago was unsettling to say the least. She wouldn't hear of my excuses not to come and God knows I tried several of them.

Her callous remarks included, "You have nothing holding you back, Annie! You have no kids, no husband at this time that I'm aware of anyway, and being a freelance photographer hardly constitutes having a job! Just put your ass on a plane and get up here!"

Good old Karyn, never mincing words Karyn, as always, she was at her finest. If not the war, at least I won the battle and drove instead of flying. I knew it wouldn't piss me off less, but it would give me more time to think and prepare for the dissonance I was walking into.

New London was ten miles away and closing in fast. My chest was tight and the coffee I had this morning was souring my throat. I needed a hotel room and pondered stopping in New London for one. It wasn't my first choice. After several calls yesterday to hotels in the Mystic area, I was shocked that there were no rooms. Since when had Mystic, CT attracted so many people. What could have possibly changed in the twenty years I had been gone? Other than The Mystic Seaport Museum, home to the C.W. Morgan whale ship, the town was quiet and quaint. The sidewalks rolled up when the stores closed at five o'clock.

Approaching New London, the signage names were familiar, but the road exits were unchartered territory. The shopping center on my left was definitely new and now had a Chuck E. Cheese. Imagine that! The one on my right had undergone a complete facelift. Everything felt foreign and extraneous. I decided to keep going. It would give me a good excuse to get out early to look for a room.

Directly ahead of me was the massive Gold Memorial Bridge that spanned the distance of nearly four miles between New London and Groton. It loomed over the Thames River. On my left was the US Naval Submarine Base. I wondered where the submarines were. On my right, I could see the Electric Boat Division of General Dynamics. Sensing that some things were unchanged, I stayed in the right lane not to miss my exit. It was so different, yet so much the same.

Exiting to Thames Street was like falling back in time. The changes were minor considering the years that had passed. The old diner that I frequented as a youth was still standing and whether it was my imagination, or not, I was, sure I could smell the bacon frying in its grease and hear the eggs crackling on the griddle.

Just a few yards ahead, I turned left to follow the river. Some of the storefronts were different and the pubs had different names, but the unexpected time warp swallowed and consumed me. On the left stood the same family owned funeral home that had laid to rest so many loved ones in my former life. It was quiet now. My gut wrenched and I fought to keep down the soured coffee. Buried memories pounded from within.

"Please, God, please..." I said aloud.

My left turn came quickly and the road I remembered well was steep, narrow and in serious need of new pavement. The old two and three story New England houses were the same. Fresh paint and new doors couldn't hide their history and decay. A few backyards converted into parking lots; took advantage of General Dynamic's parking shortage during its heyday of building submarines. "Any way to earn a buck," my father would say when he sacrificed ours. Most were barren now.

Every house on the street was white, gray, or that nondescript shade of blue that New Englanders use when they can't make up their minds to go blue or gray. That was the color of our house and there it stood.

In the driveway was an older model Honda Accord that was probably once a light cream color. The mud streaks made it difficult to decipher between the scratches and the dirt. I wasn't sure what Karyn drove these days, but with the New London County plate just assumed it was hers. Carefully, I squeezed my Lexus alongside, not daring to park behind her in the event she chose to leave in a hurry. I should be so lucky.

"Suck it up, Annie," I told myself. "You can do this."

The damp humid condensation slapped my face without mercy as I opened the car door to get out. Without looking where I stepped, I allowed my left foot to sink through the icy slush and into the mud below. I cursed as I tried to shake it off and then watched carefully as I walked toward the steps to the front porch door.

So many memories...I was back.

CHAPTER
2

I opened my hand to take the brass doorknob that I knew twisted to the left because my father installed it incorrectly, but somehow it didn't feel right. Instead, I lifted the metal knocker, corroded with age, and gave two hesitant, timid knocks. Before I could lower my limp arm back to my side, the weather-beaten door sprung open.

"Wow! I can't believe my eyes! Is it really you, Annie? You look great! How was your trip? Are you tired? Hungry? It's so good to see you!"

Well, my brother in law hadn't changed. Oh, he was pudgier making him look shorter and his hair was nearly gone. The remaining strands were wiry and gray, but he still had those steel gray eyes that could sparkle without a smile on his face. I never figured out what made him fall in love with my sister who was his total opposite.

"I'm so sorry, Annie; I'm babbling. Get in here out of the cold."

"It's good to see you, too, Bob." I just stood there, but he broke the ice, leaned forward, and gave me a warm hug.

"Well, look what the cat dragged in...if it isn't the prodigal daughter." I knew

Karyn's' voice without seeing her, but turned to face her.

"Hi Karyn, you look really great." Damn her, she did, too! I guess I hoped to find her shriveled, old, and fat, but instead she wore her 46 years well. Gray now sprinkled her black hair, but her flawless complexion still complimented her hazel eyes. Contrary to her husband's, they showed no emotion.

"You're much thinner, Annie," she said. I waited for a follow-up comment, like, "You look good," but it didn't come.

Probably sensing the tension, Bob started to take my coat and said, "Let's get in where it's warm. We have so much to catch up on and the kids will be here soon."

"I can't wait to see them," I said, and I meant it. Over the years, I had kept in touch with them on their birthdays and holidays. Especially, Sara, one of the twins, never forgot me on mine. "How are they doing?"

Bob filled me in, "Well, Susan has a surprise to tell you when she gets here and Sara, as you know, lives here. She took a well-deserved break today and went out with some friends. Tommy is working at the Senior Center."

"Since when did you get a Senior Center? What does he do there?" I always felt so sorry for Tommy. He was their youngest and had Down Syndrome. Thankfully, it wasn't as severe as it could have been, but it was a real heartbreak for Bob and Karyn.

"He's doing food prep in the kitchen. Sara's new beau, Mike, got him the job. Mike is the Activities Director there," said Karyn. "Would you like some coffee, or maybe a beer?"

"I would love a beer, but it's not even noon yet," I said trying to lighten it up a little. "I'll have coffee if it's made; just black. Thank you."

"I'll get it for you," Karyn said as she stood, and then added, "this time," as she left the room.

"She just doesn't change, does she, Bob?"

"She's okay, Annie. Give her some time. You haven't been home in twenty years. She's had all this responsibility with no help from you, or your brother. Speaking of him, he will be here tomorrow. I'm not sure if he's coming alone, or bringing MaryAnn with him."

I adored Jack. My little brother was the joy of my life from the day he was born. Jack was the glue that held me together when my life shattered. He was ten years younger than I was, but had grown to be my best friend. After graduating from the

University of Massachusetts, he released his free spirit in his paintings and lived as a pauper near Cape Cod. He met MaryAnn who shared his love for art. They went from selling art on the sidewalks to tourists to owning their own shop and now live in a very prestigious home in a country club neighborhood. Their only child, Tim, now four years old, was perfect in every way. It was the American dream.

Carrying a tray with coffee and pastries, Karyn walked back into the room just as I was saying, "What a great surprise! I can't wait to see him. Why didn't you tell me he was coming?" I looked at Karyn as I asked.

"It's important for the three of us to get together. We have some important business. It's urgent," she said without looking at me.

"What is?" I asked.

"Tomorrow, Annie, when we're all together, not now." As always, Karyn set the rules and, as always, I held back my comment.

"I notice the door is shut. Is she sleeping?" I inquired, looking at Bob.

"Yes, she naps a little every morning and then takes a longer one in the afternoon. She will be really excited to see you," Bob added.

"We didn't tell her you were coming in case you didn't show up," Karyn quipped.

Determined not to let her get to me, I sipped my coffee and tasted the cinnamon bread. "This is delicious," I said directly to Karyn.

"She made it herself," said Karyn.

"But I thought she wasn't...," I started to say, but was interrupted as the bedroom door opened and there she stood.

CHAPTER
3

Had it really been twenty years since I had seen my own mother? What kind of monster now stood before her? What demons possessed my soul that I couldn't forgive and would never forget? Would I have even recognized her in another setting? I wasn't sure. I saw no trace of the red waves that once fell freely to her shoulders. Her porcelain skin stained, drawn and lost to youth now framed with thinning white, unruly hair that hadn't seen a brush in some time.

"Oh, I didn't know we had company. You should have wakened me," she said looking at Karyn. A collision of emotions consumed me as I heard the familiar voice.

"It's me, Mom," the words choking my throat as I said them. She responded with a blank clouded stare and I couldn't tell if she heard me, or not. Her faded blue eyes looked straight through to my soul.

"Mom, it's Annie," Bob told her.

"Who is it?" she asked without looking away from me.

"It's me. It's Annie."

"How nice, dear...it's so good to see you. I hope you'll stay for dinner. Sara will make us something nice." With that said, she turned and scuffed away toward the den. "I'm going to watch some TV before dinner."

Nothing and no one could have prepared me for what I had just seen. The fiery rage I feared would surface dampened at the sight of the stranger that had passed before me. Full of questions, I looked straight at Karyn. "What happened to her? She's lost so much weight. Did she even know me? Does she know anyone? I thought she was just in the beginning stages. Oh my God, Karyn, what happened to her?"

"Where the hell have you been, Annie? Do you think this happened overnight?" Karyn's voice was soft, tight and her urge to lash out at me rising to the surface. "This isn't the reason I called you here," she added through clenched lips. "We have a bigger problem. We'll discuss it when Jackie gets in tomorrow. In the meantime, Bob will bring in your suitcase and put it in your old room upstairs. The sheets are clean and you should find everything you need, but if not, just ask Sara to get it for you. She'll be here any minute and will make you lunch. I have to go home to get a few things done. I'll see you for dinner tonight. We're all bringing something. Come on, Bob, we have to get going." With that, she stood up to leave.

"I have a room, Karyn," I lied.

"Cancel it, we expect you to stay here. We planned on it. We're expecting it. We'll talk more tomorrow. Tonight we'll just have fun." Before I could say another word, they got up and walked out.

"Fun, we'll have fun? What just happened?" I said aloud. I stood there in total shock, not sure what to do. "I can't just leave her in there alone. Can I?" I asked myself.

The door reopened and Bob walked in with my suitcase and went directly upstairs with it. Still dumbfounded, I couldn't mutter a word. When he came back downstairs, he avoided eye contact with me and before I could formulate my objection, he said, "See you later, Annie; we're looking forward to our dinner together tonight," and with that he rushed out the door once again.

Several minutes passed before the old hallway clock chimed out ten bells. It was only ten o'clock in the morning and I felt as if I'd run a 20 mile marathon. My knees were weak and the sour stomach I felt earlier was nothing compared to what churned inside me. I needed to leave and leave now, so I made my way toward the stairs to get my suitcase, muttering aloud the whole time.

"What do I care? I don't need to justify my departure. That bitch in there ruined my life. She ruined my life! Am I supposed to feel sorry for her? Did she care when Joey died? Did she care when...," but I couldn't bring myself to finish the thought. I froze in place at the foot of the stairs and my head turned toward the den. My feet followed the direction.

Quietly, I walked in behind her as she sat watching a game show. Her eyes still frozen on the television, I quietly asked, "Mom, do you know me?"

Without moving her gaze, she answered, "Yes, dear, you're that nice girl that used to visit. I hope you'll be staying for dinner. We're having your favorite."

Slowly, I edged back into the sofa chair and sat down. I couldn't stop staring at her. Thinking to myself, I wondered, "How old is she now? She can't be more than 63 years old if Karyn is 46 and I'm 38. What are those black marks? Are they bruises?" I couldn't take my eyes off her. Anger, hatred, loathing, and heartache all were ripping me apart.

We sat in silence, expressionless; neither of us taking our eyes off the other and then the front door opened.

CHAPTER
4

I'm home, Nana...," the voice shouted out. In walked Sara.

"Aunt Annie," she said excitedly and rushed to give me a huge hug. "I knew that had to be your car. Is it new? It's awesome! Can I drive it later? I'm so excited to see you!"

I loved the twins. Thanks to Jackie, I was able to see them a few times over the years with sporadic visits to the Cape and on a couple of occasions he brought them with him to visit me wherever I was at the time. Especially Sara and I kept in touch.

"Yes, yes and me, too! Look at you, Girl," I said hugging her. "You are knock-down gorgeous! It's been quite a while this time since I've seen you. What is it, two, three years?"

"It's been too long! We have so much to catch up on....Oops, almost forgot... Hey, Nana, you look rested. Are you ready for lunch? I brought you a surprise," she said and bent over to kiss her on the top of her head. My mother never changed her expression.

"Has she been like this for long?" I asked.

"Oh, she has bad days and worse days, I guess, but overall she's doing okay."

"You don't speak about her when we talk."

"You don't ask," she lightly rebuked with eyebrows arched.

Changing the subject, I asked, "So what's new with you? I hear you have a new person in your life. Will I have the chance to meet him?"

"You bet you will. He's the Activities Director at the Senior Center and he's so good looking! One day I took Nana to the doctors and my car wouldn't start when I got out. At that very moment, he was leaving the dentist office next door and when he saw my plight, he came right over and helped. Something was loose under the hood and he fixed it. Talk about fate! Oh, and did I mention how handsome he is?" He's Portuguese and you know Mom! If he's not purebred Irish like us, he might as well be an alien. At least Dad is cool about it, so she's backed off somewhat and isn't quite as rude as before. Besides, I am twenty-one and she can't do anything about it. We've been seeing each other about two months now and we're ready to take it to another level if you know what I mean." Her grin told it all.

Following her to the kitchen, I couldn't help notice how beautiful she was. She looked so much like her father's family as I remembered them. Her eyes sparkled like Bob's and even more so when she spoke about Mike.

"Just make sure you're careful," I warned her gently.

"Oh, not to worry...I'm not a kid anymore and Mike isn't my first, you know."

"Well, whatever, I just don't want to see you hurt." Little did she know the meaning of those words?

"Why don't you go get Nana for me while I put our lunch out?" she asked me.

"She probably won't come for me. I'm not sure she even knows who I am."

"She'll come...just tell her lunch is ready," so that's what I did. I went back to the den and said simply that. She got up and followed me back to the kitchen without a word.

"Hey, Nana, I have your favorite...meatball parmigiana." She responded to Sara with a huge smile and took her sandwich. "I wasn't sure what you liked, so I got one more meatball and an Italian grinder. You can have either."

"Oh, I love them both. I haven't had a grinder in years! I lived all over and they have different names in different cities. The names are submarines, gyros, hoagies and whatever else, but this is the only place I know that calls them grinders. No one makes them as good as here! Can we split and have a little of each?"

"Of course," she said smiling in the knowledge that she had pleased me.

"I have a hotel room, so I have to leave right after lunch," I lied to Sara.

"Oh, no, you can't, please stay! We have so much to catch up on and I get so lonely here sometimes. Everyone is coming for dinner and we can just hang out for a while when they leave. Please, Aunt Annie...I never get to see you. Please..."

How could I say no to that? "Okay, I will," I said giving in, "But just one night."

Without looking up from her sandwich, my mother said, "Chocolate Fudge cake with fudge frosting and don't you forget to put the cherries on top and some more between the layers."

"What was that, Nana?" Sara looked at her a little confused and then to me, "Sometimes, she says the strangest things."

"That was my favorite dessert when I was a kid," I said, while thinking to myself, "Coincidence?"

After lunch, my mother watched a little more television and then went to her room for a nap. Sara and I cleaned our lunch dishes and started getting things ready for dinner. I set the table while she peeled vegetables. We chatted more like long lost friends than relatives who hardly saw each other.

"Aunt Annie, can I ask you something?"

"Sure, anything," I told her.

"What's up with you and Mom?" I feared the moment of this conversation.

"I don't know what you're talking about, Sara. We're both busy women and caught up in our hectic lives. That's all." Karyn clearly kept our secret all these years and I, especially me, was not about to reveal it.

"No, it's more than that. It's been years. Neither one of you has been that busy. You always seemed to find time to go to Uncle Jack's house. If it weren't for him, I wouldn't have seen you either. You've never come to see Nana, your own mother, not even when Grandpa died. Mom was furious with you. All of us were."

"Sara, I've been caught up with my life and my career. I planned to come to Grandpa's funeral, but I had the flu and couldn't." She read my eyes and knew I was lying.

"I know it's none of my business, but I've had to live with it. Mom won't talk about it, the one, and only time I asked Nana, she burst into tears. I never asked again. Susan and I spent our entire lives with a mother who doesn't smile and a father who makes excuses for her. Lately, it's even worse with Mom. Something is stressing her tremendously and we don't have a clue to what. Whatever this big dark family secret is; it tore this family apart."

"First of all there is no big dark family secret, Sara. I was young, younger than you are. I had a husband. He had an accident. He died. I was heartbroken. I pursued another life; end of story!" Blood raced furiously through my veins and I fought to maintain control. Sara's eyes widened at my tone of voice and the sight of red blotches surfacing on my neck and I realized she didn't know about Joey.

Embarrassed by my outburst, I continued in a more subdued tone. "I was eighteen years old when I eloped with Joey. We knew each other since kindergarten and went through school together all the way through graduation. There was never a day when we weren't going to be married, at least so we thought. My parents always let your mother have friends over and it was no different with me, with the exception of Joey. There was always an excuse and he couldn't be included. As for his family, I just didn't exist. I never even met his father and his mother was so rude to me the couple of times I met her. We were Irish and they were Italian, so I blamed it on that, but it never made sense to me. I had other Italian friends. I even had Protestant friends. Now that I think of it, I even had a Jewish friend who was the daughter of one of my father's coworkers. None of them were a problem, just Joey and there was never a good reason, so we met in secret."

"Maybe they knew how much you loved him and didn't want to lose you." Our voices were softer now.

"No, it was more than that. Anyway, while everyone else was partying after graduation, we eloped. Joey got a job in a junk yard just outside New York City and his boss hired me to clean up their office. It was horrible and we were homesick, so we decided to come back naively expecting to be met with open arms. We really thought they'd accept us if we were married, but we returned to a raging inferno of hatred. His father refused our visit together and only met with his son. Both families were screaming annulment and it was worse than ever."

"I'm sorry. I never knew," Sara said in a whisper.

"Before we had a chance to leave again, there was the accident and Joey died. I was in the hospital when his family buried him. The cemetery is walking distance from here, but this family never even attended the funeral. His family went on with life and I never existed to them in the first place, so they never contacted me. I went away to school for a while and never came back."

"No one ever spoke about it, so Susan and I never knew."

"It was a long time ago and life goes one...not to change the subject, but I'd like to get settled upstairs and grab a short nap myself before everyone comes over if you don't mind."

"Of course, Aunt Annie?"

"Yes?"

"I'm so sorry."

"Like I said, Sara...it was a long time ago," but to me, I thought, It feels like it just happened.

CHAPTER
5

Around five o'clock, I heard voices downstairs and thought I should face the inevitable and go down to see everyone. What I really wanted to do was get into my Lexus and head south, several hundred miles south.

"What are those great smells coming from the kitchen?" I asked, making my entrance. Susan was the first to grab me in a bear hug. She was Sara's identical mirror image, but Susan was right-handed while Sara used her left. With their hair cut differently and Susan pregnant, it was easy to tell them apart.

"Aunt Annie, this gorgeous man is my husband, Eddie," Susan said making him blush.

"It's nice to meet you, Eddie," I said and shook his hand.

"Hey, no shaking hands in this family. We give family hugs here!" I needed no introduction as Mike put two big arms around me. "In case you don't know it, I already know you because Sara talks about you all the time."

The front door opened with a burst. "I'm here, I'm here," said Tommy excitedly. "We have cake!" Looking back toward the door, he said, "Dad, Dad, hurry up! Everyone is here." It was hard not to recognize Tommy. Down Syndrome carved his features at birth, yet he still held identifiable traits to tell he was Bob's son. It was also hard not to love him. His smile lit up the room. "Dad, Dad, hurry!"

"Okay, Tommy, here I am," Bob grinned entering the room. "Where can I put this pan? It's hot," he said going straight to the kitchen. Looking at Mike he asked, "Would you mind helping Karyn with the rest of the food? She has the biscuits and dessert."

At dinner, I positioned myself away from Karyn. There was lot of small talk and laughter, not to mention the questions for me. Eddie wanted to know about every feature on the Lexus until I finally gave him the keys and told him to go check it out later. I knew I safely blocked it in, at least I hoped so.

Tommy wanted to know how I liked my carrots cut and then proceeded to give me systematic instructions for making a salad at the Senior Center. It was obvious he loved his job and I enjoyed hearing about it.

Susan made her big announcement that she and Eddie were having a baby girl much to the evident delight of her parents. The three of them spent the rest of the dinner in a conversation between themselves about how wonderful daughters are. I couldn't help but notice that it was also a good excuse for them to ignore Mike.

As for Mike, I watched him and Sara closely. He was definitely handsome with russet skin, black hair and dark eyes. There was no doubt that there was a strong physical attraction between them. They couldn't keep their eyes, or their hands off each other. Sara never missed a beat though and mothered over her grandmother like the caretaker she had become, cutting the ham on her plate while Mike poured a glass of wine for Sara and buttered a biscuit for my mother. To myself I chuckled, "We'll see what the next level brings."

My mother's grin was puerile and unbroken, her eyes nomadically darting back and forth between Sara and Mike. In a total role reversal, she had become the child and they were the parents. I wondered when the headstrong, determined woman I remembered receded to the vulnerable state I now watched. Reading my thoughts, Sara said, "She's really doing fine and she's so happy when there are people around. She just loves it, don't you, Nana?"

"How long has she been like this, Sara?" I asked.

"The Alzheimer's was diagnosed about a year ago. We first noticed it when she starting losing everything and then she got lost going to New London. She went the opposite direction and headed toward Providence. We never would have known except she finally did figure it out and was upset when she got home. Still, we didn't think too much of it until we noticed she wasn't paying her bills and had trouble counting money. I was in between jobs, so Mom asked me to live here and take care of her. It's a winning situation for both of us. The medication was a big help for a while, but lately we're seeing her decline more quickly."

"She really seems to like you, Mike," I said to him.

"I think she's pretty special herself," he said. "I bring her treats from the Senior Center whenever I can." Then said to her teasingly, "You're just using me for the goodies I get you, aren't you, Mrs. Mahoney?" The grin remained unchanged. "She has a real sweet tooth and loves candy," he said to me.

"And you spoil her," Sara admonished him smiling.

With a wink to Sara, he turned to my mother and added, "Nothing wrong with that, right, Mrs. Mahoney?"

"What brought you to the area, Mike?" I asked him.

"Oh, I don't know. I had a cousin stationed at the Submarine Base here and I came to visit him for a long weekend, really liked it here, so I decided to stay for a while. Then I met Sara and I'd be a fool to leave now," he said and gave Sara a look that told it all. "I'm originally from the San Diego area."

"Is your cousin still at the Sub Base?"

"No, he's on deployment right now and when he returns, he's going to Norfolk. His fiancé is there."

Sara's eyes never left Mike while he talked. Watching her look at him with all that adoration, my thoughts drifted sadly to Joey.

The reflection shattered abruptly when my mother started singing an unrecognizable childlike tune, "Cake, Cake, Chocolate Cake, Favorite, Favorite... Cake, Cake, Chocolate Cake, Favorite, Favorite..." Tommy joined in and Karyn got up and went to the kitchen. When she returned, she set in front of me a Chocolate Fudge cake with fudge frosting and maraschino cherries on the top. I already knew there would be more of them between the layers.

Ice singed my veins while I choked back hot tears.

CHAPTER
6

Sicily, Italy

Nicoletta stood on the porch of the cottage gazing down at the three boys running toward the beach. They sported dark skin and muscular bodies. Each had black eyes and hair the color of midnight. All three had their father's build and his eyes, especially, Vinnie, the eldest, although they lacked his chiseled handsome features.

"Vinnie, where's your sister?" she yelled down looking frantically for the youngest.

"Andi didn't come down with us," he responded in Italian.

"I'm right here, Mama," the little voice behind her said. Andrianna resembled Nicoletta with her light brown hair and hazel eyes. Her skin was a rich olive and at the age of six, she was already beautiful like her mother. "I was reading with Papa."

Sal came up behind her, putting his hands around her waist, held her close and whispered in her ear, "Ti amo, Niki."

"I love you, too Sal. We're so blessed," and they stood there watching the boys.

"No, Niki, I'm blessed," and he squeezed her tighter. "Who's the other kid?" he asked noticing that another boy had joined them.

"That's Alberto. He's visiting the Cabrini's next door. I'm not sure what the relationship is, but he was here last summer and he's here again this year for a couple of weeks. He speaks several languages I think. He's a couple of years older, but he and Vinnie have gotten to be good friends. He's a nice young man, but you would know that if you were around more," she teased. "Do you really have to go on this trip, Sal? You're gone so much lately."

"I know, but this deal is important and I can't miss this meeting. We'll only be gone three weeks and the timing is perfect. I can be part of the meeting and Vinnie will get to visit the colleges he wants to attend."

Nicoletta and Sal met while attending the Sapienza University of Rome. Located in the heart of Rome, it was the largest university in Europe and it was amazing that they met at all, but they did and immediately became good friends. She never forgot the first time he asked her to dinner and then showed up unexpectedly with his little brother. His parents were the victims of a terrible accident and at the age of twenty-two, he had a toddler in his care. Niki was so impressed that he had taken the reigns of responsibility and not given him up. Their friendship grew to something stronger and shortly after graduation she, Sal, and little Vinnie stood before a priest in Rome and pledged their troth to each other. Only her family was present.

Sal insisted that they raise Vinnie as their son. He felt it would be less complicated for him growing up and she agreed. As time passed, Vinnie had no recollection of his earlier years alone with Sal and the memories formed from what they told him. His birth mother died in an accident. Niki was the only mother he knew and Sal was the father he adored. Their second son, Tony, was born early in their marriage and Louie a couple years later. Several years into their family life, their youngest, Andrianna, was born into the world. They all adored her and completely spoiled her, but they didn't care.

Sal worked for Onyx Corporation, a global pharmaceutical company. Money wasn't scarce because Sal had a comfortable insurance settlement from the accident. Still, he worked hard to climb the ladder at Onyx, but with the promotions came more and more traveling. Niki knew this trip was important to him and it was a great opportunity for Sal to spend some quality time with Vinnie who insisted on attending college in the United States. Lately, however, something seemed amiss in their relationship and she couldn't identify the problem, wasn't even sure if there was a problem.

The changes were subtle, but they were there. Sal spent more and more time on the computer. He deleted the browser history and minimized the screen when she walked into the room. His phone calls were secretive, made in a lowered voice and out of range for her to hear. His attentiveness to her was unchanged and the intimacy was still there, but something just wasn't right. She could feel it. When she questioned him, he blamed it on the stress from the job and she believed him.

Then she read the text message that changed it all.

"Call me, it's important. Love, Teresa"

With that, she hired a detective.

CHAPTER
7

When everyone left for the night, I quickly excused myself and went upstairs to bed leaving Mike and Sara alone downstairs. The rosebud wallpaper I grew up with was faded and pulling away from the walls in places. "How many dreams were born in this room?" I thought. Then chuckling aloud, I remembered the night Joey threw pebbles at my window to get my attention and instead, he met the wrath of my father. "How old were we? Sixteen?" The memories were sweet, comforting and with them, I drifted off to sleep.

Too soon, however, the nightmare crept in, the same one that haunted my sleep repeatedly since the accident. As always, I woke up soaking wet, shaking and sobbing. Waking up was always the same because I couldn't remember it. I could only recall the horrifying sounds in the dream; first the soft purr and then the screeches and howls that seared my soul, waking me in terror. They reminded me of a feral catfight I once heard in the middle of the night, a battle between two untamed felines fighting for survival, neither willing to succumb to defeat. Was it reality, or delusion? I wanted to know, to grasp the meaning of it all and yet, I wanted it to fade and never invade my mind again.

The rest of the night seemed like an eternity. I tossed and turned; I cried for all my disappointments, all the hurt and the things that could have been and should have been, but weren't. I cried because I hated my sister and I cried because the anger toward my mother ate at my insides. I needed desperately to hate her and now she was pathetic and weak, stealing my rage. I detested her very existence. I cried for the sun to come up.

Quietly, I snuck downstairs at the first glint of light. Peeking into the den, I saw Sara and Mike snuggled and sleeping together on the couch. "This house sure has changed," I thought. I couldn't imagine that happening when I grew up here. "Good for them."

I was thrilled to see the new single serve coffee maker on the counter and Sara had the K-Cups ready to go. I chose Southern Pecan, probably subconsciously because I wanted to start driving south. Just the smell of it brewing made me feel better, so I grabbed my coat and coffee and headed to the front porch.

Connecticut weather is so unpredictable. Today at least held the promise of some sunshine and the wind had died down, but still it was the beginning of April and the winter snow had melted into a dirty, wet slush. "So much for global warming," I thought pulling my coat tighter around me. "Where are the spring flowers?" A cigarette would have been nice to go with the coffee. I was sorry I quit.

Sitting on the porch, I could see the Thames River and watched a commercial fishing boat make its way into Long Island Sound. In years past, the submarines that passed in these waters were many, but the attack on the World Trade Center had changed all that. Steam billowed from one of the buildings on the river at the Electric Boat Division. I wondered about the new submarine in the dry dock. My father had worked there and so many days after school, I would sit on this same porch and wait for the four o'clock whistle to blow and I knew his shift ended. Sometimes he came right home, but most of the time he went straight to the bar across the street from the plant. My parents fought hard on those nights.

With the exception of his drinking, my father was a good man, but much older than my mother. I don't think they ever talked about how they met, or maybe I just never listened. Each had their roles and played them well. She was the doting wife and he was the breadwinner, both second generation Irish. Neither of them spoke with an accent. I couldn't' remember my grandparents. Thinking about it now, I really didn't know much about my parents. We weren't affluent, but we never lacked for anything that I could remember. When Electric Boat was between contracts to build submarines, they laid my father off like everyone else. Our friends and neighbors would struggle to make ends meet, but the only change for us was that my father spent more time at the bar. I had no reason to question their finances, so I never did.

Just as I stood up to go inside for a coffee refill, a silver BMW 650i convertible pulled into the driveway.

CHAPTER
8

Sicily, Italy

M i scusi, sto cercando di Signora Fiore," the postman asked.

"Mrs. Fiore is in town," he answered in English.

"Io non parlo inglese," responded the postman.

So in Italian, he repeated, "Signora Fiore è in città."

After being assured about Mrs. Fiore coming home soon and having a promise that she would receive the manila envelope, the postman reluctantly handed it over and unknowingly changed the lives of strangers both here in his homeland and across the ocean.

The envelope was like any other piece of mail. It was nothing more than a standard letter sized envelope with an addressor and an addressee. The return address, however, stopped the recipient in his tracks.

Marcelo Campini Detective Agency, Via Roma 1022, Palermo, Italy

Just an hour before, Mrs. Fiore asked him to do her a favor. She ran into town for an errand, but told him that she was expecting someone to come fill a propane tank. Would he mind waiting for him and she would pay him 13 Euros that equated to nearly $20.00 in US dollars, not bad for a little bit of time. The technician filled the tank and just as he was ready to leave, the mail carrier arrived.

Al stared at the envelope with curiosity. He wondered why Mrs. Fiore needed information from a detective agency. His fingers slid across the envelope inviting him to open it, but he knew he couldn't. On the other hand, could he do it? A little steam and it would easily open. What was the harm? He could satisfy his desire and reseal it. No one would be the wiser.

For several minutes, he fought with himself while his hands and fingers sensuously caressed and stroked the envelope until he gave in and opened it. In shock, he read the contents and left with the envelope carefully hidden under his shirt along with the extra Euros he found in a dresser and tucked away in his pocket.

The information he now possessed, the secret link between families, was the key to open a door of opportunity for him.

His plan came together easily and now, more than a year later, everything was going better than expected. The bitch didn't have a clue. Just a little more patience and he would have it all.

CHAPTER
9

Everything washed from my mind when I saw Jackie get out of the car. My little brother meant the world to me and I saw him so little. His features chiseled to perfection accented a smile to melt your heart. He boasted his Irish descent with jet-black hair and deep blue eyes. His face bore a strong resemblance to our father, but without the weathered, alcoholic look and he was so much more handsome. Men and women alike turned their heads when he walked into a room.

"Hey, Kiddo," he yelled. "What in God's name are you doing outside in this cold?"

"I'm waiting for my handsome little brother!" I gave him the biggest hug. "You get better looking every time I see you and, as always, you're dressed to perfection. I'm taking you shopping with me before I leave."

"Well, it runs in the family because you're looking pretty good yourself. I take it everyone is still asleep."

"Mom, yes, not to mention Sara and Mike," I said a little deviously. "She's so grown up!"

He chuckled. "That's not a surprise. Those lovebirds are quite an item these days. You should come more often and you wouldn't be so shocked." Then with his hand around my waist, he said, "Let's go inside and you can make your little brother a cup of coffee and we can wake everyone up!"

The morning was great. Mike left for work and Sara made us a wonderful breakfast. Mom kept her eyes on Jackie the entire time and just kept grinning. Jackie brought me up to date on his art business and MaryAnn's latest artwork investment. He talked incessantly about his son, Timothy. It was obvious that he loved being a dad and like everything else about my brother, it sounded like he was perfect at it. My mind erased the nightmare haunting me.

Sara entered the den where we were chatting and announced, "Mom just called and she's on her way over. Will Nana be okay with you while I get some shopping done? Mom doesn't hint around. She came right out and told me to get lost so she could talk to the two of you alone. She's always so secretive, it drives me nuts." Jackie grinned and made a playful face at her that told her it was fine. "Thanks, Uncle Jack. Call me when you're finished and I'll come back."

"Will do, Sweetie," he answered her and when she left the room he said to me, "She's been great with Mom and the few times I've met Mike, I really like the guy. He's good for Sara and he tends to Mom's needs more than her own children do. I hope Karyn doesn't screw it up for them."

"What is this all about, Jackie? Sara's right. Karyn is always so secretive about everything and has to be in control."

"I have no idea, but she made it sound serious. I don't think its Mom's health because we all know where her health is heading, but you know Karyn. Everything is always dramatic." I must have rolled my eyes because he added, "Now, Annie, you're not going to make a scene with her, are you? I have no earthly idea why the two of you are so evil to each other, and poor Mom. What did she ever do to you to make you stay away?"

"Jackie, we have this conversation every time we're together. There's nothing. I'm just a free spirit and live a different lifestyle," I lied.

"Well, I'm not buying it," he disputed and kept on about it until the arrival of Karyn halted the conversation.

"Hey, guys! It's so good to see you Jack. Hope your drive wasn't too bad," she said.

"It was great if you don't mind your alarm ringing at four in the morning and trying to navigate around Boston before the crazies get up." He meant it to be sarcastic, but with Jackie, rudeness didn't exist.

"You're such a baby, Jack," she answered. "Let's sit at the dining room table to do this. Mom can watch TV in here."

I started to protest that I was comfortable where I was, but I clearly got a look from Jackie that told me not to say another word. Grudgingly, I followed them and instead I asked, "What's all this about, Karyn? I can't believe you couldn't have told us on the phone instead of making us jump through hoops; a little overkill, I think."

Ignoring me, Karyn pulled a laptop out of a briefcase and set it on the table. Then she took out several papers and envelopes and without looking up, she simply stated, "Mom's broke."

Jumping right in, Jackie said, "Then we can all help out. Just tell me how much she needs."

"No, Jack, you don't get it. She's really broke." While Karyn spoke, she made little piles out of the paperwork and spread them out in front of us.

"Karyn, did you really drag us all the way here for this? Certainly, we could have...," I started to say, but she interrupted me.

"Just for once, Annie, will you just shut up and listen?" I started to get up and leave the table, and then she snapped, "Sit down! This is serious!"

The look from Jackie told me to close my mouth and sit down, so I did. Taking a deep breath, I asked much more calmly, "How can that be, Karyn? This family never went without and when Dad died, I'm sure he left her very comfortable."

"I wish I knew," Karyn answered. "When Dad died, I was put on all the accounts and was given Power of Attorney for Mom over everything, both medical and financial. I never had any reason to look at anything until her health began to fail. She has great insurance, so everything medical was covered and Dad's pension and social security went directly into her checking account. That's all she really needed to live on."

"I don't understand," Jackie interrupted.

"I've had some concerns that she may need long term nursing care as the

Alzheimer's progresses, so I decided to go through everything to see how we could do it. She's always been so meticulous with her finances, but with onset of her illness, everything was a real mess. She had unopened mail lying around everywhere. When I started going through it, I had the shock of my life. All the bank accounts were drained."

"Maybe she just moved it somewhere else," I said assuming Karyn was overreacting as usual. "She probably wanted more interest, or was trying to simplify everything by combining it all into one account someplace. You've probably just overlooked it."

"That's what I thought at first, but nothing surfaced, so I went back as far as I could with all the statements and nothing makes sense. For years and years, there were the same deposits made. While Dad was working, his paycheck went directly into their checking account at the Credit Union, the same with his pension and social security when he retired. After he died, Mom received her portion of his pension and social security plus a small insurance annuity payment. There's something strange though. All these years, there's been another deposit going in monthly and it makes no sense. The amount never changed. It has always been one-thousand dollars and it goes in on the first of every month. I found at least ten years of old statements in boxes because she hoarded everything and it's always been."

"What's it for?" Jackie asked.

"I don't know. It comes from a foreign bank. I've tried everything I can to find out what it is, but I keep hitting a stoned wall. I can't get any information out of the bank because they won't accept my Power of Attorney. She had over five hundred thousand dollars and it's gone."

"Whew," Jackie sighed. "No one saves a half million dollars and then loses track of it. She must have moved it. I'm just in shock that there was that much money. I knew she was comfortable, but never expected that."

Looking at both of us, Karyn said flatly, "She gave it away."

In unison, my brother and I gasped, "What?"

"That's right. She gave it away. About a year ago, she started wiring it out to some other foreign bank. When I contacted them, I got the same response. They won't tell me a thing and won't accept my Power of Attorney. They made me feel like a criminal. The statements show the withdrawals were all odd amounts, but never went over $10,000. Most of the time, she took them in cashier's checks, but sometimes she withdrew cash. Those withdrawals were always under $2,000."

"To avoid a paper trail," I thought aloud.

"When did the deposits stop?" Jackie asked.

"That's even stranger," she went on. "They're still coming in, but as soon as the money is available, the account is set up to send it right back out to the second foreign bank. It's all here in the paperwork, but I've done a spreadsheet which shows the whole thing." The three of us froze to her laptop trying to sort it out, trying to make sense of it all. Then she said, "There's something else."

I couldn't remember ever seeing Karyn cry before and these tears were real.

CHAPTER
10

A lberto Santucci was born in Milan, Italy. He was an only child and orphaned at the young age of six, forcing him to move from one foster home to another. Despite the horrendous experiences forced upon him, he viewed life through the eyes of an opportunist. He never missed a chance to learn from those around him and as a result, in addition to his native Italian, he fluently spoke English, Spanish, Portuguese and a little French without the detection of an accent. Maybe he would learn Arabic next. Moreover, why not, he was brilliant and knew it.

He wasn't bitter with the cards fate dealt him, not even with the political machine that moved him from one residence to another, none of them home. On his eighteenth birthday, he aged out of the system and finally had full control of his own future. He could relocate wherever and whenever he chose. It didn't take him long to figure out that his best opportunities would come if he surrounded himself with the right people. There was power in affluence. There was power in knowledge. Not yet, twenty-two years old and he lacked nothing, with the exception of feeling.

His soul was dead. Apathy was his best friend.

Relocating to America was easy. The counterfeit documents supporting his new identity were difficult to obtain, but with the connections he had cultivated, everything fell right into place. It was just another move to him. He didn't love it, didn't hate it. His only lust was for money, his only emotion was the thrill of power, and the envelope's contents had given him that. Like a chameleon, he could easily meld into any environment and that's where he was for over a year now, deeply entrenched in his plan and hiding in plain sight.

Looking at his bank records, he felt pride in what he had done and knew the time was near to end the masquerade. Maybe one more month to round the numbers upward a little more and then he would execute the grand finale. This would be the hard part, not because he cared, but he couldn't leave a trail of any kind.

Alberto Santucci would never be a cast off from society again.

CHAPTER
11

New York City

Vinnie was beside himself with excitement at the thought of being in New York City. This was his first trip to the United States and he wanted to see it all, starting right here in Manhattan. He had been all over Europe with his parents, but this was beyond imagination and the best part was yet to come. Accepted to the New York Institute of Technology, he was here to see the campus and make his final decision. What was the decision? He wanted to be an architect and what better place than right here in the heart of it all. None of the other colleges was even a consideration. He really wanted to live off campus in his own apartment, but knew that wasn't an option with his parents. At least, it wasn't this year, so he made up his mind he wanted to live in Affinia Residence Hall in midtown Manhattan. Per the college paperwork, it was only available for upperclassmen, but he was sure that was a minor obstacle. His father often came to New York on business and had plenty of connections. If not, Vinnie would settle for Riverside Residence Hall in Upper West Manhattan. Maybe that wouldn't be so bad after all. He would have the subway experience. It was perfect.

Sal and Vinnie were staying at the Ritz-Carlton across the street from Central Park and one block from Fifth Avenue. It was a five star hotel and Sal thought Vinnie would feel at home with the European flair. The cuisine was French culinary and the artwork was impressive, so that made Sal feel at home, as it had done on many of his trips before. Onyx was paying for the hotel, which was pricey, but it wouldn't have mattered anyway. Money was not a factor with Sal. He wanted the best for Vinnie. It would have been nice to have Niki here, but it was impossible with the younger kids. Maybe next time, he thought.

"I hate to do this to you, Vinnie, but I need some time for business today. I arranged with a friend of mine at Onyx to take you to see the NYIT campus today and then out for a little sightseeing. His name is Bill and he should be here any minute. Actually, you met him in Rome last year when Onyx had their convention there. Don't leave his sight, but if you need me, just call or text. Moreover, Vinnie, go to a nice place for lunch. Stay away from the street vendors. I don't want to have to tell your mother you got food poisoning from something unidentifiable you found on the street. Remember, Son, offer to buy lunch. He won't accept, but make the offer anyway. It's the right thing to do."

"Not a problem, Dad. I remember him. We'll be fine." Vinnie could hardly conceal his excitement.

Sal hailed a cab outside the hotel and enroute to the Doubletree near Times Square, he called Theresa.

Broadway theatres surrounded the Doubletree Suites. It was the perfect place to meet Theresa. She came to New York City under guise of seeing one of the productions with a friend. The hotel, affiliated with the International Gay & Lesbian Travel Association, had some sort of event taking place when Sal arrived. It was difficult not to notice that most of the couples were of the same gender. This made him very uncomfortable, but he knew it was unlikely he would run into anyone he knew at Onyx.

He used the lobby telephone to phone upstairs to Theresa. "I'm here, what's your room number?"

"Finally," she said and he heard her sigh of relief. I'm in Room 1233. Forget the elevator and fly up here!"

The door flew open before he had the chance to knock and she threw herself into his arms exploding into tears. It was a minute or so before they broke their embrace and just stared at each other.

"I've missed you so much," she quivered. "I know I shouldn't see you, but I just had to."

Holding her away from him, he said, "Let me look at you. I can't believe how beautiful you are. I can't believe how long it's been. Dear God, Theresa....Dear God," and he held her again. This time the tears were his.

When they finally got themselves together and pulled apart, she told him, "I made a lunch reservation for us at Ginger's on the fifth floor. I don't know what you like anymore, but the menu has a little of everything. The décor is interesting, Asian, I think. Also, it's out of the way so we won't be seen."

Smiling at her nervousness, he answered everything with, "I haven't changed, I still eat everything and we're safe here. No one knows." His face twisted into the familiar grin she remembered so well and he teased, "Unless of course, the transvestite in the lobby decides to be my lunch date instead. I may have to dump you!"

"You haven't changed, have you? I've dreamed of this day for so long and it's finally here." Theresa couldn't peel her eyes away from him.

"For you, I've never changed, Theresa. For you, I never will and we have two full weeks together. Let's get going, I'm starved!" He put his arm around her shoulders and they left the room in silence.

Theresa was right; the décor in the restaurant was fascinating to say the least. The décor paid tribute to 'The Roaring Twenties' and it was accented with several exotic pieces that were Asian. Neither, had an appetite, but they ordered anyway and included a bottle of wine chosen by Sal. After a glass from the French vineyard, they both relaxed and once they started talking, nothing could stop them. They had so much to catch up. Her excitement was his and vice versa. To them, the room was silent except for the voice of the other. The food was untouched, their eyes locked on mirror images.

Paired at birth, separated by circumstance, the bond was unbroken for the twins.

CHAPTER
12

W hat else?" Jackie was the first to ask.

Karyn was crying freely now and her hands trembled as she pulled three envelopes from the brief case and gave them to us. Jackie opened them and after we examined each of them, he said, "What's the big deal? These are our birth certificates, all three of us. We've seen them before. In fact, we all have copies."

"Look at this one," she handed us a fourth.

"It's another copy of yours," I said glancing at it.

"No, look at it again," her voice trembled.

"I am, Karyn," I said sounding more annoyed than I wanted to. Then, I froze. My eyes went to first one and then back to this one.

Jackie took them from my hands and read the first one aloud, "Karyn Lynn Mahoney born the daughter of Margaret Mary Mahoney, mother, and Peter Paul Mahoney, father, in the City of New London, County of New London, State of Connecticut, this date of..."

Karyn was staring down at her hands, her shoulders shaking uncontrollably as he read the second certificate. "Karyn Lynn O'Brien, born the daughter of Margaret Mary O'Brien, mother, and Angelo Fontinelli, father...," He stopped reading at that point, gazed wide-eyed first at me, then Karyn and back to me again. All he could say was, "What the hell is this?"

I couldn't say a word. None of this made sense. There was no way that Karyn could be the daughter of Gino Fontinelli, Joey's uncle.

"There must be an explanation. This has to be a mistake, Karyn. There's no way you're Angelo Fontinelli's daughter, "Jackie insisted. "It's preposterous. Look at you! You look just like Mom! You have her hair, her nose, her mouth. Everything about you has 'Mom' all over it."

"Not everything, Jack, look at me again," she said in a shameful whisper.

"What's different, Karyn?" I asked. "Jackie is right. You're a clone of Mom."

"Look at me, Annie, I'm not!" She looked so defeated. "Look at my eyes. Look at my eyes!"

"What about them?" Jackie asked. "You have both Mom and Dad's eyes."

"No, Jackie, I don't." She was confusing us now. "Two blue-eyed parents can't have a child with any other color eyes. Blue eyes are always dominant!"

Aghast, we stared into her hazel eyes; my brother and I could find nothing to say.

"I think I always knew," she started. "Oh, I didn't know what, but I knew something was wrong. As a kid, I thought they adopted me because the feeling of love was never there. When you came along Annie, Mom and Daddy fell all over you, especially Dad. He was good to me, but you got the smiles, played the games with him, and had his attention. You were always his little girl, not me. I was older when Jack was born, but I still felt the difference. He never looked at me the way he looked at both of you. Inside, I always knew something was different with me. Now I know and I can't even prove it. Mom is a vegetable, Dad is dead and so is Angelo!"

There was no consoling Karyn and even if I wanted to, I couldn't find the words. Joey's father, Dominick, a callous-hearted bastard, was a saint in comparison to his brother, Gino. I never met Dominick, but did meet Gino once and the memory scorched my soul. With black eyes, cold and penetrating, he told Joey to take his little toy somewhere else to play, referring to me. "How can he be Karyn's father?" I asked myself. "How could Mom have had anything to do with him?" Something was definitely wrong here. It had to be.

"I need answers," Karyn pleaded looking straight at me. "I need your help, Annie." Still speechless, I could only stare at her.

"How can we help?" asked Jack. "We'll do anything you need."

"Only Annie can help," she said looking directly at me. "You can speak to Dominick, and get the answers. He'll know and he'll tell you."

"No! You can't be serious!" I snapped back in anger. "There's no way I will ever speak to that son of a bitch! I can't believe you would even ask me to!"

"You're my only hope, Annie. He won't see me, but you're different. You were married to his son for Christ's sake!"

"Maybe you don't remember so well, Karyn, but we didn't exactly sit around any family dinners together. He never recognized me as Joey's wife. He wouldn't see me then, so he certainly won't see me now! As far as he was concerned, I didn't exist. The man hated me and I hated him more!"

Changing the subject, Jackie asked, "Does Bob know about this?"

"No, how can I tell him? How can I tell him that I'm not the person he married twenty-four years ago? For God's sake, Jack, his parents are prejudiced even against their own blood. They can't even accept an Irish Protestant, let alone a half-blooded Italian! They accepted me because my last name was Mahoney. I can't imagine the thought of them finding out otherwise and what about the twins. They'll be humiliated."

"Karyn, get a hold of yourself." Not sure where I was going with it, but continued, "You were a Mahoney. Even if this is true and I'm having trouble believing it, you were raised right here in this house as Karyn Lynn Mahoney. Nothing changes that and you have to tell Bob. He's your husband, he'll understand," and then, not really believing it myself, I added, "and so will his parents. You're like a daughter to them."

"Don't worry about the girls, Karyn. They're more together than you think. Annie's right though," Jackie added. "You've got to tell Bob. He may be able to help us get to the bottom of this."

"How is that?" I asked.

"He's a Lab Technician for Pfizer. The Groton location is their worldwide

39

research and development center. After all these years, he must have some heavy connections and know people who can help us out," Jackie said.

"I don't understand," I replied. "What does Pfizer have to do with this?"

"Me either," added Karyn.

"Their BioBank located here comprises the Tissue Bank, DNA & BioFluids repository and Pharmacogenomics lab," Jackie said with excitement.

"Jackie, what the hell are you talking about? I was very confused and by the look on Karyn's face, so was she.

"Pfizer's has one single center of expertise that coordinates the collection, processing, storage and distribution of biosamples and that is the BioBank. Bob works in the heart of it all."

"I still don't know what you're talking about, Jackie. What has this got to do with Karyn?" I asked directly to Jackie. This seemed to be going nowhere.

"Pfizer is constantly trying to discover new biomarkers in their research to develop new medicine for both existing diseases and new ones we don't even know about yet. Wow, this is great!"

"How about putting this all into English for us, Jackie? What is a 'bio' whatever and how can this help? The problem at hand is finding out about the birth certificate," I reminded him.

"Okay, I'll spell it out for you...D-N-A. They collect samples with a patient's consent and store the samples for their research. Bob works in the lab and must have access to, or knows someone else who does have access to the means of identifying Angelo's DNA and matching it with Karyn's."

Karyn stated flatly, with a roll of her eyes, "Angelo's dead. We can't dig him up."

"Of course not, but Dominick is still alive. That's where you come in, Annie. If you can get access to him and get his DNA, we can ask Bob to help us."

"No way, I'm not going anywhere near that man! I've spent half my life trying to forget the bastard," I said angrily.

"Jackie's right, this could work. I need to know for sure who I really am. Maybe we can think of a way you don't have to speak to him at all. Please, Annie, please help me." She was pleading.

"Please, Annie, do it for us? We all need to know," Jackie begged.

Hatred is a harsh word, but I hated my sister. I hated her for twenty years and now she was asking me to do something I swore I would never do. She helped ruin my life and now she wanted me to be in the same room with the man responsible for Joey's accident. As much as I despised her though, I loved my brother twofold more.

"All this is a mute point unless Bob knows and is able, not to mention willing to help. Talk to him first, Karyn, and if it can be done, I'll think about it," and then to Jackie I asked, "How do you know all this stuff anyway? You're an artist, not a scientist."

"I have a friend who is really into this, but that's not important," he answered. "You'll do it then?"

"We'll see," and changing the subject, I asked, "Does anyone want a beer besides me?"

Without a word, Karyn went to the kitchen for them.

CHAPTER
13

That night was one of the worst nights I ever had. The nightmare wouldn't end, the cats whining, screeching, sending tremors through my drenched body. My mind screamed for them to stop and I willed myself to wake, but to no avail. The sound of a distant foghorn on the river roused me and subconsciously, I blessed the unknown angler for delivering me from my hell.

I didn't have to look outside to know the weather. So typical of New England, this day would start with a heavy mist hovering low and clouding all but the closest visibility, much like the haze in my own mind. The walls of my old room provided a familiar, yet foreign comfort to me and I felt the need to veil myself in the security of this imagined womb.

Another blast of the foghorn brought me back to the reality of the morning and I wondered about the mystery of my night and pondered over the revelations of the day before. My own inability to function emotionally heightened with every hour I spent here and I knew I had to leave. I needed to run from the dysfunction, but run where, I asked myself. Where do I go from here? Was it time to move and start over once again? I longed for the answers that eluded me and I didn't want to be alone right now.

The misty vapors of fog felt refreshing as I left the silent house with everyone still asleep. Still early, there were only a few cars on Long Hill Road as I made my way to the drive-thru at the donut shop. Not remembering what Jackie liked, I bought two large coffees and bagels with cream cheese and butter wrapped separately. After yesterday's bombshell, I thought he could use a little company also and remembering he liked surprises, I steered my Lexus to the bridge crossing to New London, then exited on Frontage Road to his hotel.

Not knowing his room number, I approached the desk clerk who looked like he just crawled out of bed himself. "Good Morning, I'm so sorry to bother you. I'm Mrs. Mahoney. My husband checked in yesterday, but I am just arriving and need a room key."

"I'll ring his extension and tell him you're here," he offered without a hint of a smile.

"Oh, no, please don't do that. He got in late last night and he's just exhausted. I'd rather you didn't wake him," I told him.

"Then I'll need to see an ID," he said clearly annoyed.

"Not a problem, here it is," I said getting it from my purse and it wasn't a problem. After my second divorce, I had my surname changed back to my maiden name. My driver's license said Anne Margaret Mahoney.

After reviewing it half-heartedly, he simply handed me a key and said, "It's Room 411. The elevator is down the hall to the left."

As I approached the room, a food server pushing a cart was just about to knock on the door. "Oh, I'll take that," I told her. "Can you charge that to the room?"

"It already is, but I need your signature," she said handing me the receipt and a pen. I signed it and guessing at the tip, handed her a five-dollar bill. Her facial expression made it clear that wasn't enough, but I ignored her.

When she left, I knocked on the door, announcing softly, "Room Service".

The door opened by a handsome older man wearing a white terrycloth bathrobe and a huge smile. Behind him, the unmade queen size bed was tussled and clothes strewn everywhere. I was sure his wife or mistress would come walking out of the bathroom any second wearing a slinky negligee.

Stuttering, I fought to say, "I...I...am so sooo sorry, I have the wrong room!" My humiliation was overpowering.

His smile broadened and he said, "No, it's the right room. We ordered breakfast. You can just put it over...," but before he finished, another voice from the bathroom interrupted him.

"Is that room service, Bernie? Ask them for extra sugar." There was no mistake; the voice belonged to Jack.

Without another spoken word, the hot coffee dropped from my hands, burning my legs and feet. I let go of the cart handle as if it was a hot timber. Turning, I ran down the hall, tears out of control welling in my eyes. Behind me, Jackie was yelling, "Annie! Wait! I can explain!"

His partner, confused was saying, "I don't understand, Jack. I thought she knew. You told me she knew!"

As the elevator door was closing, I heard Jackie shout, "My wife knows, not my sister!"

The morning fog had lifted, but my tears were blinding. Somehow, I managed to get back across the bridge into Groton. Not noticing, or maybe just not caring, I drove past my mother's street, staying on Thames Street, making my way through the multitude of workers reporting for the morning shift at Electric Boat. I kept going until the road merged with Eastern Point Road. Oblivious to my surroundings, I drove along the iron fences surrounding the massive Pfizer complex, paying no heed to the numerous joggers taking exercise before reporting to work. Reaching Tyler Avenue, I took a right and drove down the hill to Eastern Point Beach located right on the point where the Thames River joins the Long Island Sound.

Not yet May and still chilly, I didn't need a pass to get into the beach. Something felt different as I drove past the empty guardhouse and it upset me to notice that the old beach house that once towered at the entrance was no longer there. So was the old white seafaring house that once stood proudly to the right of the driveway. Still resting on its stone foundation, the old weathered mansion wrapped in its massive porch remained on the point as a landmark to greet fishermen and sailors entering and leaving the river. There were only two other cars in the parking lot and no one was walking around. I parked the Lexus close to the mansion, got out and climbed the old steps to the porch without noticing the new gazebo on the lawn.

The craggy and worn wooden floor creaked under my feet and a cold current of wind whipped my face as I walked to the rear of the house directly facing Long Island Sound. I could barely see the New London Ledge House in the distance, but I paid no attention and I felt my skin tighten as the salt in the air gently dried the tears on my cheeks.

Descending the rear steps of the porch, I walked down to the rocks, careful not to slip on the algae and seaweed. Unlike everything else in my world, the stone formations were unchanged. I found a familiar rock, sat down, and felt the warmth of the sun in the granite. The only sounds to breach the silence were the squawking of the seagulls overhead and the soft splashing of the waves methodically beating against the boulders. It was a good feeling, a good feeling, to have the cradle of my youth around me once again. It felt like home.

Time didn't exist as I slept without a dream, without a care, until the soft voice behind me interrupted the tranquil slumber.

"Annie? Sis?" It was Jackie. "I went by the house and you weren't there, so I went to Karyn's house and she said you would probably come here."

"Does she know?" I asked without looking at him.

"She does now. I was pretty upset and thought maybe you had already told her, so I just blurted it all out." His voice sounded drained.

"How did she take it?" This time I looked directly at him.

"Honestly, Annie, I'm not sure. She cussed a lot and said something about the whole world going to hell and I was first in line. When I left, she was mumbling some nonsense about Irish/Italians having the best of all worlds because they could drown themselves in both beer and wine. Then she said something about getting drunk. That's when I left before she had her hands on a wine bottle in case she cracked it over my head."

"So you're saying she took it better than me?" I think I actually smiled a little.

"Yeah, I'd say she did. I'm sorry you had to find out this way, Annie. I really am," he said softly. "Can I sit down?"

"This is my rock, get your own," I said pointing to a spot next to me. "Does MaryAnn know?"

"Yes, she's known for a long time. I know this is hard to believe, but we have a great relationship. We're the best of friends, we both adore our Timothy and there's no one I would trust more as a business partner. We work so well together, just not in that way." Watching his face while he spoke, I got the feeling he was relieved to finally be out in the open.

"I feel so sorry for her, Jackie. How can she bear the thought of you with someone else?"

"It was disappointing at first, for both of us, not just her. I tried and tried to deny who I was and when it became known, it was a breath of fresh air for us equally. In addition, not that it is any of your business, or anyone else's, but it came out when she confessed to having an affair with an old business acquaintance. If not for that, I would still be struggling to hide who I really am. It's good, Annie; it's all good between MaryAnn and me, but I want you to understand, too. I need you to understand and accept me as myself. I didn't choose to be who I am. I just am who I am. I'm still the same brother who has always loved you and always will."

"Oh, Jackie, I guess I always knew. I just kept pushing it out of my mind and then when you married MaryAnn, I was sure it was my imagination. Tell me something though. Did Mom and Dad know?" I had to ask.

"I think Dad had his suspicions, but he never said anything, probably didn't want to know for sure. That way he wouldn't have to face having a gay son. As for Mom, she didn't have a clue and she sure wouldn't care now!"

I shot him the look that older sisters give their younger brothers when they're out of line, then added, "What about the rest of the family?"

"I'm not sure. I don't see them that often and when I do, I usually have MaryAnn with me. I think there's enough going on with Karyn right now, so I'd rather not make a grand announcement, if you and Karyn don't mind, but sooner or later, it will come out and so be it." Then he added, "Actually, MaryAnn and Timothy are out of town on a church retreat for the weekend and I know that there's one, in particular, recently divorced, male also going with his son who just so happens to be one of Timothy's good friends. Imagine that!" He was smiling, but not at all sarcastic.

"So tell me about Bernie," I asked.

"He's both a genius and a super guy! We've been partners for almost two years now. He's the one with all the high tech bio background that I told you and Karyn about when we were together. Why, do you want to meet him?"

"No, not really, but he is pretty cute and he looks more my age than yours," I teased. "I may give you some competition."

"Sorry, Annie," he teased back. "You're not his type! Besides, when I leave here, we're going to New York City for a couple of days to see some mutual friends and let our hair down a little."

"Lucky you," I told him, but I was serious this time. "I'm happy for you, Jackie, I really am and I still love my little brother just as much, maybe even more."

With that said, we each laid back on our rocks, letting our thoughts drift and the sunshine caress our faces.

CHAPTER
14

Power, that's what the brown pill bottle in his hand was; pure power. Caressing it, he let his thumb stroke the safety cap, slowly, gently and he smiled. He read his name on the label.

Best of all, it was so easy to get. He did a little homework, found a doctor and lied about his desperate desire to quit smoking. Before his appointment, he discolored his smoking fingers with a yellow stain and on the way, actually smoked the first cigarette of his life just for the smell of it. The physical exam was a joke and the pill pusher prescribed 150 mg. of Bupropion once a day and told him to take it in the morning. A week later, he called the office and without speaking to the doctor himself, told the nurse the cessation wasn't lessoning and had it increased to 150 mg. twice a day.

Bupropion isn't a controlled substance, however, when combined with Aricept, the popular drug for Alzheimer's patients; it can be deadly. It can cause muscle spasms and reduces the threshold for seizures, especially in the elderly.

"Well, Miss Maggie, 300 mg. of this baby for a while should do the trick," he said aloud. "A little spasm, maybe a seizure, a fall; anything could happen." Maybe he would slip in an extra Aricept to speed it up a little. She certainly couldn't tell anyone. He wondered if there would be an autopsy, but it really didn't matter. By the time they got the results, he would be long gone, back to Italy and the Cabrini's, one of his better foster families, for a short holiday. They thought he was taking some classes at the University of Massachusetts in Amherst. Fat chance, he thought. He knew he should have some remorse, but he didn't. The only regret he felt was that the money was ending.

Then another thought came to him. Maybe it was time for some other pleasures. Grinning deviously, he returned the tablets to the pill bottle, physically aroused at the thought of all of it.

CHAPTER
15

A couple of days passed with no major announcements, mishaps, or any other signs of dysfunctional behavior in the Mahoney clan. "Thank God," I thought. We all gave each other some space to absorb the revelations that changed our individual worlds.

Karyn went to work and seemed to avoid me, which was fine. Jackie was probably spending time with Bernie and I didn't mind that either. Sara took my mother to the dentist and I was beginning to feel claustrophobic in the big house, so I decided to take a drive. I got on Interstate 95, with no real destination in mind and starting driving north toward Providence. I wasn't ten minutes up the road when I saw the sign for Mystic and the Mystic Aquarium. I got off on Exit 90. The weather was beautiful and I browsed in the little shops in Mystic Village, picking up some scented soaps and a candle for myself. Still off-season, the influx of tourists hadn't yet descended on the area and I had the luxury of being alone without feeling alone.

Back in the car, I headed a little up the road to the Mystic Seaport Museum. Passing a tiny outdoor restaurant on the Mystic River, I made a mental note to come back for some fried clams, the ones with the bellies that I couldn't get anywhere else. I had no desire to tour the museum. I was here so many times as a child, it had lost its appeal to me, however I wanted to shop some more and I remembered how much I had enjoyed the maritime shop at the entrance and hoped it was still there. I was on a mission for find something special for Tommy. The shop was not only there, it was bigger and better than I remembered.

Each room was more delightful than the next and I couldn't resist the temptations they held. There was a beautiful clock set into a ship's wheel that was the perfect wedding and housewarming gift for Susan and Eddie. It was a little pricey, but after all, it was for two occasions I told myself. Then I found a baby bracelet, but that wouldn't work because what if it was boy, I thought to myself, so instead I purchased a pewter baby mug that had an area for engraving later. For Sara, I found a silver bracelet with tiny reproductions of scrimshaw delicately set, each with a different design. I knew it wasn't authentic ivory, but it was exquisite and anything but inexpensive. I found a wooden chest with a maritime carving and brass lock for Mike.

For MaryAnn, I purchased a keychain that was actually in the shape of a key. A little giddy, I chuckled to myself with a thought directed to her, "I hope you have a lot of new keys in your life. God knows you deserve them." For Timothy, I found a water coloring kit with designs of fishing vessels and whales, probably far beyond his age, but he would grow into it.

Bob was easy. He and Karyn lived in a house that overlooked the Thames River. What would be more appropriate than a set of binoculars in a leather case? Of course, there were many to choose from and I picked the most expensive. Buying for Karyn was more difficult, but I was determined that today my feelings would not cloud my mission. I found a pair of earrings with peridot stones that would compliment her hazel green eyes. Of course, I opted for the ones with the largest gems.

Still looking for a gift for Tommy, I came across a small wooden box. The lining was velvet and wrapped in flannel inside, was a brass telescope like the kind sailors used on their voyages. How perfect, I thought. I loved it!

Leaving that section, I once again found myself near the back of the store where high on a shelf I found a doll, the most beautiful doll I had ever seen. The blue velvet dress was handmade with ruffles and lace. Her hair was red, her eyes blue and her porcelain face resembled what I thought my mother must have looked like as a child, before her loss of innocence, before her fall from grace, and before I stopped loving her. I didn't care what it cost. I needed to buy it.

Of course, I couldn't forget Jackie. How could I? Especially now, what kind of gift could I give him to let him know how I felt? Unable to decide, I went upstairs where they kept the paintings, prints and books. The photographic images were impressive, but no artwork, I thought. Fingering through the pages of a book on whaling, the idea came to me and I located the perfect book. 'Billy Budd' written by Herman Melville, a classic masterpiece, was the perfect gift for my brother. I read it many times when I was young. It had all the action and power of the same author who wrote "Moby Dick", but without the length. Billy Budd, the main character was so much like Jackie, handsome, slightly effeminate, and tough. Most important was the author himself, so I combined it with a biography of Nathaniel Hawthorne, another New England author from the 1800's that I would give to Bernie when I met him. A little giddy at my own humor, I wondered if either Jack or Bernie would understand the wit; both authors reputed to be secret gay lovers.

Almost ready to check out, I passed an elaborate display of prisms. Before there was electricity, a vessel's deck was limited to oil and kerosene lamps or candles. The deck prism was a clever alternative. The transparent three-dimensional crystal laid flat on the ship's deck and its point would draw in the white light, separating it into a beautiful spectrum of colors. For myself, I chose the Cranberry Deck Prism described as an exact reproduction of Mystic Seaport's last remaining Charles W. Morgan deck prism.

Finally ready to pay for my purchases, I headed to the counter where the sales clerk was holding them for me. The young man had a huge grin when the final total came up on the register, $1,248.37. I handed him my platinum American Express card, secretly hoping he was getting a commission and told him I would be in the café while he packaged everything for me. The smells coming from the bakery were tempting me from the time I entered the shop and I could resist the temptations no longer.

Stepping to the counter, everything tantalized my taste buds and I couldn't make up my mind. Seeing the dilemma, the girl behind the counter said, "May I suggest a 'mug-up' and a Joe Frogger?"

"Absolutely!" I responded, remembering the choice from earlier days. A 'mug-up' was the mariner's nickname for a coffee break. Joe Froggers are delectable molasses cookies the size of a salad plate that the whalers stored in barrels and brought to sea because they stayed moist and fresh the entire time.

Leaving the Seaport, I made my way to the downtown area of Mystic, window-shopping on the main street, and then standing on the drawbridge just gazing at the Mystic River, daydreaming and remembering happier times. The saltwater smell and hominess of the small town brought a peace to my soul that I hadn't felt in years. Where did it all go wrong? If only Joey lived, but he didn't and it was time to face my demons and stop running, but I didn't know how.

CHAPTER
16

Mike pulled into the driveway as I was taking the packages out of the trunk. "Hey, Ms. Mahoney," he greeted me.

"Call me Annie, Mike," I told him. "Everyone else does."

"Okay, Annie, it is. Do you need some help? Looks like you've been on quite a shopping spree."

"Thanks, but be careful with this one. It's fragile," I said, handing him the large box with the clock. "What's that you've got?"

"It's just a little something sweet for Mrs. Mahoney. They had bread pudding at the Center today and I know she likes it. Can you carry it in while I've got the box?"

"Sure, not a problem, you really do spoil her. That's nice of you, Mike."

"She's a nice lady and it must be pretty awful being in her condition. I can't imagine," he said sincerely.

At that moment, Sara opened the front door for us, greeting Mike with a big smile and kiss. Then to me, she said, "Your cell phone has been ringing off the hook all day. Did you forget it?"

Until now, I hadn't even thought about it, but in my rush to leave this morning, I must have. "Do you know who was calling?"

"No, it was in your room, but I talked to Mom earlier and she said she tried to call you a couple of times. She wants you and Uncle Jack to go over there for dinner tomorrow night."

"That sounds good; I'll call her back when I get settled. I'll go upstairs now and see who else called," and then jokingly added, "No, peeking in the bags."

"That's no fun," she teased back.

Sara was right; Karyn left a couple voice messages about dinner in her characteristically serious tone of voice. "Another fun time," I thought sarcastically. Listening to the rest of the messages, I missed a dentist appointment, my broker confirmed a stock trade and a print I had framed was finished and ready for pick up.

Then Jackie's voice, "Hey, Sis....it's Jack. If you get this, why don't you meet Bernie and me for dinner around seven at the Outback Steak House? Get off on Frontage Road and the restaurant is right next to our hotel. Dinner and drinks are on me tonight! Call me back to confirm. Love ya!"

Not getting him on redial, I left him a message, "Sounds, great; see you there at seven. If you're buying, I'm starving and very thirsty!" It was already five-thirty, so I quickly cleaned up before going back downstairs. When I did, Sara was serving dinner to my mother who was already sitting at the kitchen table eating a small salad.

"Sara, I'm meeting Uncle Jack for dinner tonight, so I won't be around. I hope you didn't' have anything planned," I said looking around, but didn't see anything else cooking.

"No, that's fine. We were just going to order pizza after Nana goes to bed and have a movie night. We'd love for you to join us, but you'll probably have more fun with Uncle Jack." I had the distinct impression that she was glad that I was leaving. She and Mike probably wanted to be alone.

"Well, before I go, I have a little something for each of you and handed them their gifts.

Sara unwrapped hers first and went on and on about the scrimshaw bracelet, examining each of the designs closely. She sincerely seemed to love it, so I was pleased with my choice of gift. I helped her with the clasp so she could wear it while Mike opened his gift.

Mike seemed genuinely surprised to get a gift from me. For a split second, I thought I detected moisture in his eyes, but he quickly turned away. When he came back around, it was gone, but he studied the chest and held it like it was the first gift anyone had ever given him. "Why did you do this? It's so expensive." He said. "I'm not family."

"I just wanted to, Mike. It's not much, really it's not and I hope you like it," I told him trying to play down the cost, but it was obvious he knew the value of it. Then trying to lighten the moment, I crinkled my nose and not so seriously said, "As for being family, I think you've been around a whole lot more than I have lately!" It brought a laugh out of both of them.

After the salad, Mom didn't eat much else and pushed her plate away; then looking directly at Mike, she said, "Treat, I want a treat."

"How about eating a little more dinner first? At least eat the green beans, Nana. You like green beans," Sara told her.

The response to Sara was simply, "Treat, I want a treat."

Sara just shrugged her shoulders looking defeated and said to Mike, "You've created a monster! At least she ate her salad, I guess it is okay, but seriously Mike, all these sweets aren't good for her and that's all she wants now."

"I can't help it, she's a special lady and besides, the bread pudding is made with artificial sweetener, so it's okay." I knew he was lying.

"Mom," I interrupted. "I have a present for you, too. Would you like a present?" She didn't answer, just looked at me with her blank stare. I set the box on the table in front of her and I carefully removed the doll from the tissue delicately wrapped around it. Her face immediately lit up and she reached out to take the doll from me, the glaze in her eyes replaced with an overflow of tears. Instinctively, she cradled it in her arms, tenderly caressing its cheeks with her one free hand; the droplets from her eyes falling like wet jewels onto the blue velvet dress. In silence, the three of us watched her as she got up from the table, walked into the den and sat down in the antique rocking chair near the window. Slowly and methodically, she rocked the doll and softly started to hum an old familiar Irish lullaby that I only heard from her.

In that moment, her reality was the unreal, but the peace it brought to her was unexplainable. Who knew which of her children she was holding. Was it Karyn, Jackie, me? I would never know and at that moment, it didn't matter because on her face, she wore the love of the mother I once adored, not the scorn of the woman who betrayed me. Unfortunately, I couldn't go beyond the latter.

CHAPTER
17

Jack and Bernie were already at the bar when I arrived at the restaurant. Before they noticed me, I was able to watch them discreetly for a minute or so. This was awkward for me and I didn't know what to expect. Would they be holding hands? How would I react? Telling myself I loved my brother regardless of this newly revealed fact about him was one thing, but meeting his partner and being involved in their lives was quite another. The word nervous doesn't come close to what I was feeling.

Sitting at the bar, they looked like two executives who stopped for a cold beer after a long day. Bernie was older and more distinguished looking. He was attractive and more masculine than I expected, but then what were my expectations?

Jackie was the first to see me and motioned for me to join them at the bar. He immediately introduced me to Bernie who was already standing to meet me. He was taller than I remembered from the brief and shocking encounter that nearly sent me over the edge.

"Annie, I'd like you to meet Dr. Bernard Schneider," Jackie said introducing him.

Oh, please, call me Bernie. Jack is being a little too formal about this. All that doctor stuff is back at the lab!" He clutched my outstretched hand in a strong grip.

"It's nice to meet you, Bernie. I really am sorry about the other day, I was...," but I didn't get the chance to finish my sentence.

"Not to worry; Jack told me everything and it is all good. Let's get off to a new beginning starting with a wonderful time tonight." It was difficult not to like him and I could tell by the look on Jackie's face that he was also a little nervous and hoping this went well.

The night did go well. After a couple of drinks at the bar, I lived up to my promise of being hungry, ordering a delectable medium rare rib eye steak with the works that followed an assortment of appetizers, including the restaurant's signature fried onion. Bernie was quite the wine connoisseur and with no effort, the three of us drank two bottles.

Perhaps it was the over indulgence of wine, or just his personality, but Bernie had no shortage of words and seemed to love talking about himself and his accomplishments. He held a doctorate in biotechnology and worked for Merrimack Pharmaceuticals, Inc. in Cambridge. Currently, he was involved in the development of a new cancer drug, the research financed by a new consortium of investors. I asked him if he ever worked for our local pharmaceutical company, Pfizer, and he said he did not, however he did have the opportunity occasionally to meet several of the researchers. He explained that their work bound them in a strong fellowship with a common goal. Despite the severe competition between large corporations to be the first to register a new drug, scientists relied heavily on each other's research.

Over dessert, the conversation led into the subject of Karyn. Apparently, Jackie had filled Bernie in on the details and the idea he had to obtain DNA from Mr. Fontinelli. Bernie was all for it, but reminded us that asking Bob to involve his coworkers to run the tests was not only unethical, but would put their jobs in jeopardy as well as his own.

"So what do we do?" I asked him. "It's not like there's a do-it-yourself kit at the convenience store."

"Well, actually there is," he corrected me. "Home DNA & Paternity testing has been around for a while now. It's used all the time to verify paternal, maternal and sibling relationships. You can order a kit online for under a hundred dollars. It's discreet and confidential and you won't jeopardize anyone's job along the way. The only drawback is that it takes about a week or two to get the results. If you want, I'll get the information and Jack can order one." Both Jackie and I shook our heads in approval.

"Okay, I hate to be a party pooper," said Jackie, "but we're leaving early in the morning for New York City. We'll be gone for two nights and then back sometime Monday afternoon."

"Oh, I thought we were meeting at Karyn's tomorrow night for dinner," I said rather confused.

"No, I'm afraid I blew her off," he smirked devilishly. "Bernie and I already had this weekend planned and given the choice between an evening of doom and gloom, and a couple of days of fun, I choose the latter."

"I'm jealous," I mocked and then continued, "but if my world falls apart, where do I find you?"

"We have reservations at the Doubletree near Times Square and, Annie, your world doesn't have to fall apart for you to join us. We'd love to have a visit from you." Bernie made a strong attempt to sound sincere, but somehow I didn't believe him.

"Oh, I almost forgot," I said. "Before I go, I have a little something for each of you." I took the two books out of my handbag and gave them each theirs. "I was at the Seaport store today and picked these up for you."

"I never read this," Jackie said, "but I will now. Thanks, Annie; that really was thoughtful of you. I always like a good book."

Bernie, looking at Jackie's novel and then to his own started laughing and said, "And let me add, Jack, that she put a great deal of thought into her choices," and then to me, "Well, done, my dear...well done!"

On the way back to the house, my thoughts were on the relaxing and wonderful evening. I was glad for the company and at least the hard part of meeting Bernie was out of the way. He made it easy to accept him and I was relieved that they were discreet about their relationship, but at the same time, I was also glad that it was now out in the open. I had always been secure in my own sexual preferences and couldn't imagine what it could be like for them.

Mike's car was still there when I pulled into the driveway; not expecting to see all the lights, I was surprised to see every room on the first floor lit up. Before I even opened the front door, I could hear crying coming from the middle of the house. Sara was yelling, "I can't believe you did this. How could you do this?" She and Mike must be arguing, I thought.

Then I heard Mike say quietly, "It's not her fault, Sara. She can't help herself. Annie will understand, she will, I'm sure."

"Understand what?" I interrupted them as I walked into the kitchen. My mother was sitting at the kitchen table crying. Mike was trying to spoon feed her some bread pudding and she didn't want it.

On the table were long strands of red string clumped together in a tangled mess. Next to them was a pile of blue velvet and white lace cloth, ripped into shreds. Sara was holding what was left of the doll I had given my mother. "Look at what she did! She ruined it! I only left her alone for thirty minutes and she destroyed it. I'm so sorry, Aunt Annie. I'm so sorry; I'll pay you back for it."

At first, I didn't know what to say, and then something caught my eye. Sara, let me see the doll for a minute. It took a couple of seconds before it sunk in, but then I realized what my mother had done. It wasn't her intention to destroy the doll; she simply changed the gender by cutting the hair and making a feeble attempt to alter the dress to pants. I started to laugh, but Sara and Mike were clueless.

"She wanted a baby boy, that's all. I should have gotten her a boy doll." Well, at least I had my answer, I thought. She was rocking Jackie and I was fine with that notion. I handed the doll back to my mother; grasping it from me, she cradled him tightly, locking her eyes with mine. Briefly, I glimpsed some clarity as she stared at me, but there was also something else. I sensed sadness, fear, and an unknown emotion that I couldn't identify; then the blank stare returned.

Saying goodnight, I simply turned around and walked up the stairs to bed, to another night of demons terrorizing my sleep. Cats, crying and squealing, so loud my head hurt. Why couldn't I see them? Where were they hiding? Why couldn't I get away from them?

CHAPTER
18

New York City

Arriving at the Doubletree a little early, the front desk had a message for Sal from Theresa. She spent the day shopping and was in a traffic delay. Cursing to himself, he headed for the bar to wait for her. If she had left a message on his cell phone, he would have spent more time with Vinnie before coming over here, but he quickly remembered that she didn't dare call him on his cell. They had all the money in the world and it didn't make up for the unfairness of life.

Sipping a cold beer, he thought about Niki, how much he missed her and the kids. He had a good life in Italy, but these business trips to the States made him melancholy. Seeing Theresa made it worse. She was his mirror image, his twin, and what injustices had they been forced to suffer and why? Continents away from each other, they were forced to live as strangers and all for what? His own wife didn't know of her existence and for that, he felt ashamed. She was his sister, not his lover and yet, the truth would destroy too many lives. He could not involve Niki.

He ordered another beer, thinking of the future. Sooner, or later, the secret would surface. It had to. They weren't living in the eighteenth century; this world of global communication left nothing clandestine. If someone sought deep enough, the truth would be revealed and then what? Niki would leave him for sure, taking his sons and beautiful little Andrianna. The thought of it was unbearable; and what about Vinnie, what would he think? Would he lose him, too? It would all be nothing, wouldn't it?

"Excuse me, but I have ask," the voice said taking him away from his thoughts. "Are you with Onyx Corporation?"

"Yes, I am," answered Sal, noting that the man looked vaguely familiar.

"I thought I recognized you. It's been a while, probably a couple of years, but we met at a pharmaceutical convention in Rome. Let me reintroduce myself. I'm Dr. Bernard Schneider, Bernie, with Merrimack Pharmaceuticals. What brings you to the States, or are you living here now?"

"No, I still live in Palermo. Onyx has a headquarters here, so I'm on business. What about you?" Sal asked.

"I'm just in the City for a couple of days for a little recreation, but I live in Cambridge. Forgive me, but I don't remember your name," Bernie said.

"Sal Fiore...my name is Sal Fiore," Sal said shaking his hand. "I'm actually waiting for someone."

"Oh, I am, too. He was on the phone and I was too thirsty to wait. While we're both waiting, can I buy you a beer?"

Sal only hesitated briefly before he said, "You bet; the first two were great and I'm ready for another!" He was thankful for the disruption that broke his thoughts.

For near an hour they drank beer and caught each other up on all that was happening in their respective worlds of employment. Sal was fascinated listening to Bernie talk about the breakthroughs on the horizon, a result of cancer research and vice versa; Bernie was intrigued with the global interaction of Onyx and Sal's involvement in the sales of the newly registered pharmaceuticals. Neither of them noticed Theresa approach.

"Hey, there," she said giving Sal a hug. "Sorry, I'm late, but I got a little carried away shopping and then there was an accident right in front of my cab. Would you believe, the meter kept ticking away and I had to pay for it?"

Bernie was astounded at the resemblance between Sal and Theresa. He had just presumed, when Sal hadn't been specific that the 'someone' he was waiting for was his wife, or partner, taking into consideration the majority of clientele currently registered at the hotel. He held his hand out to greet her, but was lost for words.

"Hi, I'm Theresa Fontinelli," she said. Sal had an uneasy feeling, but was sure the name wouldn't mean anything to Bernie. It didn't.

"I'm Bernie Schneider. It's a pleasure to meet you," was all he said.

With no further conversation, Sal made his apologies and excused himself and Theresa saying they had plans. He told Bernie he hoped they would meet up again, but made no offer to leave a means to contact him.

As soon as they were outside, Sal chastised Theresa for giving Bernie her last name. "What were you thinking?" He asked. "What if he recognized the name?"

"You're too damned paranoid! No one knows who we are and besides that, no one cares anymore!" She was angry and continued, "We've got to talk about this! He's dying and he wants to see you!"

"No!" He shouted at her. "We've come this far and I will not put my family in jeopardy. I will never let them know!"

"It's ending! Can't you see that? When he's dead, it's all over and nobody cares anymore. You can come home and we can be a family again!"

"I have a family, Theresa! I have a new life and I like that new life. I don't want to lose it. Please," he was begging her, "Don't take that from me. Don't....please don't!"

"Just come see him and bring Vinnie. At least he deserves that and then you can go back to your pretty little wife and spoiled brats!" Her face was flush and she was crying.

"No, Theresa...Stop it!" His anger was a reflection of hers. "You know I can't and I will never bring Vinnie! Never!" he shouted, "Never!"

"Then why did you come here? Why did you agree to see me? Was it just to open old wounds? How cruel you are!"

"I came because you said you needed to see me. Was this just a ploy to get me back here again, so you could manipulate me? Talk about being cruel; you're cruel! Why did you deceive me?" He was furious now.

"I didn't deceive you. I just thought if you went to see him, we could all work it out before he died. He just wants to see you one more time. He wants to see his grandson!"

"I can't do it, Theresa," he said more calmly. "I just can't do it. There was another way it could have done, but he was too selfish and chose to destroy all he loved rather than share it. Now, it's too late."

"It wasn't him. You know it wasn't his plan. It was Gino's!"

"I'm so sorry, Theresa. I just can't," and she knew she had lost.

CHAPTER
19

The early evening air, crisp and brittle, snapped across me as I climbed the hill toward the Fort Griswold Battlefield. Karyn and Bob lived near the state park, so I decided to take advantage of the weather and walk the short distance to their house for dinner. The recent time change allowed me some extra time to stroll around the grounds and reminisce. The fort was a safe haven for me as a child and as soon as I reached it, I felt the soothing serenity embrace me like a warm glove.

As it had since erected in the early 1800's, the historic granite Groton Monument, the oldest of its kind in the country, stood tall and proud overlooking the Thames River. I didn't have to try the door to know a lock on it prevented access; it wasn't yet Memorial Day and besides, I had no desire to climb its 166 steps to the top. Just the thought of it invoked the unpleasant memory of leg cramps.

For the first time since I had come to Groton, I took out my camera, snapping photos of the Spanish-American War Cannon, the Civil War Memorial and the Veteran's War Memorial. The Memorial Gates were just as I remembered and, of course, it was difficult not to stop and reflect at the site where a British officer stabbed Colonel William Ledyard with his own sword as he surrendered.

The damp, dank and musty odors emerging from the small tunnel referred to as the salle port met my nose long before I entered it. Stooping down to avoid its low ceiling, I passed quickly through to the River Battery. It was breathtaking. Sprawling before me was the sacred ground of the battlefield, its soil consecrated with the blood of the soldiers who perished there. The hush in the wind rising from the river whispered in prayer to the fallen.

In the silence, there were no sounds of cannons, no shouts of anger or screams from men dying; instead, I heard the laughter of children, the giggles and sounds of happy hearts running and playing in the park. I closed my eyes to the cacophony and saw the young revelers on the battlefield chasing each other with sticks transformed into swords and cardboard turned into armor. Joey was in the group and we were fighting side-by-side, always side-by-side. I wondered how he could have been so different from his family.

The Fontinelli family was a dynasty three generations native to the area. Vincenzo Fontinelli came to America with his child bride, Elena, and the clothes on their backs. Shortly after their entrance through Ellis Island, Vincenzo came to the realization that without an education, to succeed, he would have to be strong, wise, and powerful, but he didn't yet know how to get there. He worked hard to scrape up a pittance for rent to live in a rat-infested apartment near a factory in New London. Elena gave birth to twin boys, Angelo and Dominick during their first winter in the new world. One night, the heat in the small apartment gave out and they were freezing. When Vincenzo asked the property owner if he could delay the rent payment a week to buy fuel for the furnace, he scoffed and it was then Vincenzo decided that he would no longer be the tenant. He would be the landowner, a powerful and wealthy proprietor.

With his plan in motion, Vincenzo worked day and night saving every penny to purchase his first property. When he did, it was better than the one that he and Elena were renting, but rather than move into it themselves, they in turn leased it out for a higher rent than what they were paying for theirs. Three more times they did this, each time buying a better and better property. Only then did they allow themselves the luxury of living in their cheapest unit. When winter came and his tenants asked for an extension of rent payment, he did so cheerily and willingly, as they signed his note promising to pay him interest. At every opportunity, he bought more and more property, expanding to commercial sites as well as residential, owning buildings and land throughout Connecticut and Rhode Island. Soon, his reputation for being a kind and approachable property owner and lender gave way to stories of ruthless, unforgiving loan sharking and collection methods. He was both feared and respected, as he became the man he wanted to be, a powerful and wealthy man. He wanted his sons to follow his footsteps and he succeeded, as they became even more callous, coldblooded and stronger predators to the weak than he was himself.

Unlike Vincenzo who loved his family if no one else, his sons Dominick and Angelo sired offspring, but were far too busy with their trophy wives to raise them, so the third generation ultimately became the product of nannies and daycare and so it was with Joey. The Fontinelli family spent winters in Florida and summers in one of their several cottages in Groton Long Point or Misquamicut Beach, only minutes away from the enormous family compound in Watch Hill, Rhode Island. Young children were not welcome, so Joey and his siblings spent their time with a caring Italian caregiver in Groton, rumored to be one of Dominick's many mistresses. They attended Sacred Heart; the only parochial school in Groton and because of the love and education he received outside his own family, Joey was untainted and not yet corrupted right up to the time of the accident.

I wanted to stay here and remember the good times; there were so many of them. Then, like the touch of a soft tissue, the wind gently dried my eyes when they opened and the images and sounds of my childhood were gone; only the barren battlefield lay before me in harmony with the past and the present. It was peaceful.

It was also time to go to Karyn and Bob's, so reluctantly, I left the refuge and walked the short distance to their three-story house a block away where Tommy was waiting for me on the porch.

CHAPTER
20

H i, Aunt Annie," Tommy yelled excitedly as I approached, and then with his voice escalating, "Mommy was crying and Daddy yelled at her. She cried a lot, but she's better now because Daddy yelled at her and told her to stop crying." In addition to the noticeable facial characteristics of Down Syndrome, Tommy suffered a hearing loss. He was not wearing his hearing aids.

Changing the subject, I said, "I'm so glad to see you Tommy. How was work today?" To myself, I was hoping I didn't come at a bad time.

"I like work. Mommy was crying. She's better now." He was upset, but before the conversation went any farther, Karyn opened the door. She had freshly applied makeup, hair combed and recently pressed clothes, but her eyes now dry were red and the lids swollen. I knew the look well.

"Is everything alright? If this is a bad time, we can have dinner another day," I told her.

"No, it's fine," was all she said and led me into the house.

Bob was sitting on the couch watching the news and didn't bother to get up when I walked into the room. A slight nod of his head was the only acknowledgement that he even knew I was there, his eyes remaining focused on the television.

Tommy rushed in behind us, loudly blurting out, "Mommy, don't cry anymore, please, don't cry anymore!"

Like an explosion had gone off, Bob jumped from his seat and barked, as I'd never heard him before, "Damn it, Tommy! I told you to go to your room and leave us alone. Now just get out of here!"

"Stop it, Bob! It's not his fault, he's just upset!" Karyn was crying again, and then to me, "I'm so sorry, Annie."

Caught in such an awkward moment, I could hardly utter the words and without looking at either of them, I quietly said, "I'll go and we can do this another time," and I turned to leave.

"No, don't go!" Bob snapped. "We need to get this bullshit put to rest, so we can go on with our lives." Then to Tommy, more calmly, he said, "I'm sorry, Tommy Boy. Daddy's had a bad day and I need to talk to Mommy and Aunt Annie. Please go to your room and play your video game until dinner. Okay?"

"But," Tommy started to object and then Karyn stepped in.

"Do as Daddy says, Tommy, the grown-ups need to talk. I'll call you for dinner in a little while." Reluctantly, he climbed the stairs to his room as Bob turned off the television and motioned for Karyn and me to sit down.

"Annie, I'm sorry you had to walk into this tonight, but maybe you can put some sense into your sister because I sure can't!" He glared at Karyn while he spoke.

"It's the only way, Bob! I have to know," Karyn's eyes were begging with him while I just sat there in silence and listened.

"Let me see if I have this right, Karyn. You want to put us at risk, put my job on the line and send your sister into the pit of hell, all because you want to verify what you already know is true. Oh, and let's not forget to mention the total humiliation to this entire family when it gets out that you are Angelo Fontinelli's daughter!"

"Bob, that's not fair! I don't know for sure. I can't believe it!"

"Yes, you do, Karyn! You saw the birth certificate. You know it's real and I think you've always known. God, I knew the day I met your parents and saw the color of their eyes. I just presumed that they adopted you and it didn't matter to me. Now it even makes sense about Sara and Susan. There's no history of twins in

Hidden Mirrors

either of our families. Angelo and Dominick were twins, for God's sake. Don't you understand? None of it matters. It didn't matter then and it doesn't matter now!"

"It matters to me, Bob! It matters to me!" I could only listen as they argued.

"How can you ask your sister to get involved with that family again? Gino Fontinelli was the devil himself and by the grace of God, he's dead and buried. Leave him there!"

"Dominick is alive, Bob. If I just had his ...," but Bob didn't let her finish.

"His DNA, yes, I know! Then I can put my job on the line to have it checked for you. No way, Karyn, no way will I do that!"

Not knowing where I was going with this, I interrupted at this point, "You don't have to do anything, Bob. We can use a paternity kit."

"So you're willing to do this? Is that what I'm hearing Annie? You're willing to meet with Dominick and ask him for his DNA, just like that?" Now he was glaring at me.

"Well, no," I stammered, "I didn't say I would agree to meet with him, I just said there are paternity kits that can be used."

I still didn't know where this was going and looking at Karyn, I saw a glimmer of hope in her eyes because she thought I was defending her. I wasn't. There was no way I was willing to meet with Dominick Fontinelli or any other member of the notorious breed.

"Annie, all we need is some DNA, that's all." She was pushing hard.

"What would you like her to do, Karyn? We don't even know where the man is and if we did, should she just knock on the front door and ask if she can swab his mouth? Get real, will you?" Bob's face was crimson, his voice taught and strained. I had never seen him like this before.

"He's right, Karyn. I can't possibly think of a way to get close to the man and if he knew for one minute that it was me, I'd be ousted out like the morning garbage."

Karyn was so serious and persistent. "I did an internet search for news on him and found out that he has been in and out of the Dana-Farber/Harvard Cancer Center in Boston. If he is really that sick, we may not have much time."

Again, Bob interjected, "Okay, Karyn, so now you want her to march into the hospital and do what, pretend she's a nurse? You have to put this to rest. It's not going to work! I won't allow it!"

"You won't what? Are you saying you won't allow it? Who the hell are you to...," I didn't allow her to finish.

"Karyn, you have to calm down!" Now I was shouting. "I can't just walk into a hospital room and start touching him. What if there's family there? Don't you think there might be a nurse or two in the vicinity? What will the man himself do? Do you think he will just invite me in for a cup of tea and nice conversation? This whole thing is insane."

Karyn's face suddenly lit up and she said exuberantly, "Forget about the hospital because I have a better idea. Annie, you're a photographer. We can set it up so he thinks you are doing a story on him and you're there to take some photos for your article. Everything I've ever read about him says he's an egomaniac. He'll jump at the attention, especially if he knows he's really sick."

"Don't you think a man of this stature will have her checked out before he invites her into his home? He will recognize the name, Annie Mahoney, right away and it will be a total disaster. It will never work," Bob objected.

"Actually, my pseudonym is still Anne Daley. I never changed it after the divorce to my second husband because my career was taking off and I was afraid my work would be unrecognizable under a different name. My photos are all marked with a simple "AD". Even the book I just published, I authored under that penname and it's a technical textbook, so there's nothing personal in it, not even a photo of me on the book jacket. I've moved so many times and in twenty years, my last name has been Mahoney, Fontinelli, Daley, Harrison, and now Mahoney again. Even I can't keep up with it sometimes."   Bob threw his arms up as if in defeat and Karyn took my comments as a willingness to do this for her, so I quickly added, "It's irrelevant though because I'm still not going to do this, Karyn."

"Even you said it, Annie, he'll never figure out who you are." She was clearly excited and feeling back in control.

"What if he does recognize me?" I was still not about to give in to this bizarre, madcap request.

"Actually, Annie, it's been twenty years and we all change in that time and I thought you never actually met him face to face. If anything, he probably saw a photo of you lying around. With an adequate disguise and your credentials, you could probably get away with it." I hoped Bob was serious with these comments and then speaking directly to Karyn, "Let me ask you this, Sweetheart; if Annie does this and we can prove that Gino was your father, where will it go from there? What will you do with the information? Surely, you can't let the Fontinelli family know. That's not your intention, is it?"

"Of course not, Bob! I just need to know for myself. Once I know for sure, it's over, I promise. She can just get a hair sample and leave."

I interrupted, "I haven't agreed to this, you know. Angelo may, or may not, be your father Karyn. Anyway, he's dead; you'll never have the displeasure of meeting him, but Dominick was my living hell in case either of you have forgotten. Please don't just assume that I am willing to walk into my hellish past and face this monster under any circumstances. That best news I heard tonight is that he is sick and you can believe that my nighttime prayer before closing my eyes this evening will be that he suffers long and brutally. Besides, I should have been heading south two days ago. I can't believe I'm still here." I bit my lip and held back the words I really wanted to say to Karyn. My gut yearned to tell her how she ruined my life and now had the audacity to ask me to help her. What had she done to help me?

"Please, Annie, now I am asking you to do it for me." Was this really Bob saying this? His anger drained away and he no longer carried the look of defeat, just a resolve to put it all to rest. "Karyn and I are too emotionally involved at this point and our faces are too familiar locally, or we would do it ourselves. As a favor to me, I am asking you to help us find the truth, so we can all get on with our lives and put it behind us. Please, Annie, do it for me, for Sara, for Susan, for Tommy, and for your sister; your only sister. Then you can run away, go back to your life, whatever and wherever that may be. We'll never ask you for anything ever again. You have my word."

"Oh, God," I moaned. "I'll do it." Karyn cried and Bob put his arms around me and held me in a brotherly embrace.

"Can I come out now?" The voice came from the top of stairs, "I'm hungry!"

"Yes, Tommy Boy," Bob chuckled. "We're all hungry, come down and we'll eat."

"I made roast beef tonight," Karyn said to me, "Rare, just like you like it."

"Too bad Jackie isn't here," I responded.

"Yes, Jackie, just Jackie would be nice to have for dinner," Karyn said, without hiding the sarcastic reference about Bernie.

Holding back the dirtiest look of my imagination, I thought to myself, "Well, Karyn, the bitch is back!"

No one mentioned the plan the remainder of the evening and after dinner, I brought out the gifts I had for them. Karyn, still emotional held her earrings for the longest time before putting them on. She sincerely appeared to appreciate them and Bob loved the binoculars. I teased him about checking out the neighbors, especially the women.

The best of all, however, was Tommy! Down Syndrome often leaves its mark with narrow upward slanted eyes, but when he opened the wooden box, and unwrapped the telescope within, those eyes rounded wider than I thought possible. He was remarkable and the perfect child, the perfect nephew, and in my heart, I knew I made the right decision both with the gift and to meet Dominick. I would do it for Tommy.

Bob offered to drive me home, but it was such a short distance and still a beautiful evening, that I decided to walk. Mentally, I felt drained and welcomed the night air, but I still had one more question before I left.

"Karyn, did we have a cat when we were children?"

"No, never, Dad was allergic to them. Why do you ask?"

"No reason, I was just wondering. Thanks for the dinner. The roast was delicious and cooked to perfection. I'll talk to you tomorrow." With that said, I left.

CHAPTER
21

S al spent the greater part of his first week in the city dealing with his schedule at Onyx Corporation, Vinnie and Theresa leaving little time for anything else. His sister was persistent to the point of annoyance that he visit his father, but he held fast fearing that the charade would be discovered and those he loved would walk out on him forever. He couldn't bear it. His wife meant everything to him. After all, she was the one who pulled it all together for him and gave him the home and family he desperately craved at a time when he was alone and isolated from all he knew.

He called Niki every day, but more than the miles spanning between them he felt a different kind of distance and couldn't figure out why. Little did he know that she was making attempt after attempt to reach the detective she hired, but to no avail. She checked her bank records, he cashed the deposit check payable to him, but his office didn't answer and on the last few tries, all she heard was a recording telling her that his voicemail was full. Hiring a detective was new to her and she did her homework discreetly, checking out his reputation and the length of time he was in business. She was positive he was legitimate and confident that he would get to the truth about Theresa, but now he was missing for what felt like weeks, or was it months? Afraid to inquire with the police, or even his neighbors, she resolved herself to the fact he swindled her until she heard on the news that he met his fate while on holiday. The details were sparse, but the report stated that his automobile veered out of control and he crashed into a trench. He left no family behind. Perhaps it was fate, she told herself, and perhaps there was a reasonable explanation for the text message from Theresa. She decided to wait until Sal returned to ask him. Until then, she just worried a little less knowing that his brother, their son, Vinnie, was with him and Sal would certainly not stray while in his company.

In the meantime, Vinnie was having the time of his life, enjoying every aspect of the city, including some his father forbade. Already he made a couple of friends while touring the school and much to his surprise, Sal agreed to let him spend time with them, so the last couple of days were given to drinking beer, smoking a little marijuana and meeting girls. Vinnie was in heaven, with the mere thought that living here permanently was the singular thing to make him happier and that was most definitely in his near future. The one and only guilt he felt was a slight twinge that his father was working so many hours, both day and night, but after all, this was a business trip for him and Vinnie was lucky to be there.

On this particular night, the meeting at Onyx ran over, so Sal met Theresa a little later than usual for dinner. Theresa insisted that they take a cab to Greenwich Village; she wanted to see a different part of the city, so Sal agreed. Neither of them was familiar with the area, so they relied on the taxi driver who drove around several blocks before suggesting they get out on 2nd Avenue where there were many restaurants, both moderate and expensive. It was a clear evening and perfect for walking, so they took time to stroll the avenue, people watching and enjoying the company of each other. Pausing in front of Candela Candela, Sal argued that he didn't come all the way from Italy to eat Italian food, but Theresa argued otherwise telling him it was an Italian-Cuban restaurant. They had two distinctive chefs, one from Italy and one from Cuba, so the dishes created were uniquely tropical and Mediterranean. How could he argue with that? Besides, they advertised a Mojito Bar, so it had to be good! The choice was an excellent one and they spent the evening reminiscent of childhood times and she caught him up on everything and everyone she could think of, intentionally avoiding any conversation of their father. He shared with her the extensive photo gallery he kept on his phone, bragging about his three sons and precious little Andrianna. There were several pictures of Niki and Theresa watched sadly, as he beamed when he spoke of her. She was happy for him, but it was heartrending not to share in the life of her twin, and all because of what and because of whom? Life was cruel to them. They had to suffer the sins of another, unspoken sins not known to them. It was unfair, yet they obeyed.

Greenwich Village has a population of approximately 1900 people with the number of families actually living in the village only around 500, most of which were home for the evening. Not yet, the season, however, the streets were moderately bustling with tourists. The odds of seeing a familiar face were not worth the wager to a betting man. Known for its Bohemian lifestyle, the Village is a fascinating and interesting place to visit at any age, thus, it was also on Vinnie's list of places to visit. Unbeknownst to Sal, who thought Vinnie was attending a production on Broadway, the older model taxi pulled to the curb and out stepped three young men already semi-intoxicated and bound for a good time.

Stepping out of the car, Vinnie was no more than twenty feet from Sal and Theresa, neither of whom saw him. Sal had his arm around his sister's shoulder, they were laughing and he was hailing a cab of their own. Vinnie stopped dead in his tracks when he saw his father, his father with his arm around a woman not his mother.

"Hey, move," said one of his companions, trying to get out of the cab behind him. "I can't walk through a door!"

"Zitto!" Vinnie snapped back in Italian. "Shut up!"

"Don't cop an attitude, asshole! We're just trying to get out and your share is $12.00," the young man said motioning for Vinnie to pay the driver. Vinnie just stood there, his feet frozen.

"Listen, Pal," the driver yelled to him. "You heard your friend, you owe me twelve bucks!"

Vinnie shouted out to Sal, "Attenzione, Papa! Attenzione!"

"Pay up, or I call the cops!" Vinnie pulled out his wallet and paid the driver, but when he turned back to the street, Sal's cab pulled away.

Confused and angry, assuming something that wasn't real, Vinnie broke into a run chasing after them not noticing that his wallet dropped to the ground, only seeing that the taxi quickly turned down another street and drove out of sight. Crazed, he ran into the street trying to catch them; he put himself into the direct path of another taxi. The blunt force knocked him unconscious, his body caught under the front wheels, his blood running profusely across the pavement. He saw nothing and he heard nothing, nor did Sal and Theresa as they drove away. Bystanders gathered, some shouting for help, others just curious wondering if he would die while they watched. His companions didn't see the accident occur around the corner from them, but at the sound of sirens, they jumped back into the cab, leaving the scene in fear of an arrest for underage drinking and possession. An emergency vehicle arrived quickly and transported Vinnie to the nearest trauma center, Bellevue Hospital, but it was two miles away and the traffic congested. The EMT's worked desperately to control the bleeding and keep the life of the unidentified young man from ebbing away.

Crashing through the Emergency Room doors, three members of the hospital staff met the gurney that transported their newest John Doe, a young white male in his early twenties with black hair and internal hemorrhaging.

CHAPTER
22

Lying in the hospital bed with poison dripping into his arms, staring at the ceiling, left little for him to do except think about his life. Already, he was here for four days and not one visitor. Granted, Boston was a good distance away, but out of three children, not one of them saw fit to check on him. His daughter would be there, but she had some urgent business and needed to be out of town for a while which was probably for the best anyway because she drove him crazy, just as her mother did. His eldest son whom he hadn't seen in years was in California doing God knows what and Dominick had to admit that he didn't really care; he was never much of a family man. His second son lived in Italy, his life dead to him, and there was, of course, the grandchildren he would never meet. For that, he should feel remorse, but he didn't.

His thoughts drifted to his brother. Gino was the strongest twin, both emotionally and physically, and that made it all the more difficult for Dominick to understand why he died first, why his heart just gave out one day. He always thought he would be the first to die, not Gino, but now he was soon to follow. The cancer ate away his insides bit by bit and he was now in a program called Chemo Quality of Life, according to the doctors. He might have beat this, but he was too stubborn to see a doctor until it was too late, blaming his stomach pains on too much wine, too much spice, too much stress; like everything else, he placed the blame elsewhere, refusing to take ownership. Now, he wouldn't live long enough to have a heart attack and die dramatically like his brother, instead he would just shrivel and die, once again the weak one. That disgusted him.

Dominick and Gino never got along and yet, he missed his brother more than ever now. As children, their father set them as rivals at every opportunity. It was Vincenzo's way of making them stronger, more competitive and hungrier for what they wanted. Still, they were mirror images and bonded stronger than their father understood. They had matching goals and when they chose different paths to reach them, they haggled and fought, until Gino won; he always won. Cheating, lying, and bullying each other were a way of life for the two ruffians, but they shared everything and each would die to protect the other and so it was when Gino decided to have his way with the Irish girl.

Years ago, Dominick buried the details of that day in the back of his mind, but the act itself stared the two of them in the face their entire lives. For all the ruthless and uncaring things that each of them had done over the years, this is the one they paid for and they each paid dearly.

Vincenzo played cards at the Italian-American Club every Wednesday evening and he often brought the boys with him, but more often, than not, they chose to skip out, going to the cemetery right up the road to hide out and play amongst the tombstones. It was a game to see who could find the markers with the oldest dates and with every bit of brute strength, they often did their best to uproot and vandalize what they could. At other times, they just sat leaning on a stone and talked about girls, or planned some other trouble to get into. The Catholic Church held a teenage Catechism class at the same time on Wednesdays and each week they watched the same group of girls walking home, so the game began. They waited behind the stoned wall of the cemetery and when the girls passed by, they jumped out and scared them, then laughed as they screamed and ran home. Sometimes, they threw spitballs, even sticks, but every week the girls still passed because it was their only way home. Then one night, they waited patiently, but there was no sound of the girls and they were about to give up, when Gino noticed one of them on the other side of the street. She was walking home by herself, and probably in fear of the weekly abuse, decided to cross the street to keep some distance. Gino would have none of it.

Like a bolt of lightning, he darted across the desolate street and grabbed her before she had a chance to run. Dominick screamed at him, "What are you doing? You're hurting her!"

She kicked and screamed trying to free herself from him, but either no one heard, or no one wanted to get involved because no help came and Gino easily dragged her to the cemetery. Dominick stood back, watching his brother as he tore her clothes, stripping her, stuffing her panties in her mouth to silence her. Like a beast out of control, he punched her and raped her while his Dominick did nothing. She was moaning and whimpering like a pained animal when he got off her and turned to Dominick. "Go ahead, it's your turn," he told him.

Dominick clearly remembered telling his brother that he wouldn't do it, but Gino never accepted refusal, especially from his twin. Dominick gave in and he, too, had his way with her.

When they were finished, Gino kicked her in the ribs while she lay on the ground sneering, "You tell anyone, Bitch, and you're dead! Do you understand me? You're dead!"

Neither of them spoke about the incident after that night, but they stopped joining their father on Wednesdays, choosing to stay at home in New London with their mother. For them, it was over and they would certainly never see her again.

Three months later, however, their father came home, drunk as usual, but a little meaner this time. He called the boys down to the basement and with no explanation, beat the daylights out of each one of them individually until they hovered in the damp corners afraid to ask why. He told them.

One of the card players at the Italian-American Club was also a parishioner at the Catholic Church next door to the Club and that night he shared a very sad story about a young Irish girl, only 16 years old, who was raped and beaten in the cemetery one night while on her way home from Catechism class. He said they are a good family, even if they're Irish and they mind their own business. The father is a cop and never hassles anyone. They are crushed this happened to their only daughter and to make matters worse, she's pregnant and they are mortified.

Vincenzo had a look of anger in his eyes to match the devil himself. Looking at his sons, he snarled through gritted teeth saying half in English and half in Italian, "Questo non è accettabile! Having fun is a good thing, crossing the line is irresponsible, an inappropriate action caught is unacceptable. Il padre è un poliziotto! You little assholes! The father is a cop! Do you hear me? Un poliziotto! Do you think I need trouble from the cops? Is that what you think? You will make this right! Pagherete tutta la tua vita! You will pay your whole life! I mean it, your whole life!"

Vincenzo never told them what he did to make it right and they were too afraid to ask him, but they did hear that the Irish girl married a local man, moved into a house near the river and gave birth to a daughter. Neither of them inquired further.

On their twenty-first birthdays, Vincenzo gave each of them a bank savings passbook showing deposits of hundreds of dollars at a time. He told them that this was their share of the family wealth, that was growing rapidly, and as long as they worked as hard as he did, it would continue to grow. Gino was the first to notice questionable monthly withdrawals made from the account, in the amount of, $500.00 each. It came out on the first of every month. Dominick also had the repetitive transaction.

Gino made the foolish mistake of asking, "What is this monthly withdrawal, Papa?" His father backhanded him across the face and walked away. No further words were necessary; they knew what it was.

After Vincenzo died, the payments continued to go into the offshore account and were delivered to the now Mrs. Mahoney on a monthly basis. Dominick fought hard to focus. He tried to calculate how much money they gave her over the years. One thousand dollars per month for years was a bundle of it. He was too tired to think. He took up Gino's half after his brother passed away, so she continued to receive the $1,000.00 per month. He wondered if the money made a difference in her life; it was just a pittance to him. He couldn't spend what he had in a lifetime, especially now with so little time left.

"That's right," he thought aloud. "So little time left and I'll be damned if I'm going to lie in bed with this shit going in my veins." He was dying and this wasn't going to help him live any longer. Which was worse? Dying alone in a big empty house, or dying lonely with strangers? He rang for the nurse.

She came right away. "Can I help you Mr. Fontinelli? What do you need?"

Thinking to himself, he wondered how many patients wakening from surgery were scared to death by her ugly face. She was too homely for words. To her he demanded, "Take this crap out of my arm, I'm leaving here. Get my clothes and my driver."

"You can't do that, it's important that you...," she started to say before his arrogance cut her off.

"Just do as I say! You do it now or I'll have your job! Do you hear me?" His face twisted viciously, his words spitting out through clenched teeth. She turned and left to do as he asked.

CHAPTER
23

The cell phone felt foreign and cold in my quivering hand. On the table was a telephone number I was unprepared to dial, unwilling to speak with the swine who would answer. I desperately wanted to wait for Jackie to return from New York City, but he called to say he was staying a couple more days. I envied him.

My brother and I spoke at length about the plan Karyn, Bob and I designed and at first he sounded hesitant, but then agreed this would be the best way to get in to see Dominick. This afternoon, I went out and purchased a prepaid telephone so there would be no way for him to trace the number with Caller ID. At least we all agreed on this one thing, hiding my identity was the utmost priority. Too many people met disastrous consequences when confronted with the wrath of the surviving Fontinelli brother and I intended to avoid that at all cost.

Queasiness came over me as I dialed the number, a wrong number. I had to retry. God, I felt sick, but a sense of urgency overcame me and I redialed with a new strength, somehow mustering up the fortitude to obtain what I wanted, a determination to get answers.

A woman answered, "Hello, Mr. Fontinelli's residence, May I help you?"

"Yes, my name is Anne Daley. May I speak with Dominick Fontinelli?" My voice sounded strong, but the vocal cords were taut and the palpitations in my chest beat as if my soul was fighting the devil to get out.

"I'm sorry, but he's resting. I can take a message." She was soft spoken and professional, probably a caretaker I thought.

"Well, I'm in and out of the office, so it would be impossible for him to call me back. What's a good time for me calling him again?"

"He's not a well man, so it's difficult to say when he's resting and whether, or not, he is up to speaking on the phone." It was apparent that she had instructions to screen his calls and I needed to overstep this gatekeeper.

More confident now, I used a firm tone and said, "I'm a freelance photographer and reporter with an assignment to interview Mr. Fontinelli. I am under commission to do an article on him that is of interest to several media outlets, including a well-known national magazine. Of course, if you think he's not interested, I won't waste any more of your time."

"Excuse me, what did you say your name was and who do you work for?" She bit the hook and I knew I had her full attention.

"I'm Anne Daley and I'm freelance. I have the appropriate credentials that are verifiable and I'm willing to give the information to Mr. Fontinelli, but only Mr. Fontinelli."

"Please hold, Ms. Daley, let me see if he is awake."

There was a long silence while I silently prayed, "Oh, please, God, help me with this. Let this be the right thing to do." The anticipation and sheer terror were unbearable.

"This is Dominick Fontinelli," he hissed rather than spoke. "I understand you want to speak to me, so speak."

I inhaled deeply to avoid stuttering and introduced myself again, "I am Anne Daley and I'm a freelance photographer and reporter. I'm commissioned to write an article about you and want to set up an appointment to meet with you."

"Why would you want to do something like that?"

"Mr. Fontinelli, you're the largest landowner in the region and if we count the number of properties rather than acreage, you're definitely one of the largest individual owners in the nation. I would like the opportunity to share your story with thousands of readers who will find it fascinating."

"And of course, you want to make yourself a little money along the way," he said with the raspy voice that sent chills through me like the fiend I knew he was.

"Yes, there's no falsehood here, of course, I'll make some money if the story sells. I'm under a small commission to get it started and if it's any good, it has the potential to be very profitable for me," I lied.

"And just what do I get out of all of this, a headache?" He sneered.

"No, sir, you'll be quite famous and you might even have your photo on the cover of a national magazine. Does that work for you?" I played to his ego.

"Let me think about it," he hesitated and I feared I was losing him.

"Mr. Fontinelli, you're one of three candidates for this story. I called you first because I am personally intrigued with your success, but I will be very honest with you. I am freelance which means I don't receive a paycheck unless I sell the story and I could really use one of those right now. If you say no, this is not a problem, I will approach the second candidate and I am confident I won't have to approach the third one. If you're interested, we need to set up an appointment now. I'm only in the area until the end of the week."

"Are you any good?" There was a hint of sarcasm in his voice.

Feeling I had him now, I said with confidence, "You bet I am, just run my name through the internet and you'll see firsthand what I've written and the photographs that I've sold. Trust me, I'm good."

"Come here the day after tomorrow at ten o'clock prompt. If you're late, don't bother ringing at the gate. If you don't have the address, just run my name through the internet and you'll see firsthand where I live." His sarcasm was overbearing.

Before I could finish with, "I'll be there," the dial tone buzzed in my ear, the phone frozen to my hand and I stood motionless caught up in shock, astonished at what just happened.

Behind me, I felt the presence rather than the sound and turned to see my mother standing there clutching the doll that had undergone a gender change, her right arm twitching mildly. I hadn't noticed this before. In the past, I've heard an adage that the eyes are the mirrors of one's soul, yet staring deeply into hers, I saw only emptiness, the mirrors buried somewhere in the abyss of her mind, her soul veiled in the reflection of hidden mirrors.

CHAPTER
24

New York City

When Sal returned to the hotel after dinner with Theresa, he wasn't overly surprised that Vinnie hadn't returned. It was still early considering the city's nightlife and Sal felt a little guilt at not spending more time with him. He promised himself that tomorrow they would catch a ballgame together. Onyx would have to do without him for a few hours and he only met Theresa in the late afternoon or evening. Turning on the news to wait for Vinnie, he poured himself a glass of bourbon, but before he took the first sip, his head nodded back and he gave in to a deep slumber.

Still clouded with sleep, he woke to an intense urge to urinate and headed to the shared bathroom in the two-bedroom suite. Only when he finished did he think to check in on Vinnie, wondering how he did not hear him come in. The bed was empty. A quick glance to the small clock on the dresser told him it was 4:00 a.m. Where was Vinnie? He should have been back hours ago.

A mother's keen intuition is reputed, but both parents feel the terror that comes with a missing child. His nerve endings tingled when the hairs on his arms stood straight. His chest tightened and his midsection ached as if a knife was pushing into his gut. He felt the ominous threat of losing his son and panic came over him. Self-confidence normally second nature to him, was now lost to the thought that something horrific happened to Vinnie and he didn't know where to begin to look for him. Why hadn't he listened more closely when Vinnie told him about his new friends? Why can't he remember what play they went to see? Why? Why?

He picked up the hotel phone and dialed 9-1-1. Almost immediately, the dispatcher answered. "Is this a police or medical emergency?"

"My son is missing!" He didn't recognize the pitch in his own voice.

"What time did he go missing, Sir?" The canned voice asked with little expression.

"I don't know. I expected him back to the hotel by midnight and he hasn't shown up."

The voice, mechanical and robotic asked, "Do you have reason to expect foul play?"

"No, it's not like him to be late. I know something has happened. I'm sure of it."

"May I have your name, Sir?"

"My name is Salvatore Fiore."

"And what is your son's name?"

"His name is Vincenzo Fiore. We call him Vinnie."

"What is the name and location of your hotel?"

"It's the Ritz-Carlton across from Central Park."

"Okay, Mr. Fiore, since this not an emergency, I'm going to transfer you to the 19th Precinct. They're located at 153 East 67th Street. You will probably have to go in to file a report, but you can speak with them first. I'm going to transfer you now."

Sal lost his composure when he heard that this was not an emergency. "How can you say this isn't an emergency? This is my son we're talking about, haven't you heard a word I've said? It's not like him to stay out like this."

The voice, no longer mundane, answered him with more feeling, "I know you're upset, Mr. Fiore. The New York City Police Department deals with these situations all the time and I know the officers in the 19th Precinct will be able to assist you. I'm going to transfer you right away, so you can get started."

Now in total distress, he waited for what seemed to be an eternity before someone answered the phone. Again, he explained the problem, and again, the call transferred to someone else. This time the officer told him to stay at the hotel and wait to see if Vinnie showed up. He was probably out partying with some friends and would come back at any time. If his son didn't return by noon tomorrow, he should go in to file a report, but in the meantime, he gave the officer his name, the hotel phone number, his cell phone number, hotel address and room number. The officer promised to call him if anything came up.

He had to do something, but didn't know what. All the times he came to New York City and he still didn't know the city. Does anyone know the city? Where would Vinnie go? Who went with him? How did he get there? Why didn't he call? So many questions with no answers and now he is supposed to just sit and wait.

Sal spent the next few hours calling every associate he knew at Onyx to ask if they knew who Vinnie went out with that evening. He woke every one of them, but any annoyance they felt quickly dissipated when they heard the alarm in his voice. There's an unspoken bond shared by parents when it comes to the loss of their progeny. Finally, he got through to Bill, who escorted Vinnie on his first day in the city. Bill suggested that he contact Riverside Residence Hall in Upper West Manhattan because he remembered Vinnie met some young people there on the day they took the tour of the school and apartments. He was sorry that he didn't know their names or have a telephone number for him.

Sal acquired the phone number from the automated Information Directory and called, but no one answered even after several tries. He slammed the receiver down, damning the city that never sleeps. The six-hour time difference made this the opportune hour to call Niki, which he did every morning at this time, but he couldn't bring himself to dial the number. Niki would have to wait. She was against this trip from the beginning and now this. How could he tell the woman who loved and nurtured his son from the first day she met him that there is no clue to his whereabouts? This was a discussion for later, he decided. Instead, he called the Doubletree Hotel; he wanted to speak to is sister.

The miasma of last night's hangover hazed her mind heavily and she barely heard the phone ring. First, she reached for the alarm clock, trying to shut it off, and then realized it was the telephone so she answered in a barely audible voice, "Hello?"

"Sis, it's me...I need some help," the pain in his voice overtook him and he choked on the words. "Vinnie never came back tonight and I don't know where to look for him."

"Did you call the police?"

"Yes, but they're no help. He hasn't disappeared long enough for them to consider him a missing person. I've called everyone I know at the company and I'm getting nowhere. I don't know where to turn." His sobs were audible.

Completely awake now, she clung to his every word. She never met Vinnie yet he was her flesh and blood, a derivation of her lineage and her despair equaled that of a mother. Fearing the worst yet hoping for the best, she groped for words to comfort her brother and found none. Bloodlines ran deep in their ancestry; had they not, they wouldn't be in this situation to begin with.

"Do you want me to come over there?" He couldn't see the tears they shared.

"No, we can't take the chance. I don't want to be alone, Theresa. I'll come there. I need to go into the 19th Precinct this afternoon if he doesn't come back and I know he won't. I feel it. Something dreadful has happened and it's my entire fault; I wish I spent more time with him."

"Leave a message and tell the front desk where to reach you if he shows up. Let's just hope he's sowing some wild oats and he'll crawl in with a hangover and a huge case of remorse. We've all done it, maybe it's just his turn and we're overreacting."

"He's a good kid, Theresa. I would expect this from his younger brothers; they're holy terrors, but not Vinnie. Niki and I refer to him as Saint Vincent. I'm scared, really scared."

Her concern was apparent. "Speaking of Niki, have you called her yet?"

"No, there's six hour time difference, so she expects a call from me every morning when I wake up because it's her afternoon. I couldn't bring myself to call her today. If I lie, she'll hear it my voice and if I tell her the truth, she'll never forgive me for bringing him here. She loves him like a son even though she didn't give birth to him, but what makes it worse, Theresa, Niki thinks Vinnie is my brother; she doesn't know that he is really my son. We agreed to raise him as our child because he was so young when we met and Nike felt it would be less confusing for him. As for Vinnie, he has no recollection of anything, so he remembers only what we tell him. I never told Niki the truth because she fell in love with me thinking I was responsible for my little brother after our parents died in a car accident. I was this big hero to her and I needed that desperately. There's no way I can tell her the truth at this point; we have three more children. She's a great mother and wife; I can't lose her now. It's all mayhem and out of control."

"We'll work it out somehow, but just get over here as soon as you can. Trust me, we'll work it out." Already, she knew whom they needed to call, but she also knew her brother would not approve.

"I'll be right over. Will you go to the police with me?"

"Of course, I will."

Sal left a note in the room for Vinnie in case he returned and gave a message to the Desk Clerk instructing Vinnie to call his cell phone right away. Silently he prayed this would turn out to be nothing, but in his heart, he felt otherwise. The fear mounted inside him as every minute ticked away.

Arriving at the Doubletree, he literally rushed through the lobby to the elevator. As the door opened, Bernie was exiting alone and Sal literally bumped right into him, nearly knocking him over.

"Hey, my friend," said Bernie. "What's the rush? You look like there's an alien chasing you, but then this is New York City." Bernie was laughing.

"I'm sorry," Sal stammered. I have a little problem and need to get upstairs right away.

Seeing the seriousness in Sal's face, Bernie lost the humor and asked him, "Is everything okay? Can I help?"

"No, I'm fine. My son didn't come home last night and I'm in a bit of a panic, that's all. I'm sure he's just at a party."

"Never having children myself, I can't imagine what you're going through, but I'm sure you're right. I pulled a few shenanigans as a youngster myself and I still have the scars to show for it. I gave you my number the other night. Do you still have it?"

"Yes, I have it someplace."

"Then call me if there's anything I can do. My partner and I would be more than willing to make calls, search, or do whatever it takes to bring your young man home."

"I'll remember that. Thank you."

As the elevator ascended with Sal on in, Jackie met up with Bernie in the hallway. "Hey, who was that? He looked familiar."

"That's the guy from Italy I met at the bar the other night. It's a sad situation actually; his son accompanied him here on a business trip and now the son is missing. The father is frantic."

"He just looks so familiar."

"Well, maybe you were screwing around in Italy and that's where you met him," Bernie said in a half jest.

"No, he must just look like someone I know. Hope he finds his son. I can't imagine anything happening to Timothy."

Deep in thought, both men walked to the restaurant for breakfast, neither of them spoke, feeling a compassion for the father in distress over losing his son. How lucky they were.

CHAPTER
25

Karyn and Bob nearly begged me to come to dinner again, but the thought of sitting with them and discussing my meeting with Dominick the next day was intolerable. I chose instead to invite Tommy for a picnic in the park and he ecstatically accepted. Sara loaned me a small cooler and I packed it with a couple of grinders, some fruit, and apple cider. There's nothing better than Connecticut's apple cider, especially when it's fresh and ice cold. It was Tommy's favorite and mine too.

Washington Park was close enough to walk, but I chose to drive rather than hike the large hill and I knew Tommy would appreciate the ride also. Although he was physically in good shape, he walked with a slightly rigid gait so the incline was difficult for him.

I parked the car near the picnic area and we walked up the hill to a table Tommy chose for us under a heavily budded tree near the craggy cobblestone wall. The smell of spring filled the air inviting us to inhale deeply. Oak pollen teased our nostrils and eyes, a gentle reminder from Mother Nature that she is always in charge.

The sprawling 32.9-acre park, its land donated by George Marquardt, to the City of Groton in 1931 was more beautiful than I remembered it and I looked around for new additions to the recreational area and was pleased with what I saw. Standing atop the hill, I counted three baseball fields, two softball fields, and admired the updated tennis courts and basketball hoops. The pavilions and restrooms were new, the playgrounds expanded and more enticing. I reminisced about sledding down the hill, ice-skating for hours and fireworks on the Fourth of July. I thought about Joey without sadness, just the good times.

Tommy and I ate leisurely, enjoying each other's company and I was all ears listening to his stories about work and his winning achievements with Special Olympics. I can't remember when I gave this much attention to anyone other than myself and I enjoyed every minute and wished it would never end.

After we ate, Tommy talked me into sitting on the swing set with him and before I knew it, my legs were suspended and pumping as fast as possible. I was swinging as high as I could with the rush of cool air beating my face and laughing more than I remember laughing before. I was a child again; an innocent carefree child lost in a world of incorruptibility before the harsh tentacles of life strangled my soul and stole my future. Maybe there was still an essence of purity still buried within me; I longed to find my former self and rid my heart of its consuming hatred.

Dusk came too quickly and it was time to end this beautiful day, so we packed up our belongings and I drove Tommy home. As he was getting out of the car, he reached over giving me the strongest hug and said, "I love you, Aunt Annie. This was the very bestest day ever! I want to do it all the time."

"It was the bestest for me, too, Tommy, and I love you, too." I didn't have it in me to tell him that I planned to leave as soon as my business with Dominick was finished.

Arriving back at the house, Sara and Mike were already eating dinner at the kitchen table. My mother was with them, with one hand on her doll lying on the table next to her. Her frail body rocked back and forth in the stationary chair as if she sat in a rocker. Sara was trying to get her to eat, but she didn't want it and I heard Mike promise her a great dessert if she ate at least her vegetables. The sight intrigued me and I marveled at Mike for taking such a proactive role in my mother's life. Of course, he did it to impress Sara, I thought, but he didn't have to do it. His feelings seemed so natural and genuine. I was impressed and happy for Sara having someone so special in her life.

"Hey, Aunt Annie, we started without you, but there's plenty on the stove for you. We ate a little early tonight because we wanted to eat with Nana. She's not eating much lately and we're a little worried, so Mike and I thought that she might eat more if we ate with her, but it doesn't seem to be working."

"She does look a little out of sorts tonight and I notice that one of her hands has a tremor that she can't seem to control. Has this happened before?"

"No, it's something new. The doctors told us to expect changes, but we keep hoping the progression will slow, but lately she appears to be failing rapidly. She has another appointment next week and I'll talk to the doctor then about the tremor if it doesn't stop. Can I fix you a plate of food?" Sara looked tired.

"I'm still stuffed from my picnic with Tommy. We had a late lunch in the park and he was a bad influence on me because I ate too much. If I get hungry later, I'll heat something up. Right now, I think I'm going to watch a little news, take a hot shower and hit the bed early. I'm exhausted. He wore me out, but it was fun."

"That's fine, what are your plans for tomorrow?"

"Not much, I'm going to Rhode Island to see an old friend, so I won't be back until later. You don't have to save dinner for me," then to Mike, I asked, "How was work today?"

"It's always great. I really love it there and I've gotten to know the seniors that come in for the activities really well now, so it's a lot of fun." I loved his attitude.

"That's super. Well, I'm heading off to the other room for the news and then upstairs. I'll see you both sometime late tomorrow. Good Night."

"Good Night."

It's not that I didn't want to spend some time with them; the truth was that it was difficult for me to be around my mother for any length of time. Alzheimer's is a cruel disease, and yet, it is kind in another way because it erases the pain and heartache of life. There was no eradication for the anguish burdening my heart everyday and her Alzheimer's shrouded the woman I abhorred. In a strange way, I felt cheated because I was unable to give her the measure of hatred she deserved.

On my dresser sat my crystal prism, its delicate colors dancing without restraint on the walls and ceiling like little ballerinas dressed in neon. The tiny specks of radiance were mesmerizing and I watched them until my body gave in to the comforting warmth of the mattress and my eyelids surrendered soothingly into slumber. I slept without dreams and woke only to the sound of the alarm clock reminding me of what I must face today.

CHAPTER
26

Sicily, Italy

Niki sat on the veranda sipping her espresso wondering why Sal didn't call her this morning. It wasn't like him to miss a call to her, so she decided to phone him. She hated disturbing him if he was working, but she worried about him when he was out of town. Now, she had Vinnie to worry about also. There was no answer so she left a message and then called the hotel, no answer there either. She left another message.

She thought about Vinnie and the fine young man he was becoming. There was not one day of trouble from him, not like his two hellion brothers. She smiled at the thought of the other two who were trouble from birth, but thankfully, nothing serious yet. The day she met Sal's little brother, she knew she could raise him as her own and that's what she did wholeheartedly. If she gave birth to him herself, she could not love him more. Many times, she questioned the decision that she and Sal made regarding his birthright. Maybe they should have told him that he was really Sal's brother and not his son. Would it have made a difference? At the time, Sal thought the difference would be huge once they began having their own family because he feared Vinnie would not feel as if he fit in, so she agreed and they decided together to keep it simple. Sometimes, however, simplicity is multifaceted and becomes complex. The older Vinnie got, the more difficult it would be to tell him and now she prayed he would never find out she was not his real mother. It would kill her to lose his trust, and worse, his love.

The musical ringtone on her phone startled her out of her thoughts and with a sigh of relief, she was thankful Sal called her back. Without looking at the display screen on her phone, she blurted out, "Buongiorno, Innamorato! Mi manchi terribilmente!"

"Scusami?" The woman on the phone was definitely not Sal. "Signora Fiore?"

"Sì, questa è la sig. ra Fiore," Niki was embarrassed at her presumption that it was her husband calling and blurting out that she missed him terribly.

In Italian, the woman explained that she was calling from the Marcelo Campini Detective Agency in Palermo. Unfortunately, Mr. Campini met with a terrible accident; however, his staff was committed to notify his clients and bring closure to the accounts so they could settle his estate. The agency was wondering why Mrs. Fiore did not pay the invoice when she received the information she requested.

Rather annoyed, Niki explained that she never received the information and only found out about the detective's demise because she did some internet investigating on her own. She went on to tell the woman how rude she was to ask for payment for something she never received.

The woman apologized and offered to email the information as an attachment with Mrs. Fiore's permission. Niki, still agitated, agreed and said she would send payment upon receipt of the information.

It wasn't long before Niki's laptop flashed to tell her she had a new email so she made another cup of espresso and sat down at the screen. Expecting one, two pages maximum, she was surprised to see so many attachments and began opening them one at a time.

Nervously, she read the first, a cover letter summarizing the research on all activities for Salvatore "Sal" Francesco Fiore. The agency verified his employment, his position with the employer, and his daily activities. After thorough scrutiny of his telephone records, email access, internet history, and bank and credit card statements, even following him for several days, the agency determined there was no indication of infidelity. Niki breathed a huge sigh of relief.

Reading on, however, the letter explained that an inadvertent finding that went outside of the realm of their investigation, did uncover a few discrepancies that may be meaningless; however, in the best interest of their client, it was their obligation to present the discoveries.

The agency, in fact, did verify Sal's university degree, the marriage to Niki and the birth of their three children. Prior to his time at the university, however, there was no evidence of the existence of Salvatore Francesco Fiore and no records of his parents and the alleged automobile accident. In addition, based on supplementary information provided to them by Mrs. Fiore, there was no record of the birth of Vincenzo Fiore. An international search, however, did uncover documents that may, or may not; pertain to the parties in question. Although the agency was not in a position to certify the authenticity, they stood on the supposition that the documents presented were legitimate. The information provided was now in the hands of Mrs. Fiore and it was her responsibility to review them and decide the pertinence.

The letter went on to thank Mrs. Fiore for the opportunity to serve her and asked her to contact the agency if they could do more for her. Wishing her the best of luck in her endeavors, the signature presented was that of the late Detective Campini.

Niki stared in disbelief at the words jumping off the page to her. There must be some mistake, an oversight of some sort. She was more concerned with the relief that came when the detective agency found no evidence of infidelity. More out of curiosity than anything, she went on to open the first of the attachments, an Official Transcript of Name Change. The espresso cup slipped from her hand, the delicate china shattering on the terrazzo floor at the very moment her cell phone rang. It was Sal. She didn't answer; she couldn't answer, not now. Instead, she opened the remaining documents and then called the airline to do what she needed to do. He could wait.

CHAPTER
27

The drive to Watch Hill was less than one hour from Groton, but I allowed myself ample time to ensure I was there exactly at ten o'clock. The northbound traffic on the interstate was light, but my mind was elsewhere and I missed Exit 92 toward Stonington and Pawcatuck, forcing me to backtrack. When I reached Westerly, Rhode Island, I pulled into a convenience store for a cup of coffee, but I was unable to drink it; my nerves bundled, the smell of it sickening.

Watch Hill, situated on a stubby peninsula that juts into Block Island Sound is widely acknowledged as one of Rhode Island's most affluent and beautiful seaside villages. The desolate downtown area gave it an eerie atmosphere, which strengthened the trepidation of what was to come when I saw Dominick. Most of the shops were not yet open for the season, but a few local residents were taking advantage of the beautiful spring day. I left the town driving past the marina that would fill to its limit shortly, but now, there were few yachts. I maneuvered my Lexus through the winding streets and headed to the hillside passing century old summer cottages, each one more intriguing than the last. It was as if I stepped back in time.

As I drove along the beachfront, the mansions became more and more impressive, but my thoughts were on only one, the Fontinelli estate. I found it easily and drove slowly up the hill to the sprawling seven-acre mansion perched high between the bay and the ocean.

The massive barricade, a combination of sculptured concrete wall and elaborate fence, discreetly and aesthetically hidden behind hedges, barricaded the fortress from the rest of the world. An enormous iron gate stamped vainly with the initial for Fontinelli mandated I proceed no further. I was petrified, but rolled down my window and stretched my quivering hand toward the button on the freshly painted speaker. Before I made contact, the gates slowly opened with the invitation to proceed along the snaking driveway lined with tall Leyland Cypress trees. Scattered among them, newly planted Empress trees with their embryonic buds promised the beauty that was yet to come. My window still down, I crept slowly along; my pounding heart drowning out the chirping of the birds and the distant thunder of ocean waves crashing on the shoreline below.

A caretaker met me as I approached the colossal manor and directed me to park in the circular driveway. As he opened the door for me, I hoped he didn't notice my shallow breath, my chest too tight to breathe normally. Prudently, I wiped the perspiration from my upper lip and hoped my heavily applied deodorant would handle the sweat ripening under my arms.

"Good Morning, Ms. Daley, I am Victor. May I help you carry anything?"

"Yes, thank you, I have a camera and recording equipment," I said as I opened the trunk of the car.

He led me to the front door of the mansion where a distinguished looking middle-aged woman greeted us and said to the caretaker, "I'll take her from here, Victor. Then to me, "You must be Ms. Daley. I'm Mrs. Foster; it's a pleasure to meet you." I immediately recognized the voice from the telephone. "Please come in, Mr. Fontinelli is in his library. Follow me."

I trailed behind her through the marbled foyer that opened to a huge Greeting Room overlooking the ocean. It was elaborate to the point of being gaudy with highly polished wooden floors that creaked when we walked. The area carpet in the center of the room was ivory, accented with a rose-colored tapestry couch and chairs that looked as if no one ever sat in them. Looming over the ornate fireplace was a giant oil painting of a beautiful woman with jet-black hair and eyes to match. My breath caught in my throat seeing the strong resemblance to Joey. I only met his mother a couple of times, but never really spoke to her.

Noticing my interest in the image, Mrs. Foster simply stated, "That's the late Mrs. Fontinelli. She passed several years ago."

I followed her to the end of a long dark hallway with a gleaming marble floor; its walls decorated with paintings of Italian landscapes gently illuminated with accent lighting to bring out the bright colors. We passed several rooms, most with closed doorways until we reached the library and she knocked quietly on the oversized double mahogany doors. A gruff voice behind them bellowed, "Come in," and we entered.

Behind the desk was a thin, frail man who looked older than his years. He wasn't the man I remembered in photos, but he was still intimidating. His once olive complexion was now sallow offering a hint of jaundice and the deep dark circles under his eyes dominated his ruddy features. He was completely bald from the chemo treatments. So much for the hair sample, I thought to myself and I wanted to turn and run.

"I see you found my humble abode with no problem, Ms. Daley, and you're on time, too." He had a voice that sounded like a razor scratching sandpaper. His eyes were cold and difficult to read and I avoided a direct gaze for fear he could read my thoughts, my feelings, for fear he would recognize me somehow from one of Joey's photographs.

"Yes, I found it with no problem. It's nice to meet you, Mr. Fontinelli," I lied.

"You look a little familiar to me," he said. "Have we met before?"

My greatest fear was about to become reality; he would recognize me and it would be all over, but I was committed to this now and replied, "You've probably seen my work or my photo in a media byline."

"Yes, you're probably right and I did, in fact, do some research to verify your legitimacy. So, Ms. Daley, am I what you expected? Did you expect some big Italian wise guy with a heavy accent?"

"No, I've done my research on you also and I'm aware that you were born and raised in this country, so I didn't expect you to have an accent. I've also seen you on the news more than once."

"Oh, are you referring to my little court house scuffle last year with the State Attorney's office?" I knew he was referring to a recent tax evasion charge, but like everything else, they dismissed it and he came out smelling like a rose.

"That, and a few others," I replied trying hard to swallow my sarcasm. "Perhaps, we should get started." I wanted to get out of there as quickly as I could.

"Before we start, let's take a walk and I'll show you around. I could use some fresh air and we can talk while we're taking a little stroll. Leave your equipment in here; we won't need it just yet."

He got up before I had the chance to say anything with the expectation that I would follow him and, of course, I did. He was obviously a man who was always in charge. Following behind him, I looked desperately for an item, any item that was solely his and would have his uncontaminated DNA. I saw nothing outside the library and I was not in a position to pocket anything from the library, not yet anyway.

Dominick gave me a tour of the first floor of the three-floor mansion, each room ornately decorated. He pointed out the staff quarters, but we didn't enter, so I presumed there was staff in house. I wondered if Mrs. Foster lived there fulltime. These rooms were adjacent to the oversized kitchen with its highly polished stainless appliances, all of them industrial quality. The dining room could easily sit twenty people at the formal table and he bragged that with extensions, the table was able to sit twenty-eight formally and up to thirty-six with less formal dinnerware. In addition to his library, there was a small Reading Room, a Television Room set up like a movie theater with a screen large enough to cover more than half the wall. The area around it held several smaller ones for viewing multi channels simultaneously and several comfortable reclining chairs filled the room with the strong smell of new leather. They looked untouched.

We passed through the Greeting Room again to proceed to the wing on the opposite end of the house. In an attempt at conversation, I asked him about the woman in the oil painting. "How long ago did she pass away?"

"Several years ago, at least twenty-five, I keep the painting there because it's a good fit for the wall." He was so callous. I remembered when Joey lost his mother. It was a day of mixed feelings for him; they weren't close, but she was still his mother.

Her death ended all hope of them ever forming a bond as mother and son.

"Did she decorate this house? It appears to have a woman's touch."

"Yes, most of it, with the exception of the library and my personal quarters upstairs, it was her design. The Television Room is new; Mrs. Foster took care of that and her husband who also lives on the grounds helped with the Billiards Room I'll show you later. It's a smoking area, so the entrance is from the veranda outside to avoid the smell of cigars coming into the Main House.

"It's all beautiful, Mr. Fontinelli," and I meant it.

"This corridor leads to two identical guest suites; each has his own sitting area and balcony. One faces the bay, the other the ocean."

They were beautiful, one very masculine, the other decorated in floral patterns. I noticed that every room had a vase of fresh flowers with no other personal touches. With the exception of the oil painting, there were no photographs, or memorabilia of any kind. I thought it strange, but the man himself was more than peculiar.

"The second floor has five more bedrooms and the third floor is completely devoted to my personal living quarters. There are three sets of stairs, one large elevator and a utility elevator that accesses each floor."

"Do Mr. and Mrs. Foster live on the grounds?" I asked him, but to myself I was wondering how I could slip into his library, or up to the third floor.

"Yes, they've lived here for more than fifteen years. Why do you ask, are you looking for a job?" I couldn't tell if he was trying to be witty, or just sarcastic.

"No, I was just curious," I said with a forced smile.

"They live in one of larger cottages on the grounds. He is my chauffeur; she is the brains and runs the entire place, including me. I also employ a fulltime cook, two house cleaners, and a groundskeeper. Everyone else is part time or contractual as needed. Would you mind if we sit on the patio for a bit? I'm a little tired."

"Of course not, it's beautiful out today. I would enjoy it." I was amazed at how easily he offered information so far. "I'd like to start recording our conversation because I want what you tell me to be accurate. I'll go back to the library and get my things."

"No, Mrs. Foster will bring them," he said as he pulled a small black remote from his pocket. As he pushed the button, I heard a soft chime resonate throughout the first floor, and to my disappointment, Mrs. Foster appeared.

Anticipating his request she asked me, "Would you like me to bring your personal items, Ms. Daley?"

Dominick, answering for me told her, "Yes, get them and also send in something cold to drink, ginger ale for me and whatever Ms. Daley would like."

"Ginger ale is fine. Thank you."

A few minutes later, I had my equipment and a second woman carrying a tray with our beverages and small muffins met us on the patio wearing a gray uniform and a starched white apron. He said nothing to her, not attempting to introduce her.

"Try a muffin, they're fresh from the oven," he said, but I thought it strange because we were just in the kitchen and the only smell from the two ovens was strong disinfectant.

"No thanks, maybe later." I was too nervous to eat.

"Your loss then, they're good," but I noticed he didn't take one either.

"So, tell me, Ms. Daley, what do you think of this view?" We sat at a table near an Olympic size pool overlooking the calm waters of Narragansett Bay.

"It's magnificent; does the pool get much use?"

"Not much anymore, this one is fresh water, there's a salt water pool on the other side of the house that's smaller, but has more character. I prefer the ocean; it's unpredictable, wild and free."

"Is that how you see yourself?" I asked aloud, but adding to myself, "And it can be cruel, like you."

"Oh, maybe in my younger years, but it's a little difficult to be wild and free in my condition!" He gave a half laugh and started coughing.

"If you're not up to this, I can walk around, take some photographs today and we can reschedule our appointment." I prayed for him to agree knowing that once I had what I wanted, I would not come back.

"I'm fine, Ms. Daley," he lied, "It's a beautiful day and I don't have that many of them left, so I have no intentions of wasting one precious minute. Let's get started."

"Alright, the recorder is turned on, but it's for my memory, not yours so just forget it's there. Tell me a little about your youth. What were your parents like?"

Without taking the time to think, he started talking about his upbringing, mentioning his brother Angelo and their disputes. I expected him to paint a bed of roses, but he was candid and blunt, speaking with vacant eyes and no emotion until he described his mother. His voice softened somewhat and a slight smile curved his otherwise grim face when he mentioned her. The longer he talked, the more curious I was to learn about this man that I knew to have no heart.

It was a little before noon when a young girl wearing the same uniform as the earlier servant brought us each a cup of minestrone and an antipasto. She poured fresh glasses of ginger ale and left a basket of warm rolls with a strong aroma of garlic. "Will there be anything else, Sir?"

With a deadpan glance, he simply answered her, "No," and went on with his story while we ate. The food was delicious and I found myself intrigued as he spoke, but the loathing I felt remained. Shortly after lunch, she returned with biscotti and demitasse cups of espresso flavored with a hint of anisette. The meal was delicious and I surprised myself by eating all of it while he scarcely touched any of it.

"Why do you think you and your brother were such rivals? Did something specific happen?"

"No, it wasn't one thing in particular," he said thoughtfully and then went on to tell how his father forced them to compete in an effort to make them stronger. They brought home a stray dog once and asked to keep it, but their father told them the dog could only belong to one of them and the other could have nothing to do with it. He flipped a coin and Dominick won the dog. A few days later the dog was gone and Dominick always wondered if his brother caused the disappearance, but didn't ask because the answer would be a lie anyway. He spoke of whippings, alcohol and nights without dinner, the ones when his mother snuck food to them after her husband passed out.

"You must have a deep hatred for your father," I stated.

"Of course not, he was the greatest man that walked this earth!"

"I'm sitting here listening to stories about alcohol abuse, child abuse, and God knows what else, but you're telling me he was a great man. How can that be?"

"He taught my brother and me that to succeed in life, we have to go after what we want, take it, and keep it close. You can't sit back in life and let someone else take what is rightfully yours, can you? Look around you, what do you see? I am successful because my father taught me. He was a great man."

"Did he teach you to take what's not yours, what should not be yours? I don't understand."

He gave a deep sigh and said, "You remind me of someone and I just can't think who it is. Are you sure we've never met?"

"I'm sure," I lied again and was thankful I asked no questions about Joey, at least not yet. "Like I said before, my photographs are widespread and my own photo accompanies every byline. Tell me how you became involved in your father's business?"

Before he could answer, Mrs. Foster walked out on the patio and said to him, "Excuse me for interrupting, Sir, but you have a phone call and the gentleman says it's urgent that he speak to you."

"Everything is urgent in business. Take his name and tell him I'll call him back. He probably owes me money."

"He sounds quite upset; you may want to speak to him."

"Okay," he told her and then looking at me, he added, "I'll be right back. Maybe you have to use the bathroom while I'm gone. Mrs. Foster will show you."

Finally, I thought, there's a chance to take something with his DNA, but I was quickly disappointed when Mrs. Foster walked me to a sterile guest bathroom and waited right outside the door for me. The library wasn't possible because that's where he went and the third floor was definitely not an option, at least not now. When Mrs. Foster led me back to the patio, the young servant girl was holding the tray with our used eating utensils and cups, so the chance for getting something from there was also gone. As I sat down, she replaced our glasses with fresh ones and left just as he arrived again with Mrs. Foster trailing behind him.

"Ms. Daley, I'm afraid we are going to have to reschedule our meeting. I have a slight crisis that needs my immediate attention. Please return the day after tomorrow at the same time and we can have lunch together again. I'm sorry for the imposition. Mrs. Foster will show you the way out." With that said, he simply turned and reentered the house without waiting for me to reply. It was sometime around two o'clock in the afternoon. I was there four hours and failed to get what I needed.

CHAPTER
28

A lberto sat in his efficiency sipping a cold beer and thinking about the phone call he just made. What an ingenious plan he had! Why hadn't he thought of it earlier? He milked one cow dry and now he had the whole herd, but it was time for him to speed it up with Miss Maggie. He noticed her tremors after he increased the dosage, but he needed a full force seizure to put her out of her misery. If his new endeavor played out, the insurance money was just a drop in the bucket, but he wanted it all. He was on a high from the greed and tomorrow he would meet with the old man and let him know who was boss.

Big deal he called in sick today, the stupid job was just a front anyway, but he had important things to do. He needed to go to the bank and transfer some money, then make sure the insurance agent had an updated address for the beneficiary, long lost nephew Albert Santucci. As far as the agency was concerned, they never met the nephew and he planned to be long gone before they had the opportunity. He already rented an apartment in New Jersey where he would go later. There could be no glitches.

Almost forgetting, he had another call to make. "Hey, Sweetheart, I can't make it over tonight. I have some kind of stomach bug, so I called in sick."

"Oh no, I hope you're feeling better. Do you want me to come over there?"

"No way, the last thing we need is for me to pass it on. I'm just going to hit the bed early. Tomorrow is my regular day off, so I'm going to sleep in and I'll call you when I get up. I'm sure I'll feel better by then."

"Okay, if you insist, but I'd feel better if I could be with you."

"I know, but I'll see you tomorrow. I love you; give Nana a big kiss for me."

"I will and I love you, too, Mike. Be well."

Ending the call, he said aloud, "You bet I will be well, Sara," and he opened another beer.

In the meantime, Dominick Fontinelli was also pondering the telephone call. Who was the young punk who insisted on seeing him tomorrow, or he will let the world know the Fontinelli secret? Just another wise ass, he thought, but he knew better than ignore him. His father was right; he would pay for his dirty little transgression the rest of his life. Was there never an ending to the night in the cemetery; he cursed his brother and envied him for dying first.

Well, he needed to find out what he was dealing with so he knew how much blackmail the son of a bitch would demand. This opportunist wasn't the first, but with luck, he was the last. There was no way this could go public; he still had children to think of and they would never accept a half-bastard sibling demanding a share of their heirloom.

He knew what to do, so he made a call to his trusted nephew. His brother's eldest son, Tony, had the resources to trace the telephone call and much like his father had no qualms about putting matters to sleep. Tony was not privy to this particular skeleton in the cupboard, but no matter, Dominick was confident this matter would go away like all the others.

A short while later, Tony called him back, "Sorry, Uncle Dom, he used a prepaid phone and there's no time to trace the site of purchase. I'll be there in the morning when he shows up and we'll take it from there. Do you know what he's threatening?"

"It's just a little matter from the old days with your father, nothing to worry about. I'll see you in the morning. Stop at the bakery and bring some cannolis and sfogliatelle; throw in a couple napoleons, too. Make sure they give you fresh ones from the back; I don't want any crap that's been sitting in the case."

"Will do, Uncle Dom, I'll see you in the morning."

"Be here early, and Tony, make sure there's no problem with this one. I'm getting too old for this stuff."

"You bet I will and I'll be there early."

Dominick's thoughts went to Anne Daley. It was too bad the bloodsucking rogue called and broke up their session. He liked talking about himself and she was a good listener, yet he could not shake the feeling that he met her before, but where?

CHAPTER
29

New York City

A young officer wearing a name tag, D. Smith, and a look that said she just graduated from the Academy took the report at the police station. Her inexperience infuriated Sal who knew better than let his anger show. She apologized that they had her, but Sergeant Burns called in sick this morning and she was filling in for him at the last moment. Fumbling over words to show some compassion, she said, "I'm so sorry for your loss, Mr. & Mrs. Fiore."

Sal lost it. "He's not dead, you idiot, he's missing! I need you to find him. I need you to find him right now!"

"I'm sorry," the police officer replied in a near whisper fearing her colleagues would overhear her blunder and ridicule the rawness of her remark.

"And this is not my wife, this is my sister," Sal gritted through his teeth. "My wife is in Italy and doesn't know yet."

"You need to contact the boy's mother and keep her informed in the event that your son or someone else gets in touch with her."

Sal knew she was referring to a kidnapping; he hadn't considered that possibility until now. "I've tried calling her all morning, but she isn't answering. She's probably getting her hair done, or something," he said not believing his own words.

"Well, I think I have all the information I need to get this started, if not, we'll call you. We would prefer that you stay local in case something comes up."

"I'm not going anywhere; I won't leave without my son!"

"If we find anything out at all, we'll contact you right away," Officer Smith told him.

The dismissal was curt and professional, but Sal had trouble getting up to leave. He felt helpless faced with the harsh reality that he was unable to find his son and he wanted to stay at the police station to ensure they did their job and made this case their top priority. The need to take charge engulfed him, consuming all sense of reason and common sense. He remained glued to his seat until Theresa took his hand and gently prodded him to leave. "Come on, Sal, we need to go and let them do their job."

Seeing the tears in his eyes, the young officer assured, "Really, Mr. Fiore, we will do everything we can to find him. This is a big city, but we're a strong force and there won't be a stone left unturned, I promise you."

Reluctantly, he followed Theresa, looking over his shoulder to see what Ms. Smith would do with the paperwork and she was already speaking with an older man in plainclothes who was reviewing the report. Reading his thoughts, Theresa said, "This is their job, Sal, let them do it. They'll find him; you'll see."

Why couldn't he believe her? Nothing was okay anymore and he needed desperately to speak to his wife. Where was she? Where were the kids? Why didn't she answer his calls? Why was he even here? There were so many questions with no answers.

Sal called the hotel for messages and there were several. His false hopes, however, shattered quickly when none of them was Vinnie, just corporate colleagues and that chap named Bernie from the Doubletree.

Unable to do nothing, Sal and Theresa decided to go on the hunt themselves, starting a walk down Broadway. They stopped into every shop, box office and lobby that was open, showing Vinnie's photo and asking if anyone had seen him. Of course, no one remembered; too many people passed through the productions every day.

From there, they tried some of the less formal pubs and eateries, places young people would enjoy, but again they had no luck. Their efforts seemed hopeless.

"Let's call him, Sal. He has connections and can help." Theresa expected an angry objection to her suggestion, but felt the need to offer it anyway. "We have no choice."

Sal, however, torn between finding his son and the fear of losing his wife and other children simply replied, "Not yet, Theresa, not yet, okay?"

"Okay, but we both know he can help us and I'm so afraid the longer we wait, the harder it will be to find Vinnie."

"I know, but not yet, okay?" He was exhausted, both mentally and physically, but not ready to give up.

"Well, then let's get something to eat and come up with a plan. Did you try Niki again?"

"Yes, she's still not answering. I even tried the neighbors, but I'm just getting their voicemail, so I left a message there also. Not like I have enough to worry about, now I have to worry about the rest of my family."

"She's probably out having fun with the kids, trying to do something special for them while their older brother is on vacation with you. Maybe they're at the movies or doing whatever you do over there for entertainment. Come on, you must be starving, I am."

Reluctantly, he followed her knowing he needed to eat, but he had no appetite. They stopped at a small deli a couple of streets off Broadway. Sal didn't bother to look at the menu, just showed the server Vinnie's photograph and asked if she remembered him being there. No, she never saw him before. He ordered a cup of black coffee and told her he wasn't hungry.

That was unacceptable to Theresa who handed the menus back to the young woman taking their order and said, "He'll have pastrami and Swiss on rye with dark mustard; I'd like tuna on toasted whole wheat with tomato and light on the mayonnaise. We'll share an order of fries."

Sal's head was down and he was rubbing his temples in a circular motion. His eyes were moist when he looked up at his sister. "I feel so helpless, Theresa. I've devoted my entire adult life to his protection and I let him slip away. God, I can't let anything happen to him, I'm so scared."

"What if he didn't go to a play and wasn't in the area of Broadway? What if he and his friends decided to go to a party instead, maybe we should check with the school."

"I tried Residence Hall where he met some guys when he toured the school, but I never got their names, like the fool I am, so I didn't know who to talk to when I got there. I flashed his photo around, but didn't get anywhere. It won't hurt to try it again; maybe we'll meet some different people. It's just not like Vinnie to lie to me."

"Maybe he didn't lie, maybe they just changed plans and you weren't around for him to tell you, or he didn't think it was a big deal."

"He knows the rules! I have a phone, Theresa, and he has a phone, so that's not an excuse. He's a good kid, he wouldn't lie to me."

"I'm not calling him a bad kid; I'm just saying that he is just that, a kid! Don't you remember how you were, always sneaking off?" She meant her last comment to be lighthearted, but the glare from her brother told her it was not appreciated, so she backed off and said, "Come on, eat up and we'll go to the school."

"I'm not hungry," he replied pushing his plate away.

"I don't care if you're not hungry, there are starving children in Africa, so I've been told anyway, so just eat something. I'm not leaving here until you do." She smiled at him, a very sad smile; the fear and anguish in her eyes matching his own.

"I'm glad you're with me, Sis, I couldn't bear it alone," he said as he picked up half of the sandwich and took a bite. Do you mind if we stop by my hotel first? I'm desperate for a shower and I need to pick up my other phone that has my overseas contact numbers in case I have to start tracking down Niki."

"Not a problem, you're actually going to let me be seen with you there?" She was smiling when she said it, but she knew the repercussion if they were discovered.

"Yes, but we'll be in and out. Make sure you don't open the door for anyone, including Vinnie, actually, especially Vinnie! We'll deadbolt the door from the inside and you can hide in the closet." Sadly, he was serious, not joking he when told her that, because he, too, knew the consequences if their secret was uncovered.

The ride to the Ritz-Carlton was silent, both of them deep in thought wondering about Vinnie and his whereabouts. They each knew the importance of finding a missing person early, the longer it took, and the more unlikely the ending would be a happy one. Theresa's hand was in her jacket pocket clenching her cell phone tightly knowing the call they needed to make, the one she needed to make before it was too late.

The concierge met the taxi and opened the door for them when they arrived. He politely nodded to Theresa, but remembering Sal, he greeted him with, "Good afternoon, Mr. Fiore, I take it you've had a pleasant day, Sir." Sal could only nod and handed him a generous tip, then led Theresa to his Premier Parkview suite on the twentieth floor overlooking Central Park in full spring bloom.

Theresa let out a whistle when she entered the eleven hundred square foot suite, and said, "Not bad, my dear brother! You must be doing quite well for yourself," but of course, she already knew his worth matched her own; she was just less ostentatious, preferring modesty over flamboyance. These accommodations had to be well over twelve hundred dollars per night, which she thought was excessive regardless of one's wealth. She quickly made a tour of the floor plan noting the open door to Vinnie's adjacent bedroom that connected it to the otherwise one bedroom suite. Aside from some personal toiletries, the closet and dresser drawers held everything else neatly tucked away. It looked untouched.

While Sal took his shower, Theresa waited for him in the Living Room, occupying her time looking through the telescope located near one of the large windows with a view of the park below. She wished she waited for him in the lounge.

Seeing his wallet on the table, she couldn't resist the urge to open it. She wasn't interested in the cash or credit cards; her attention went to the family photo. She had never met, nor seen images of his wife, or any of the four children. Niki was just as beautiful as he described and their little Andrianna looked just like her. The three boys were handsome and resembled her brother at their age, especially the oldest that she knew was Vinnie. Quickly, she put the wallet back before he came out and caught her.

To her relief, no one knocked at the door and shortly, he came out dressed in fresh clothes and looking a little less scruffy, but still tired. "Are you ready? Let's go," he said picking up his wallet, room key and two cell phones. "I already called for a taxi, so it will be ready for us when we get downstairs." She followed him out the door and down the hall.

Waiting for the elevator to arrive, Sal put his arm around his sister's waist and gently kissed the top of her head, "Thanks again, Sis. When this is over, I need to make some changes. I've given up too much and I won't give you up anymore. I don't know how, but we've got to find a way to stay in touch."

Theresa started to answer, but before she had the chance, the elevator door opened, revealing a tall, attractive woman and the only word Sal could mutter was "Niki?"

CHAPTER
30

My meeting with Dominick left me emotionally drained, yet it wasn't what I anticipated. He was nothing like what I expected, whatever that was in the first place. My memory of him was like an old faded photograph, but seeing him in person for the first time after two decades of photographs forced me to face the harsh reality of time and the cruelty of life as it passes. I wondered what strength and power, if any, remained under his dying, rotting flesh. Seeing him, I feared him less, yet hated him more for allowing him the power over me to steal my youth and my soul mate. He spoke so openly and freely to me when we were together; was it the loneliness or the imminence of his mortality? I wondered.

Jackie called to say he was back from New York City and said he would meet me at the house for dinner. I asked him if Bernie was joining us, but Jackie explained that Bernie needed to get back to work, however, Karyn and Bob were joining us, along with Susan and her husband. Wow, I thought sarcastically, another family dinner! Would this never end? Oh well, at least with everyone there, Karyn would be unable to scrutinize every word between Dominick and me. We already spoke on the phone and I wasn't up for more of it.

Everyone arrived around five-thirty and Sara gathered all on the back patio to enjoy the beautiful spring evening. The smell of chicken on the barbecue and the voices of mindless chatter filled me with loss and regret for the family and children I never had. I felt as if I carried the brunt of life's cruel joke, always the buffoon smiling on the outside and crying within from the pain and rage I couldn't squelch. Where do I fit in life's giant puzzle?

Sara and Susan carried out bowls and platters full of food that everyone contributed with the exception of me I realized. Even Jackie brought several bottles of wine. Was I that thoughtless I asked myself? Yes, I guess I was.

"Hope everyone has an appetite," Susan announced, "because there's enough food here for the entire neighborhood! Grab a seat and dig in before Mike eats it all now that he has his appetite back."

"Where's Mom?" Jackie asked.

Sara started toward the doorway to find her, but Mike stopped her and said, "I'll get her, so you can keep doing what you're doing." He gave her a sexy wink. I envied their future together.

After a short while, Mike came back onto the patio with my mother clinging to him with one arm and holding her doll with the other. Karyn snipped, "She hasn't put down that damn doll since she got it! She looks ridiculous, Sara. You should get rid of it when she's sleeping."

"No, way will I do that," Sara snapped back at her mother. "I don't know what she's thinking, but to her it's real. She loves it and it's not hurting anyone." Karyn didn't respond, her silence confirming her disapproval.

Skillfully changing the subject in an attempt to lighten the atmosphere, Eddie asked, "Where's Tommy tonight, on a hot date?"

"He has dinner once a month with a group he belongs to and he won't miss it for anything. He tells me he has a girlfriend there who is just like him and they are in love so they sit together." Bob answered with a little chuckle and then added, "She brings him cookies, homemade cookies, he tells me."

I couldn't resist adding, "Well, she's going to have to fight me for him because he's pretty special in my book!"

"Yes, he is special. We worry about what will happen to him when we're gone," Bob said glancing over at Karyn. "We've made arrangements for him financially and there are some really nice group homes, but it would break my heart to see him torn away from family."

Without a split second thought, I blurted out, "That'll never happen. I'll make sure of it." As soon as the words left my tongue, the table was silent and all eyes were on me. "Look, I know you all think I'm selfish and I'm out just for me. There's not one person at this table who knows me well enough to say a damn thing. I like my privacy, but that doesn't make me a bad person just because I don't want to live here in this hellhole of a town with each one of you knowing my business and telling me what to do every minute."

"Well, excuse us, Ms. Annie, for being below your standards. It must be nice to live in your glass tower counting the money your ex-husbands keep pumping into it. Some of us just aren't that lucky, or are we, now that you've graced us with your company." Karyn's rage, directed at me opened the floodgates and I let loose.

"Karyn, you're nothing but a condescending bitch and I've put up with you my whole life. Well, I don't have to anymore, do I. I left town the very minute I could so I didn't have to listen to your haughty pompous bullshit and as for my ex-husbands, that's a real cheap shot, isn't it? I'm glad you and Bob are so perfect, but it didn't work out for me. I lost my true love, and then I married an abusive prick followed by a lying cheat! I deserve every penny I get from them and furthermore, I have a very lucrative business of my own and that's my main income! I'm not a bloodsucking leech like you."

"Now, that's a cheap shot," Bob interjected, "Karyn's a hard worker."

"Stay out of this Bob," I shouted. "This isn't about you!"

"Oh, poor, poor Annie, slobbering in her pity, nothing ever changes with you! How long has it been, twenty years, more? Will you never get a life and get on with it? We're just a little sick and tired of hearing how you lost your one and only love and how the accident ripped away your life. Why don't you lose your bullshit? Your whining makes me want to vomit!"

"How dare you mention the accident? You stood right there and let them steal my life! You watched that evil wench sitting at the end of this table pull my soul from me and you never said a word; you just watched her take it away."

"Don't you dare call her names, Annie, you selfish bitch, who do you think you are? That night is over; it's been over for more than twenty years! She didn't take him away; he was dead and you wouldn't let go. He's still dead and even now, you can't let go! Go home, wherever that might be, just get the hell out of here! "

"You need me, remember? I'm the one you begged to do your dirty work; did you forget already? At the snap of your fingers, I came running when you called."

"I don't need you, I never did and I never will. Gee, if my memory serves me correctly, you didn't come running, you crawled here when I called. I needed your help and I had to beg you; even then, you took your sweet time getting here insisting on driving. Why was that, Annie, to show off your fancy Lexus or to make me wait? Whatever happened to crap like sisterly love and blood is thicker than water?"

"You were jealous of me from the day I was born, Karyn. When you had the opportunity to watch me bleed out, you did. I saw you! I saw the look on your face that night. You gloated knowing what happened and I hate you for it! I hate her for it!"

"You're right, Annie, I did hate you! You were Daddy's little girl, always Daddy's little girl. I loved him, too, and I thought he was my father!" As soon as she said it, I could tell she regretted it, but it was too late and I didn't care. Bob had his face buried in his hands unable to look at Sara and Susan, their faces twisted in shocked expressions.

"Well, now you know, don't you?" I felt a rush like never before, knowing my words stabbed her. I wanted her to hurt, to watch her life hemorrhage away while she ached with the pain of it. "You're a half bred monster, the daughter of scum; it's no wonder Daddy wanted nothing to do with you and that mindless whore."

"She's not a whore, Annie, and Daddy loved her! We don't know what happened yet, do we? Furthermore, if I am Gino's daughter, then I have the same foul blood as your precious Joey; did you stop to think about that? Did you?"

"Don't you dare mention his name, Karyn; he was nothing like you and nothing like his father!"

"You're nothing but a fucking bitch, Annie! How can you be so heartless?"

I stood up, pushed my chair from the table, glared at her with eyes exposing every ounce of hatred I could manifest. "I don't need this bullshit," I muttered. I'm out of here and I hope you rot in hell with the prick that sired you!"

Jackie jumped to his feet and shouted, "No, Annie, don't go!"

Karyn barked bitterly to his objection, "Stop protecting her, Jack, and let her go. She didn't want to be here in the first place and she's put her feelings on the table. Let the bitch go!"

Jackie started to follow me, but I pushed past him and walked out the front door while everyone else sat with gaping mouths, stunned by the performance laid before them. My Lexus was wedged in the driveway, but I managed to maneuver it free. The metallic scraping sound told me I didn't quite clear the lamppost, but I didn't care. I drove over the lawn to the road, leaving tire tracks in the grass as I sped away.

My skin burned with anger, but my eyes were dry and I felt no remorse, only relief at the release of the pent up emotion I carried for so long. I only had the clothes on my back and the purse I grabbed from the foyer table when I ran out the door, but I didn't care. Everything else was just material and I would shop for new clothes and personal items. I refused to go back. In a couple of days I would call Jackie, but tonight I planned to get a hotel room and leave before daylight to head south.

In an effort to calm down, I drove to Eastern Point Beach, not leaving my car, I just sat in the parking lot watching the river and taking in the smells and sounds of the beachfront. The familiar rank smell of seaweed washed on shore was strangely pleasant and soothing, taking some of the burn from my flushed face as I inhaled it deeply. The pounding of blood in my veins and the throbbing in my head slowly appeased as I calmed to a more relaxed state of mind. I still couldn't reflect on the argument, wanting only to forget and run; tomorrow would bring just that. Until then, this was my hour to say good-bye to one of my favorite places, the beach, and when I was ready, I left for another.

I drove a very short distance to Avery Point, once home to a U.S. Coast Guard Training Station, the location now dedicated as a branch of the University of Connecticut. Passing through the stately entrance, I admired the old Branford House overlooking Fisher's Island and Long Island Sound. In my youth, I toured the 31-room mansion now part of the academic institution, surprising myself with the recollection of the two-story fireplace and the winding staircase of imported Italian marble. I parked the Lexus and got out to walk around the grounds, heading to the massive rocks beaten relentlessly for centuries with crashing waves that polished their smooth, shiny surfaces. A young man and woman were each flying colorful kites from the point; she laughed when his crashed to the stones below leaving him with a vibrant tangled mass of shredded silk. For the first time that day, I smiled, and in my heart, I wished the strangers a good life, willing the argument with Karyn to fade to a distant place. I drove away, leaving behind another farewell.

Determined to find a hotel in New London for the night, I took Shennecossett Road driving past the Yacht Club, following it to Thomas Road along the railroad track. I decided on one more good-bye, so I followed Poquonnock Road to Mitchell Street heading toward Washington Park where Tommy and I had so much fun. Along the way, the massive granite archway of the Colonel Ledyard Cemetery beckoned me to enter. Close to my home, I played here as a child, along with Joey and other classmates, as did generations before us. My parents had no family buried here, my mother refusing to enter, calling it an evil place, the home of the devil himself, yet she had no problem with other cemeteries. Even now, I didn't wonder why. Until Joey I had no family buried here either, now it was no longer a playground, it was place to grieve and say good-bye.

Dusk was settling when I drove under the arch, following the short road ahead lined with the tall budding trees eerily standing guard as sentinels over the dead. With the exception of some newer monuments marking the graves, there were few changes and I knew the turf well from my childhood. I parked the car close to the mausoleum and walked toward the wall where I knew I would see his grave for the first time. Never told why Joey's family chose this cemetery for his interment, I always hoped it was their last minute acceptance of our marriage and out of respect for me, yet I knew otherwise. The proximity to my home was their way to punish me with the constant reminder of his death, but I fooled them, didn't I, when I left town forever.

I don't know how I knew where the grave was located, but I did; someone must have told me at some point. The only thing I knew for sure is that this was my first time here since I was a child. Reverently, I walked between the burial plots, smiling slightly at the memory of Joey telling me I would die in twenty-four hours if I stepped on a grave. I believed him. I always believed him. The grass was muddy and brown from the spring thaw with a few patches of new green growth trying to find its way to the surface. The moist earth receded with each of my footsteps adding to the silence; even the birds bedded for the night.

Suddenly, frozen in place, I saw the marker to my left. I was on the backside of the tombstone, yet I knew without a doubt the inscription on the other side as I slowly walked around to its face. I felt nothing. Why did I feel nothing? Shouldn't I cry, or throw myself down on the grave sobbing? There was just emptiness and then I raised my eyes to see the words etched deeply into the polished marble.

I read the words aloud, "Joseph Salvatore Fontinelli, Beloved Son, and," but before I could finish, the light around me faded, my legs became wobbly, no longer supporting me and my body went limp as I collapsed to the ground in a faint, hearing only the crying of cats, their pitiful, helpless cries. I remembered, Oh my God, I remembered.

CHAPTER
31

Alberto Santucci was happier than any man had the right to be he thought while driving to Watch Hill to meet the man envied by any aficionado attracted to power and wealth. The Fontinelli family was an icon for the American dream and Alberto one of its greatest fans for as long as he could remember. As a child, Alberto would daydream that one day Social Services would contact him to say that one of the brothers, it didn't matter which one, wanted to adopt him, only him. In his fantasy, a private jet picked him up and took him to America where he lived in their compound and they grew to love him more than the children they sired. Singing loudly with the radio, he imagined he was going home because now that Gino was gone, Dominick needed him more than ever and he would be the good son.

Reaching the giant gate to the mansion, he pushed the button and waited for a response, but none came. He rang three more times and still there was silence. About to get out of the car, he was startled when the passenger door opened and a large burly looking man in his forties got in the seat next to him and in a deep commanding voice said to him, "Mr. Fontinelli is waiting for you, drive up the hill."

When they approached the mansion, the man instructed him to park the car facing the exit and without question, he obediently turned the car around to face the direction from which he came. Then with no further words, he followed the man through the front door down a long dark hallway passing the rooms with closed doors. The mansion was eerily quiet and dark with shades drawn and curtains closed. It felt as if he and the man were alone and although he knew the envelope in his hand was all the power he needed for protection, he was nervous entering a world of unknown.

At the end of the hall, the large double doors to the library were already open revealing a large mahogany desk entirely wiped clean with the exception of the leather desk blotter, a marble penholder and a telephone. There wasn't a piece of paper in sight. A leather chair with a high back faced the wall away from him. The raspy voice of its occupant said, "Thank you, Tony, please wait outside," and the man left, closing the doors behind him.

As a schoolchild called to the principal's office, Alberto stood before the desk with a white knuckled grip on the envelope waiting for the leather chair to swivel around and reveal its tenant. His legs were weak and his knees wobbled, but he dared not sit. Slowly, the chair turned exposing the man he had seen only in photos.

Alberto didn't see the frail, sickly man before him, instead his eyes locked to the eyes of evil; he knew it, he felt it and he was scared. He knew Dominick was sizing him up and he needed to get back into control, or get out before this went any further. He chose the former and without invitation sat down. Dominick's eyes followed his movements with disapproval and they each maintained their silence trying the read the other.

Without hiding his annoyance, Dominick was the first to speak and mordantly asked, "To what do I owe the displeasure of our meeting, Mr. Santucci?"

Alberto's confidence rising, he answered, "I believe I have something of interest to you, Mr. Fontinelli, something that perhaps you would not want made public."

"My dear little man, you are not the first to uncover my little discretion from many years ago and you probably won't be the last. At this point, it really doesn't matter if it goes public, but to avoid embarrassment to my daughter and son, please just get to the point and tell me what you want. I'm a busy man."

"Hmmm, I believe this information, if it goes public, will carry more legal ramifications than embarrassment. It's more like a major cover-up," Alberto explained in a caustic tone.

Dominick, still feeling he had the upper hand, snarled back at him, "What happened was many, many years ago; my brother and I have supported her and her little bastard daughter, keeping them comfortable. The woman kept her silence as agreed and she will continue to do so, therefore, our little meeting today is a total waste of time for both of us." While he spoke, he opened a desk drawer, pulled out an envelope, and continued, "For your inconvenience, however, I'm prepared to help offset the cost of your trip here, knowing that this is now a dead discussion. I understand the price of gasoline is quite high these days." With that said, he slid a thick envelope toward Alberto who suddenly appeared to be confused.

"Mr. Fontinelli, I don't believe we are speaking of the same matter. I know nothing of the woman and her daughter to which you refer. I'm here about something else, someone else entirely. I'm not quite sure of your motives, but I know there are some people that would be very interested to know about your grandson, perhaps his mother for one."

Dominick's pallor went ashen, his hand squeezing the envelope of money until the seal began to split. For a moment, Alberto thought the old man stopped breathing and was having a heart attack. Visibly shaken, Dominick fought for composure, and knew well what information the young man uncovered. The secret, if revealed, would destroy his dynasty and implicate his son legally, all for a decision he made decades ago.

"Have you nothing to say, old man?" Alberto knew he made the homerun with this one and he wasn't about to let it go. "I think this is worth much more than the pittance you hold in your hand. Perhaps you'd like to reconsider the price of gasoline."

Finally able to speak, Dominick said with less authority, "Before we go any further, I'd like to know exactly what documents you have to support your allegations."

"Not a problem," he answered. "I've got them right here. Of course, these are copies; the originals are in a very safe location." He laid the manila envelope on the desk, removed the documents and laid them out before Dominick so he could see them.

Dominick's hands shook uncontrollably as he picked them up to read, one by one. It was even more devastating than he imagined; they were all there, birth and death certificates, marriage certificates, name changes, adoption papers, passports, all there at his fingertips. The entire paper trail was in his hands. He had to stop this and he knew only one way.

Knowing he had total control, Alberto said, "I believe our little meeting is now a formal Finance Meeting, don't you agree?"

"I am willing to triple what I...," Dominick started to say, but was abruptly interrupted.

"No, I don't think you understand. You're going to do as I tell you to do, not what you are willing to do. I'm in control here, not you; do you get that, old geezer? I'm in control. I want five-hundred thousand upfront and another two million wired to my offshore account. If the money doesn't hit my account in two days, this goes public, very public, get it?"

"I don't keep that kind of money in the house. I can give you one hundred today and arrange for the remaining four hundred tomorrow. I will need three days for the wire. How will you assure me that this matter will never surface again? "

"I am a man of my word. After I receive the wire, I will destroy the original documents and you will never hear from me again." Alberto fought to hide his excitement and surprise at the ease of it all.

Dominick pushed a button under the desk, the doors opened and Tony walked in and asked, "Do you need me, Sir?"

"Yes, Tony, I've made a financial agreement with Mr. Santucci for a special purchase. Please arrange to meet with him tomorrow sometime to deliver the funding. In the meantime, please go to my quarters and return with his down payment of one hundred thousand."

"Of course, I'll be right back." Tony didn't appear to be in the least bit surprised, having been part of many dealings with his uncle. He had the combinations for every safe Dominick owned and access to the entire empire, which would one day be his and his alone. His uncle would never allow his oldest son, Peter to have control and his daughter was out of the question entirely.

The two men were silent waiting for Tony to return. Alberto was mentally counting his cash and Dominick was planning how to eliminate this problem altogether.

Neither even glanced at the other until Tony returned with an envelope containing fresh clean one hundred dollar bills and handed it over to his uncle who in turn passed it to Alberto without counting it.

Dominick simply said, "That will be all, Mr. Santucci," and dismissed him like a servant.

When Tony returned after escorting Alberto off the property, Dominick told him to sit down because he needed to talk to him. Tony listened intently while his uncle laid out the details of the night in the cemetery. The story he failed to tell was how the sins of the fathers tangled a web so tight that it strangled the lives of their sons. That would come in time when Tony was ready for it, not now. As Dominick spoke, Tony noticed how fragile and frail he was becoming as the cancer ate him away and he silently prayed an enigma wanting this to be over soon so he didn't suffer, yet wanting him to live forever. He loved his uncle like the father he lost before him, knowing there was nothing he would not do for him in the future, nor had not done for him in the past..

"Tony, this has to go away quickly. Do you understand?" Dominick's eyes said it all; there was no need for further words.

"Of course, I'll take care of it right away, Uncle Dom," and Dominick knew he would. "Hey, did you bring the cannolis and sfogliatelle?"

"Sure, they're in the fridge. If you want, I'll get you some. There are a couple of the napoleons you asked for, too and they're fresh."

"No, that's okay; I'll have some later with a little espresso. That reporter is coming back tomorrow, so I wanted to make sure there's some for her, too."

"Since when do you care what a reporter eats? Are you getting soft in your old age, Uncle Dom, or looking for a new girlfriend?" Tony loved to tease his uncle.

"Don't be a smartass! Take a good look at this body; my days with women are over. Seriously, though, she's doing an article on me and I want to make sure she's not upset over anything. I don't want her to write anything bad. It's driving me crazy though because I could swear I've seen her before. Maybe I'm just getting old and they all look alike now."

"If that's the one you had me check out for you, she's pretty famous. You probably just saw her book or something," Tony told him.

"I guess you're right. Anyway, I'm going to go take a nap. Take care of that matter for me as soon as possible. Ok? Oh, if you get a chance, stop by tomorrow and meet the reporter lady. Maybe she's not married and you'll get lucky."

"Maybe I'll do that. Go get some rest and I'll call you when everything's settled."

CHAPTER
32

New York City

When the elevator doors opened, the last person in the world Sal ever expected to see was his wife and there she was in the flesh, more beautiful than ever, but her eyes were stone and piercing right through him. Without a spoken word, he knew instantaneously that this was the unveiling of his paradox and for a moment, he froze, just staring at her in disbelief until he was finally able to mutter, "Niki, what are you doing here?"

All English to the wind, she was holding nothing back, venting her pent-up thoughts from the transatlantic flight. "Ci siete, voi sporco Farabutto!" she said angrily calling him a scoundrel. Then with eyes locked on Theresa asked if she was his dirty little whore, "Chi è questo, la tua puttana piccolo sporco?"

"Niki, calm down, I can explain, but tell me what you're doing here! What's going on? I mean, I'm so happy to see you, but it's such a surprise." He stepped forward to give her a hug, but she pushed him away with a hissing sound.

"Ti stai chiedendo me cosa sta succedendo? Come OSI?" She demanded how he dare ask her what was going on.

"English, Niki, please speak in English," Sal never saw her with this much anger before. His Italian was fluent, polished, and without accent, but it still required more thought and concentration for him than English did and under the circumstances, he just couldn't do it.

Stunned by the altercation, Theresa kept silent taking a step back from the crazed woman she never met. Her gut feeling told her to stay out of it until her brother made an indication otherwise. She wanted to leave, but knew this was the point of no return and wondered about the outcome because when this was over, so many lives would change. What would become of them? What was next?

Adjacent elevator doors opened and an elderly couple started to get out, but seeing the quarrel between Sal and Niki, they cautiously stepped backward allowing the doors to close and take them to another floor.

Fearing a public display, Theresa interrupted her brother, "We should probably take this out of the hallway."

"Who is this whore?" Niki demanded to know.

"She's not a whore, Niki, she's my sister and she's right, let's get out of the hall; let's go to my room where we can talk privately."

For the first time, Niki looked directly at Theresa and noticed the strong physical resemblance, but continued to glare at her with hatred. "I won't go anywhere with you; it's lies, nothing but lies. I want to see Vinnie, my son. He is my son, isn't he, Sal?"

"Please, Niki, let's go to Sal's room," Theresa pleaded in an effort to remove themselves from public view. "We can all talk there."

"Get away from me, you whore!" Niki's face was crimson, her anger escalating out of control. "I want to see my son!"

Sal stepped forward to take her arm, but before he could do so, she swung her handbag aiming for his head. Instinctively, Theresa grabbed the purse, but not before it connected squarely with his left cheek.

"Stop it!" Theresa yelled, "We're making a scene and we can't afford this right now. We've got to go to the room and talk; we're running out of time if we're going to find Vinnie!" With that said, she turned and started walking back down the hall to Sal's room and the two of them followed her.

"What do you mean, running out of time to find Vinnie? What's happened?" Niki was clearly upset, but she followed Theresa and Sal to the room, a mother's look of terror on her face. Once they were in the room, she demanded angrily, "What's happened to my son, you lying son of a bitch?"

"Calm down, Niki, I can explain everything," Sal said, still not knowing exactly how much she knew and fearing the worst, which she confirmed with her next comment.

"I know everything," she yelled. "You've lied to me since the first day we met, about Vinnie, about you, about everything! How could you, Sal? How could you? That's not even your name, is it? Who are you? Why the lies, Sal; I would have loved you anyway! All these years and I don't even know you and what about Vinnie? You came to me with your baby brother and together we agreed to raise him as our son; now it turns out he really was your son. Where's his mother? Do I lose him now, too? Why did you lie? Why?"

"I never planned on any of this, Niki, honestly I didn't. I had life mapped out for Vinnie and me, then you came along and I knew I had to be with you. One lie led to another and then another, before I knew it, I was in so deep and there was no way out. I tried to tell you many times, but knew you would leave me and I couldn't' bear it. You're my world now; we have a beautiful family together! I'll tell you everything, Niki, but you can't leave, you've got to promise me that." Sal was pleading with her, but she just looked at him with total disgust. "Let me start by introducing you to my twin sister, Theresa. We've been in touch, but it's been many, many years since we've seen each other."

"I don't care about her! First, tell me where Vinnie is; why do you have to find him?" For the first time since entering the room, she spoke in a softer voice, but her eyes remained bitter and cold.

"I don't know where to begin, Niki," he said, tears forming in his eyes.

"Try starting where you lost my son because he is my son, you lousy bastard, you can't take him away from me now; you can't!" She, too, was crying, but her tears were those of anger, not compassion.

Leaving out his personal history and the truth of his identity, Sal started at the point when he arrived in New York with Vinnie to look at the university. He told her he arranged for Vinnie to see the school and when he befriended some of the other students; he let Vinnie go out with them a few times. The other night, Vinnie never came back from the theater he attended with his new friends and the police were notified and looking for him. He told her that he and Theresa were about to go to the school to look for him themselves when she got off the elevator.

"You let him go with strangers, total strangers? How could you be so stupid, Sal? Damn it, I don't even know what to call you!"

"Sal, my name is Sal, and they weren't strangers. They were friends of someone's son who works at Onyx that I know well." That wasn't entirely true, but Sal knew better than admit he had no clue about the identity of his son's companions when he disappeared.

"He's just a boy, how could you let him roam freely in this city?"

"Niki, he's my son; I would never put him in danger intentionally! I knew these people from Onyx."

"Do you even work at Onyx, Sal? Do you work there?" Her voice was rising again.

"Yes, I work there, but not in the capacity you think," he answered, but before he could explain, his cell phone rang and praying it was Vinnie, he answered it immediately.

"Mr. Fiore, this is Officer Smith from the 19th Precinct. I took the report on your son."

"Yes, yes, I know who you are. Did you find my son?" Sal's patience was all but exhausted and he had no time for polite conversation.

"No, Sir, we haven't found him, but his wallet and passport were found. I'm afraid there was no money and the credit cards were stolen."

"You idiot, he had no credit cards and I could give a damn less about the money! Where is my son?" Niki and Theresa just stared at him while he vented his rage at the young officer on the phone. "I want to know where my son is!"

"As I said, Sir, we haven't located him, but the wallet was found in Greenwich Village, not on Broadway where you said he went to the theater. Could he have been in Greenwich Village?"

"Of course not; he had no reason to be there. Some bum probably stole it and somehow it ended up there! Stop chasing rabbits, Officer and find my son!"

"We're working on it, Sir. I'll call you as soon as I have any additional information." It was apparent Sal intimidated her with his rage on the other end of the phone. Before she could end the call, Sal slammed closed the cell phone ending it for her.

"We were in Greenwich Village that night, Sal. Could he have followed us?" Theresa asked her brother.

"Of course, not, why would he? He was going out with his friends and he didn't know anything about you. Besides, he was long gone before I came to pick you up."

"Where's his mother, Sal? Who is she?" The color in Niki's face, now gone, left her looking tired and drawn. She wanted answers, needed to know it all and Sal knew it was time to come clean, but he couldn't do it.

"You're his mother, Niki, the only mother he's ever known. There was an accident, a bad accident before he was born. He was saved, she was not."

Sarcastically she asked, "Was it the same accident that killed your parents?"

"No, they didn't die in an accident," he explained, knowing she already knew the truth. "My mother died when I was a teenager and my father is still alive and lives in the States. I'm an American, as American as apple pie, so the cliché says. I went to Italy after my son was born to begin a new life and run my father's international operations. He has interests all over Europe, one of them being Onyx in which he's a major shareholder, but now he's retired, so I'm his eyes and ears, incognito most of the time. It was a way to start over and protect my son."

"What are you protecting him from? Who are you protecting him from?" She was full of questions.

"From a dirty deed my father did as a child, from life itself, I guess," Sal tried hard to find the right words. "Sometimes I wonder myself; it just doesn't make sense anymore. After the accident, his mother's parents wanted to keep the baby, but my father insisted otherwise. They threatened to expose the truth of his deed, so he used his power and bought them off as he always does. In everyone's best interest, my father decided that I needed to take my son away and of course; it was also convenient to my father for me to run his affairs at the same time. Looking back, it was all about my father; it's always all about my father."

"That's not true, Sal," Theresa interrupted. "He's not as bad as you make him out to be."

"How easy for you to say, it wasn't your life he changed. It was mine." Sal spoke to Theresa, but looked directly at Niki as he spoke, trying to read her feelings, but unable to do so.

"What's your real name, Sal?" Niki asked almost in a whisper.

"My legal name is Salvatore Francesco Fiore. Joseph Salvatore Fontinelli is dead and buried."

CHAPTER
33

The pounding pain in my head throbbed until my whole body ached from it. Make those cats stop crying, please, I screamed to myself, but their howls and whines went on and on with no end. I couldn't bear it anymore; they needed to stop before my head burst. Who is there? Mom, is that you? Why are you crying? You're so young, so beautiful. Where am I? Please, please, get rid of the cats! Make them stop!

"Annie, you're in a hospital," my mother said softly to me. You're so young and beautiful, I thought. "There was a bad accident and you're in a hospital."

I can't speak I thought to myself. Where's Joey, where's Joey? I can't think straight, I can't speak. Why can't I speak? Oh, God, where's Joey? Please Mom, bring Joey to me. There's something in my throat. It hurts to swallow. Why can't I speak? Mom, get Joey for me, please. Get Joey!

"Sweetheart, I have some bad news; Joey died in the accident. The doctors did everything they could, but he didn't make it; he's gone." She was lying; she had to be. Joey wasn't dead. We were leaving town again, taking our baby and leaving town! Oh my God, the baby, where's my baby! My stomach is flat; where's my baby?

"Annie, listen to me, you've been hurt badly and you're losing the baby, too. He's a little boy, a beautiful little boy, but the impact was too much for him and he is bleeding internally. He's not going to make it, Annie. The doctor is here with him, so you can say good-bye, but he's gone, Annie; he's gone."

He's so small and the blanket is so warm. My precious baby, oh my God, my precious baby next to my heart; where are your tears? Why won't you cry? You're beautiful, like an angel. I'm going to hold you forever and keep you safe. Joey, where's Joey? He needs to see our son. He's so beautiful, so beautiful. Why is my mother crying when she should be so happy? He's beautiful.

"It's time to let him go, Annie," she said reaching for him. "You need to say good-bye to him. Kiss him good-bye." She reaches to take him away from me.

Is that my sister standing behind my mother? She's smiling. Why isn't my mother smiling? She should be smiling like my sister, happy like my sister.

No, no, don't take him away from me! Don't take him away! He's mine; give him back to me! My screeches escalate to the pitch of the cats, they resonate in harmony with the cats; we are one, we are the same. My screams are theirs; their cries are mine. Make them stop. Please, make them stop!

I don't know how long I was unconscious at the gravesite, but when I woke, there was a trickle of blood streaming from my forehead to my cheek, cleansed only by my tears. My clothing bore the signs of the moist dirt and my head ached from the impact against the monument. Every muscle and nerve in my body shook with sobs as I remembered the pain of years ago, years that melted into nothing with the memory of losing my husband and child.

Slowly, I got to my feet, pushing myself up against the cold granite of the stone, again reading the words engraved in the marble, "Joseph Salvatore Fontinelli, Beloved Son", and "Baby Fontinelli". Who bought this stone? It read "Son", not "Husband" and "Baby", not "Vincent" as we planned. He didn't even have a name; my poor, sweet baby didn't even have a name.

Exhausted and spent, I pulled myself together and drove back to the house. Thankfully, the house was dark and the driveway, clear of all cars, including Jackie's car. I can't describe my feelings because I felt drained, yet relieved of a burden somehow. The pain of remembering was deep, but the burden of only partial memories was far worse. I needed to heal; I needed desperately to heal and now I could. First thing tomorrow, I would go back to Dominick's and get what Karyn needed. Then, I would face him with the truth because I was no longer afraid. No more games, no more rage and hatred, just the truth and I would follow where it led.

I desperately needed a shower, but with no one home decided to grab something to drink first, so I went into the kitchen. On the table was a note addressed to me. It read, "Annie, hopefully you'll be in early and get this. Mom had a terrible seizure and the ambulance is taking her to Lawrence Memorial Hospital in New London. You're not answering your phone and I'm worried. If you see Mike, tell him Sara has been trying to reach him also. Call me ASAP! Love, Jack".

When I left the house in such a hurry, I only grabbed my purse, leaving my cell phone upstairs in my room. I skipped stairs running to the second floor to get it. Besides, a call from my agent and a number I didn't recognize, there were six calls from Jackie, two from Sara and one from Karyn. I didn't bother listening to the messages and just dialed Jackie's number instead.

"Oh, thank God, you called," said Jackie with a sound of relief in his voice. "I've been worried sick about you, all of us have."

"I'm fine, really I am. Tell me what happened. How is she?" I didn't want him to hear the fatigue in my voice.

"Not good, Annie, it's not good. We're still not sure what happened, but after you left, everyone was upset and Mike offered to take her to sit on the front porch with some dessert to get away from it all. The rest of us stayed on the back patio trying to figure out what went wrong and Mike ran back to get us saying that she was having some kind of fit, as he put it, and she fell down the front steps and hit her head on the pavement. By the time we got there, she was laying on the sidewalk in a full-blown seizure, so we called an ambulance first and then her doctor who met us here at the hospital."

"How is she now? What are they saying?" I asked.

"She's getting lots of attention to say the least, but she's unresponsive. It's complicated because they don't know why she had the seizure in the first place and now she has the head trauma from the fall. Her doctor said they won't know anything for a while, but he's being straightforward that it doesn't look good for her. There's definitely something going on and he's concerned about the coma now. Do you remember how to get here?"

"Not a problem, it's on Montauk Avenue. I remember how to get there. I'm going to take a quick shower and I'll be there. Call me if anything comes up in the meantime, okay?"

"Sure, I'll call. Annie, are you okay?" He asked with apparent concern.

"I'm good, Jackie, and Jackie?"

"Yes?"

"I'm sorry, really sorry about tonight and everything else. Is Karyn there?"

"Yes, she's with Mom, hasn't left her side."

"Good, I'll see her when I get there, and there will be no problems," I promised.

"Please, Annie, no more problems. We don't need them right now," he told me firmly.

"I know," I said with sincerity. "I'll see you in a bit."

CHAPTER
34

Back in his apartment, Alberto hurriedly threw his belongings into a duffle bag, only taking what he absolutely needed for a couple of days until he could reach his new apartment. He would have plenty of time, and money, to shop for new clothes and anything else he desired. He doubted anyone would find this apartment and connect it to Mike, the son of the Portuguese fishing family. He never took Sara here and as far as she was concerned, he lived at a different address with a nonexistent roommate. He was as proud of his plan as a peacock strutting with open feathers and hummed loudly while he packed.

Everything was already playing out as planned, but the unexpected quarrel between Sara's snobby aunt and her mother, the grumbling crank, was a bonus for sure. It was so easy to play the caring Mike and take the old woman out to the front porch while they acted like the selfish bitches they were.

His dear Miss Maggie, which he now uncaringly referred to her as, was such an easy target and tonight was perfect. She salivated seeing the chocolate cake and devoured the contents of two additional capsules of Bupropion without tasting the pharmaceutical. It didn't take long for her to start rocking away in her chair with that damn doll of hers. He chuckled when he thought how he helped the forward momentum of her sway just enough for her to plunge down the steps. If anyone was looking, they would think he was trying to stop her from falling, not pushing her into the pavement. How clever he was, how clever he was indeed!

The cell phone rang interrupting his thoughts and he cursed Sara for being the pain in the ass she was. He easily slipped away during the commotion with the ambulance and everyone jockeying to get to the hospital. He would be glad to get rid of her, clinging to him all the time like a rock around his neck. Her cuteness was beginning to make him sick.

He decided to ignore her call as he had the three for four previous ones, but unconsciously glanced at the number. It wasn't Sara; it was a Rhode Island number, maybe Dominick Fontinelli with the details for his pickup tomorrow.

"Hello," he answered cautiously.

"Mr. Santucci, this is Tony Fontinelli," the gruff voice on the other end announced. "My uncle was able to secure what you requested a little earlier than expected. Can you meet me later this evening?"

"Of course, tell me where to be and what time," Alberto could hardly contain his excitement.

"Well, my uncle wants to meet with you personally to hand it over and suggested I pick you up by helicopter. Unfortunately, I can't be there until around nine o'clock if that's not too late."

"That's not too late at all. Where do you want to meet me?" Alberto would have gone anywhere for this.

"Okay, I'll be there to pick you up at the Groton-New London Airport and we'll meet my uncle at his estate. You can stay in the guesthouse this evening and he'll send you home with his driver early in the morning," he said.

"Are you sure he wants me to stay over? Isn't he afraid someone will see us together?" Alberto asked, nervous about the plans, but excited at the same time for the opportunity to stay at the mansion.

"There's no need for us to be clandestine, Mr. Santucci. It's strict business and my uncle is very comfortable with it. So, will you be able to meet me at the airport at nine o'clock?" He asked.

142

"Yes, I'll be there," Alberto affirmed, "and please tell your uncle thank you for the prompt attention."

"Yes, I'll tell him," Tony said thinking what a naïve fool he had on the other end of the phone. "Oh, I almost forgot, take a cab so you don't have to leave your car in the parking lot overnight."

"Okay, will do," answered Alberto, trying to hide his excitement as he ended the call."

He could hardly contain himself waiting for the time to arrive to meet Tony and receive his reward, his well-deserved reward for all his sacrifices and hard work. Finally, he had come of age in his own right.

As instructed, Alberto took a taxi to the airport getting there early as Tony anticipated. The terminal and restaurant were not open, but also as Tony predicted, he would not be able to stay to himself and wandered around in full view of the employees and others still around. He was handsome and had a look that drew stares and Tony wanted him seen.

Promptly at nine o'clock, the black helicopter with the Fontinelli monogram set down and Tony stepped out to meet Alberto directing him through the gate to the tarmac where he boarded the luxury helicopter. Onlookers openly stared with envy as the handsome young man accepted his invitation to board the personal helicopter of the Fontinelli family.

The leather seats fit like a glove and he immediately nestled in as if he was riding in his personal aircraft. Once settled, Tony gave the pilot the sign to lift off and the quick ascension brought Alberto's stomach to his throat like the thrill of a roller coaster. He was born for this, he thought. Then Tony reached into the cabinet next to him and pulled out a magnum of champagne, already opened and chilled. He poured them each a glass and handing Alberto his to drink, he toasted, "To your health, Mr. Santucci." Oh yes, Alberto thought, he was born for this.

The taste of the champagne honed his taste buds and whetted his appetite for more and Tony gladly accommodated him. The methodical whir of the aircraft blades and the savor of the sparkling wine relaxed him, lulling his senses and with his last thought knowing he was born for this, he drifted into a deep peaceful sleep.

As Alberto slumbered without a care, Tony gathered the champagne bottle, his own untouched glass of wine and Alberto's glass with traces of sleeping aid. Several miles out over Long Island Sound, Alberto's naked, weighted body fell into fathoms of ocean, discarded like yesterday's garbage along with the remaining champagne.

The next morning, the helicopter returned to the airport and the young man who disembarked in Alberto's clothing had the same build, but wasn't nearly as handsome. One woman, who admired his good looks the night before, clearly remembered that he looked rather rough the next morning as if he partied all night. How lucky, she told her friends. As for the decoy, the drunken college student was just happy to get a lift back from Fisher's Island. What luck that he met Mr. Fontinelli's personal pilot! He not only gave him a clean set of clothes to replace his alcohol-stained ones, but also provided cash for the cab called to pick him up. The Fontinelli's were a generous and giving family.

CHAPTER
35

New York City

Following New York City's tragedy on September 11, 2001, Bellevue Hospital was one of the busiest medical facilities, treating those who survived and identifying those who did not. Rosa Gonzalez thought about those days as she tended to the young man under her care in the Intensive Care Unit. Medical staffing was short and the victims were endless, but she and her colleagues gave selflessly until they had no more to give, all the while feeling powerless that they were unable to help more injured, to save more lives. It was days like those and days like the one today, that she cursed herself for choosing this profession. Not particularly an outwardly religious person, she did believe in God, but could not understand his plan.

Now in her forties, she was a veteran nurse with over twenty-five years experience and tenure just shy of two months with Bellevue Hospital. The doctors changed, the patients changed, but never the sickness, the injuries, the atrocities that occurred daily; there was no end.

Gently, she wiped the sweat from the brow of the young man and wondered about him. The chart listed him as a John Doe, but his manicured nails, styled hair and the expensive clothing they cut from him said otherwise. He belonged somewhere, but where did he belong? She admired the fight in him, knowing he should have died at the scene, but did not. The surgery yesterday went well, if you can measure success with removing one kidney and patching another to prolong the inevitable if there was no transplant. As a John Doe, he didn't have a chance. Speaking to him aloud as if he could hear, she asked, "Where do you belong, Son? Where do you belong?"

Exhausted as always, and not wanting to wake her husband when she arrived home shortly before eleven that night, she curled up in her favorite chair and turned the news on with low volume. Her full attention was on the bowl of strawberry ice cream in her hands until she scraped it clean and she was ready to turn off the television and go to bed. The remote in her hand pointing at the set and her finger on the power button, she caught her breath with the News Alert. There he was, the John Doe, staring at her from the screen with round, black eyes and a wide grin, healthy and alive like he should be. Quickly, she turned up the volume just in time to hear about the young Italian student who went missing while visiting schools in New York City with his father, a prominent Italian businessman, and there are no leads or any indication of foul play at this time. The news commentator requested that anyone with any information please call the number listed on the screen. The empty bowl dropped to the floor as she reached for the telephone to call, yelling to her husband to wake up.

Once they received the information, it didn't take the 19th Precinct long to verify with Bellevue that they did indeed have an unidentified John Doe matching the description of the missing Italian student. They immediately notified Sal, asking him to meet them at the hospital for a positive identification, so he, Theresa and Niki set out for Bellevue, putting his explanations to his wife on temporary hold.

Two plainclothes officers, already there, met them in the lobby when they arrived, one of them looking like the person Sal saw reviewing Officer Smith's report at the precinct. He was the one who explained that they needed to wait for an escort to the Intensive Care Unit.

As they spoke, a professional looking woman in her mid-fifties approached them, held out her hand to the one of the detectives and introduced herself, "Good evening, I'm Linda Wright, Bellevue's Director of Corporate Public Affairs."

"Thank you for meeting with us on such short notice, Ms. Wright. I am Detective Barnes, this is my partner, Jim Blackman, and this is the boy's father, Salvatore Fiore." He didn't introduce Theresa and Niki.

She acknowledged with a handshake to each and asked, "Is the boy's mother also here?"

"Yes," Sal said, "This is my wife, Nicoletta Fiore and my sister, Theresa Fontinelli. Can we see my son now?"

"Before we go upstairs, it's very important for me to tell you. This young man is in the Intensive Care Unit and badly injured. The report we received from the Emergency staff at the scene said he ran into moving traffic in Greenwich Village and a taxi hit him. I have not personally seen him yet, but the supervisor on staff told me his face has several bruises from hitting the pavement. It is quite swollen and lacerated. The injuries that you'll see, however, are minor compared to the internal trauma. He was pinned under the front wheel of the vehicle in such a manner that our surgeons were forced to remove one kidney and the damage to other one is severe."

"Oh my God," Niki cried aloud, holding her hand over her face.

"One more thing," Ms. Wright continued. "We are all assuming that this is your missing son, but in the event that it is not, it's important that you let me know right away and you must leave right away. Do you understand?"

"Yes, of course," Sal told her.

"Also, if it is not your son, I must ask that you not divulge anything about this young man to the media, or anyone else. Medical confidentiality is of the utmost importance."

"We understand," said Sal. "Can we see him now?"

"Yes, but I'm going to ask that only one of you officers and his parents accompany me. It's the Intensive Care Unit and visitors are limited. If it is your son, Mr. & Mrs. Fiore, you will have to adhere to visiting regulations for his well-being."

"Yes, yes," Niki said in a half whisper.

"Okay, good," she added, "Follow me. Before we enter the room, you will need to sanitize your hands and don a gown and mask. It's a further protection for everyone." She held a small walkie-talkie to her lips, pushed a button, and announced,

"We're on our way up."

Neither Sal, nor Niki looked at each other as the elevator escalated upward, each of them buried in their own thoughts. The doors opened to the sterile smells, unique only to a hospital. Her stomach already upset from the fatigue of her transatlantic trip and the stress of learning about her husband, Niki fought the acid reflux burning against her throat. For Sal, the smell and sounds brought back memories of his mother's final days many years ago. He remembered feeling numb, not like today.

A middle-aged man in scrubs met them as they disembarked from the elevators. Ms. Wright immediately introduced him as Dr. Hartmann, the young boy's surgeon.

"Please follow me," he told them. He brought them to a small room where they donned yellow gowns made of paper and were asked to wear caps and foot covers for their shoes. Under different circumstances, they would find humor with their costumes, but not under these.

Sal thought he prepared himself mentally for anything, but when he walked into the room, the sight of the helpless young boy lying there overwhelmed him and he gulped aloud. His throat tightened and for a minute, he could not speak. Niki's weight pushed against him and he felt her tremble, but only had eyes for his son.

"It's him," he said softly. "It's my son, Vinnie."

"Are you sure?" the detective asked. "It's difficult to tell with all the bruises and bandages."

"Yes, I'm sure," he answered and then more firmly added, "I would know my son anywhere, Detective. Do you think I wouldn't recognize my own son?"

"I'm sorry, Mr. Fiore, I have to ask. We need to be absolutely sure," the detective explained compassionately.

"Will you leave us alone with him, please?" This time, Niki spoke.

"Yes, of course, if that's okay with Ms. Wright," he answered.

"That's fine. Please stay with your son. I'll speak with you later. If there's no problem with you, Doctor, I'd like to send up his aunt also," Ms. Wright said looking at the surgeon for approval.

"Yes, you can send her up, but only for a short time," he answered and then to Sal and Niki, he said, "Your son is very critical. We had to remove his right kidney and the left one is failing due to the severity of the trauma. It's imperative that he receive a transplant. I would like to screen both of you for a possible match and if you are not, we can expand outward to siblings, relatives, etc. Lastly, we'll try other options, but we have no time to waste. That is, of course, you would be willing to be a donor."

"Yes, of course, Doctor," said Sal.

When Niki didn't respond, he looked at her and asked, "Are you also willing?"

"I'm not his birth mother, Doctor," Niki choked on the words.

If the doctor was surprised, he didn't show it and answered, "Not to worry, we'll check you anyway if you're willing. Do we know where the birth mother is? I would like to screen her also."

"She died in childbirth," Sal told him. "Right now, there's just us, but money is no object, Doctor. Whatever the cost, we just need to find one."

"Mr. Fiore," the doctor stated firmly, "Having the financial means cuts through a lot of red tape, but let's make no assumption that it guarantees we will find him a match. We all die at some point and we all have the opportunity and the capability of donating our organs, but unfortunately, most people do not. We live in a selfish world, a very selfish world."

"I'm sure it will make the difference, Doctor, and I'm also sure you will find him what he needs no matter what it takes, or how you have to do it." Even Niki had never heard this tone of voice from Sal before. He spoke the words like a threat, his look challenging the doctor to argue otherwise.

"We'll do what we can, Mr. Fiore. Spend some time with your son and I'll leave instructions for you at the nurses' station. When his aunt gets here, please ask her if she's willing to be screened." He turned and walked out of the room, not waiting for a response. He was a surgeon, not a social worker, not a psychologist and his low level of patience did not include an amiable bedside manner.

Sal and Niki stood on opposite sides of Vinnie's bed looking down at his swollen, battered face. Sal clenched his fists in anger, the wrath directed back to him for letting this happen. Niki patted his forehead and gently stroked his arm careful not to disturb the tubes. The only sounds were the methodical bleep of the monitor above his head and the soft gushes of air as he breathed with the help of the clear tube pressed against his face.

"I'm so sorry, Niki, so sorry for everything," Sal looked up at her across Vinnie, but she said nothing, her eyes refusing to look directly into his.

Before he could say more, Theresa entered the room. Vinnie was an infant leaving the country in his father's arms when she saw her nephew last. Now, she openly gasped at the sight of him. "Oh, my God," she repeated, "Oh, my God!" Then before Sal could ask, she said, "I already told them at the desk that if he needs a kidney, he can have mine. I guess they have a list going, so my name is in the hat now, too."

Hearing this, Niki looked up at her with swollen eyes and whispered, "Thank you, thank you so much," and then she looked away.

"Niki, I know we've never met, but I also know how much my brother loves you," Theresa told her.

"Not now, please, not now," Niki, responded. "Maybe in due time we can talk, but not now."

"Okay," and then Theresa looked at Sal and said, "Look, I know you don't want to, but we have to call him. He can help, Sal."

"How can he help, Theresa? Is he going to steal a kidney for us? I know what he is, who he is! I've been running his overseas operations for years. I know exactly what kind of man he is and I don't want any of my sons to be part of his life. I want them as far removed from his dirty little dynasty as possible! "

"Look at him! What happens if none of us is a match for him? He's your son, Joey! He has connections; he'll get him what he needs!"

"Only as a last resort, Theresa, only if we're not a match for him, then we'll call. You can call and for God's sake, do not call me Joey again. My legal name is Sal!"

Niki silently took in their communication, more and more surprised at their physical resemblance. She felt as if she always knew Theresa; the whole thing was so strange. She even felt she could actually like her, but she could not forgive Sal for his deceit. Now she was apprehensive about what his father's overseas operations really were and just how much her husband was involved in them.

CHAPTER
36

The ride to Watch Hill the next morning was poles apart from the first one. This time my entire demeanor was different, nearly euphoric and at peace. I knew what to expect and I had the inner fortitude to achieve the goal I set out to do. In the cemetery the night before, I faced my demons and knew I would win against the goliath of a man I was about to challenge. I was prepared to guile every way I knew to set the record straight. I was amazed at my composure.

This time I didn't have to ring when I approached; the massive gates opened as if they had eyes of their own. I followed the long driveway to the house and parked in the same space as before, looking around for Victor, but he was nowhere in sight. Mrs. Foster opened the front door and greeted me as I approached it.

"Good Morning, Mrs. Foster," I acknowledged her first.

"It's nice to see you again, Ms. Daley," she responded amiably. "Please come in, Mr. Fontinelli is expecting you. He's already on the terrace enjoying the sunshine and having his espresso." I followed her straight to the patio this time, disappointed that we avoided the library. "May I get you some espresso, or would you prefer a café latte or regular coffee?"

"Just regular black coffee would be nice," I answered.

"Of course, I'll get it right away. Please join Mr. Fontinelli," she said opening the door for me.

"Good Morning, Ms. Daley," Dominick greeted me in a voice sounding even raspier than before. "I hope your drive was a pleasant one, after all this weather is truly remarkable for this time of year."

"Yes, the ride was fine and I can't get enough sunshine."

"Well, sit down and join me. I'll have Mrs. Foster get you some coffee."

"She's already doing so. I get the impression she is really on top of everything around here."

"Oh, yes, and bosses me, too," he said, "I don't know what she's going to do when I'm gone."

"I thought you said there's a Mr. Foster," I answered.

"Yes, she's married to Victor, but the two of them have been part of this estate for so long; it's going to be a tough transition for them to go into retirement. I believe you met Victor the last time you were here."

"Yes, I did. She looks too young to retire."

"In age, maybe, but I've made sure they'll be fine financially. Enough about them, what would you like to ask me today? As a sick man, I'm afraid I don't know what time I have left for small talk." It sounded as if he tried to make a joke, but somehow it didn't come out right with his somber expression.

"I'd like to know about your family," I told him knowing he had no idea just how much I really wanted to know.

"I thought we talked about them last time. I told you all about my father, my mother, and my brother. There's not much else."

"What about your own children, Mr. Fontinelli. It's my understanding that you have three of them. Is that true?"

"Oh, yes, my children, how could I forget them?" This time he was not joking, just sardonic and cynical.

"Well, let's see," he paused. "The eldest son, Peter, was his mother's favorite, clung to her every minute. When she died, I think a little of him died with her. He loves to live well, off my money, of course, the same as she did; there's not a party too lavish, or a car too expensive for him. I lost count of his houses and cottages, but when he's not jet setting somewhere, he seems to like Los Angeles the most. The last I heard, he was on a safari somewhere in South Africa. He calls every now and then."

"Does he work for you?" I asked.

"Are you kidding? He hasn't worked a day in his life, unless if you consider vacation planning a job! His interest in the family business extends to how much he will receive when I'm dead and gone," he replied.

"Is he married?" I already knew he was not, but felt I needed to ask.

"What, that one? I can't imagine him settling down with a wife, but good grief, he certainly has enough women wanting him. Of course, it's for his wallet and once they had it, you know the rest of the story."

I wanted to ask, "Like your wife?" I didn't though and instead asked, "Does he have any children?"

"I already told you that he never married," he seemed annoyed.

"Well, in this day and age, it's not uncommon," then I was impelled to add, "Actually in any day and age, these things occur, don't you agree?" It was a baited question, but he didn't flinch.

"I suppose, but not in this family; it simply would not be tolerated." Now it was clear, he was annoyed.

Mrs. Foster arrived with my coffee and a fresh espresso for Dominick. She also had a plate of Italian pastries that she placed directly in front of me.

"Try a cannoli or sfogliatelle," Dominick said. "I prefer the Napoleons myself, but they're all good. My nephew picks them up for me."

"They look delicious, but I'm really not hungry," I protested politely.

"I insist that you try these. In fact, let's take a little of each, so you can taste the ecstasy of Italy itself," he said as he sliced them in small pieces, giving me a little of each, but taking none for himself.

"This is good," I said, tasting the filo and custard.

"That's called sfogliatelle," he said. "It's like a little heaven on earth I think. I'm hoping heaven is made of these."

I smiled, but in my mind I was thinking, "I wonder what they have in hell because that's where you're going!" Aloud, I said, "That would be nice. Now, what about the other two children you have?"

"Hmmm, my dear Theresa, St. Theresa herself," he said with a half smile. "Now, that is another one who never worked a day in her life."

I couldn't help interjecting, "Mr. Fontinelli, you gave your children a life of affluence and you put them down for not working. I don't understand."

"Ms. Daley, I do not put them down for not working. I am disappointed that they do not want more in life. They settle for what I give them as if it's enough when there's so much more to get. They miss the excitement of the hunt, waiting instead like chicks in a nest for someone to bring them food. They'll never soar like an eagle; they'll never feel the rush of adrenalin that comes with the triumph of the win."

"When does enough become enough, Mr. Fontinelli?" I asked aloud, but I was really thinking, "How selfish and greedy can you be?"

"One can never have enough, Ms. Daley. The riches are just the prize; it's the game, the challenge of achievement. You're quite successful; I'm sure you understand."

"I understand the satisfaction of achieving a goal, but I don't understand greed."

"Are you calling me greedy, Ms. Daley? That's a little odd for someone with the audacity to interview a man of my stature?" His eyes stared through me and I knew he was playing me, but I didn't know why. I thought it was best to move on.

"We're getting off track. Tell me some more about your daughter," I said hoping to change the subject.

"Well, as I said, she is truly Saint Theresa reincarnated. If left up to her, she would give every penny away for one cause after another. She devotes all her time to fundraising and I am the first on her list of benefactors every time. When she walks through the door, her hand extends toward the check. I keep a special account just for her causes. The paintings in the hallway to the library are all auction purchases from her various fundraisers. There's not a painting there I like, but I keep buying them to help out my Saint Theresa."

"Does she live here?" I remembered Theresa well, but lost touch with her after Joey's death. Before I left town, I called her a few times, but when she didn't return the calls, I got the message. Over the years, I often wondered what she did with her life. It must be terrible losing a twin.

"No, she has her own place closer to Misquamicut Beach. I've never been there, but I'm sure it's modest. I have a place in Palm Beach for the winter, but she prefers Boca Raton which is just south of there."

"Yes, I know where it is," I told him. "Is she married?"

"No, she was engaged once to a fine young man from the Hamptons, but it didn't work out. She called him stuffy and said she would rather live alone than in his structured prison, whatever that meant and before you ask, she does not have any children," he said with an odd look on his face. Then he added, "You're different today, Ms. Daley, more confident. I can't help but feel there's more to this interview than you let on."

I looked him directly in the eyes and lied, "Of course not, I have no idea what you're talking about." I sensed the end of my charade was near, so I continued with, "Is it true that she was a twin?"

He took a moment before he answered and then said, "Yes, she was a twin. Her brother, Joseph died in an accident at a young age."

"Was he married?" I never took my eyes off him with the question.

"No, he was a young man who drove too fast and hit a tree. That's all, nothing more, just youth gone awry."

His lack of emotion angered me, but I hid it and asked again, "So, he never married?"

"What did I just say, Ms. Daley? Joseph was a young man when he died. There was no wife and again, I will add before you ask; there were no children. I have no grandchildren."

"So, you only had three children, is that correct?"

"Yes, I only had three," he said derisively.

"What about your brother? How many did he have?"

"Two, he had two of them. His son, Antonio works for me and is more like a son to me than he is a nephew. He's quite handsome, I must add, Ms. Daley. Maybe you would like me to introduce you to him."

"You prick," I wanted to say aloud, but instead I smiled and said, "No, thank you, I'm not interested. You said there were two children. Is that right?"

"Yes, he also had a daughter, another socialite, married and divorced several times, lives in Chicago. Her latest husband is a minor politician, I think, probably some kind of crook like the rest of them. She and her brother keep in touch, but I haven't heard from her in years."

"So, that's all he had for children, just the two of them?"

"Yes, that's what I said, isn't it? He had two children and I had three children. Do you need a calculator?"

I ignored the sarcasm and asked, "Did either of you have any other children outside of marriage?"

The flush in his face crept like a slow wave to his balding skull and he snapped, "Ms. Daley, I agreed to an interview, not an inquisition. Of course, we did not have children outside of our marriages. My brother was deeply in love with his wife, as was I with mine. Her eternal beauty stands over my fireplace for all to see and admire."

I had to ask, "The question is not about love. Was he faithful to her and what about you?"

"There were no other children! Now, let's get on to something else. I'm getting tired."

"Mr. Fontinelli, a marriage between two people is based on something. It may very well be love, or it may be a contract bringing together two fortunes. Beyond that, it could be that each has something the other wants; perhaps the woman is a trophy wife and the man has enough money to keep her in the quality of life she desires. I'm not here to judge. Every marital union has its own story; I'm just trying to learn yours, to document the biography of a very successful man." I feared my lie would anger him, but it appeared to have the opposite result as I played to his ego.

"You're an interesting lady, Ms. Daley and you certainly have guts. If I were a younger man, I would like to know you on a different level."

"I think you just answered my question about your relationship with your wife without revealing any details." I said, giving him a half smile.

Smiling back, he replied, "Perhaps I did, but in the very least, I would certainly employ you in some capacity or another. Some unions are stronger than others and in retrospect; I believe I lost a good one with you."

He was flirting with me! I wasn't good enough for his son, but now he wants to fix me up with his nephew and tells me he missed something himself by not having a relationship with me! In my opinion, this man was a dysfunctional pervert on every level. I felt sick to my stomach and knew I needed to change the subject. "You look tired. If you need to rest, I can roam around and take some photos if you don't object." I decided to delay telling him the truth about me, at least for a little longer.

Before he could answer, Mrs. Foster came out to the patio and interrupted us. "Theresa is on the phone, Sir, and she says it's urgent."

"Here we go again, Ms. Daley, and now you see it firsthand. Saint Theresa herself has interrupted us on both your visits with her emergencies," and then to Mrs. Foster, he added, "Tell her I will call her later. I'm in a meeting and cannot be excused."

"She really sounds upset about something and said to tell you it's about an overseas matter that you need to be aware of right away. She said you would understand."

"Okay, I'll take it in the library. Please stay with Ms. Daley as she takes some photos of the property. I gave her a tour on her last visit, but she wants to take some photographs," and then to me, he directed, "Please do not photograph the staff, or any personal items with the exception, of course, the portrait of my lovely belated wife. We are private, here. After lunch, you can photograph me in the library."

"I'll be glad to stay with her, Sir, and your lunch is nearly done. It will be ready to serve in thirty minutes. We have a cold shrimp pasta salad for you today with fresh fruit and hot rolls," Mrs. Foster informed him and to me said, "I hope that is to your liking, Ms. Daley. If not, I will be glad to bring you something else."

"That sounds delicious," I lied because I hate shrimp.

"Please excuse me while I take my call, Ms. Daley. I'll join you shortly," he said while rising to leave. I noticed he had difficulty getting out of the chair, looking weak and exhausted.

I really wanted free reign of the grounds, but his orders were explicit to Mrs. Foster and it was apparent he wanted me escorted. He touched nothing while we talked with the exception of the demitasse cup served with his espresso. I needed to slip it into my purse, but how could I do it with Mrs. Foster with me? Then I had a thought.

"Could we walk down to the tennis courts, Mrs. Foster? I'd like to take some shots looking up at the house."

"Of course, the pathway is beautiful this time of season, follow...," but before she could finish her sentence, I stood up, hitting the demitasse cup with my camera. It fell to the cobblestone, smashing it to pieces.

"I'm so sorry," I gasped. "I can't believe I just did that, how clumsy of me!"

"You're not hurt, are you? Don't worry about the cup; it's nothing. Please don't touch a thing and I'll get something to clean it up before someone gets a cut. I'll be right back, and really, Ms. Daley, it's nothing."

"I'm so embarrassed," I said as she left. As soon as she was out of sight, I dropped down searching for the piece that touched his lips. Oh, please let it be here, I prayed to myself. There it was! I picked up a section of the rim approximately two inches wide that was sure to be the right piece with his DNA. Carefully, I slipped it into my camera bag just as the patio doors opened and she came out carrying a dustpan and broom.

"This will just be a minute," she said, "And we'll get on our way."

"Mrs. Foster, I must apologize, but I'm suddenly not feeling very well. I've been fighting something and I think this little upset just triggered it. Please give my regrets to Mr. Fontinelli, but I feel that I need to leave and reschedule for another time."

She seemed surprised that I would leave so abruptly. It was unlikely that anyone before me ever slid out on an interview with her employer and that fact only added to the credibility of my excuse.

"Of course, Ms. Daley, but can I get you anything? Perhaps, you need something to settle your stomach, or ease a headache. We have everything here and if you want to lie down for while, it's no problem." She was so sincere that I felt sorry for her.

"No, I think I just want to get back to my hotel. I'll call him in the morning. Please tell him how sorry I am."

She believed me and walked me to the front door all the while wishing me to feel better. I couldn't leave fast enough.

CHAPTER
37

New York City

Vinnie was unaware of the silent vigil surrounding him as his parents and an aunt he never met, or even knew existed sat somberly at his bedside, each quietly praying for him to open his eyes. Niki stared only at her son, purposely avoiding any eye contact with either Sal or Theresa. Sal, on the other hand, sat close to the bed with his face buried in his hands while his sister's tears shed softly, rolling down her flushed cheeks. An occasional nurse stopped in to check his vitals, to readjust the monitor settings and medicate him, but there were no words.

The shift changed at seven o'clock and a different nurse walked in on them. "Good Evening, I'm the night nurse on duty tonight. My name is Rosa Gonzalez. Are you his parents?"

"Yes, we are," answered Niki in a whisper.

"Well, I'm so glad he finally has some visitors. I was worried about him, such a fine looking young man and he had no one. When I saw the television and his face was so bright and brilliant staring out at me, I called right away."

"We're so thankful for what you did. I don't know how I can ever thank you, Ms. Gonzalez." Sal spoke from his heart.

"It was God's will, but now we need God's will to wake him up," she said turning her attention to Vinnie checking the drain coming from the surgical cut just below his ribs.

Dr. Hartmann, who walked to the bedside without acknowledging the presence of anyone else in the room, joined them. He removed the bandage on Vinnie's midsection revealing an incision nearly twelve inches long. Niki and Theresa both looked away, but Sal watched his every move. "This looks good," the surgeon said to Rosa and watched as she redressed the area.

"What do you think, Doctor?" Sal asked him.

"I think he's going to die without that transplant, Mr. Fiore, and he can't have that transplant unless we can get him to wake up. That's what I think."

"Will he wake up?" Niki asked softly.

"We certainly hope so. After a radical nephrectomy, we need to get him sitting up on the side of the bed and walking. He needs breathing exercises. The longer he stays like this, the higher the chance of pneumonia and infection."

This time Theresa spoke, "A radical what?"

"A radical nephrectomy, also called an open kidney removal. For this procedure, we cut the tube that carries urine from the kidney to the bladder and blood vessels and remove the entire kidney. Normally, we keep the adrenal gland and lymph nodes in place with the exception of cancer, but in this case, the trauma to that area was so extensive that I removed them also. I chose to make the incision on his belly, rather than his side because of the location of the injury," answered Dr. Hartmann.

"What about the other kidney?" Sal asked.

"I did a simple nephrectomy on the other kidney, removing just part of it, along with some muscle, fat and tissue. I also removed one of his ribs in preparation for a transplant. This side will take the new kidney. It has less damage. Now if you'll excuse me, I have other patients." Dr. Hartmann turned his back and walked out.

Rosa, seeing the looks on their faces said, "He may not have a good bedside manner, but he is the best of the best. Your son was lucky to get him because he was on vacation, but the other surgeon on call had a personal emergency and could not come in when called. It was God's will."

"Well, God better wake him up soon," Theresa, said cynically.

Rosa looked at Niki directly and said, "Keep talking to your son aloud; let him hear you and pull him out of this. Touch his hand; let him feel you. Let him know you're here. There's something special about a mother's touch. I've been around many years and I've seen miracles you can't imagine, but you have to believe and not give up." Then to Sal, she asked, "Have you seen Dr. Baker yet?"

"Who is that?" Sal asked.

"She's the Neurologist assigned to your son and she's also very good. I think you'll like her bedside manner much more. You may have missed her today though because she normally does her rounds in the morning," Rosa told them. "I will see you in a while. I have another patient who needs me now, but just buzz me if you need me."

"Okay, we will and thank you, Rosa. Again, I don't know how I can ever repay you," Sal said.

"You already have, Mr. Fiore, just by being here. I'm so glad he has someone now," she said with compassion. "He'll be fine. You'll see." She left the room.

Before they had a chance to say another word to each other, a middle-aged woman with a stethoscope hanging over her white physician's coat walked into the room donning plastic gloves as she entered. "Good Evening, I'm Dr. Baker. Are you his family?" she said cheerily.

Sal stood up, holding out his hand to shake hers, which she ignored. Embarrassed, his arm fell to his side and he said, "Yes, I am his father, Sal Fiore and this is my wife, Niki and my sister, Theresa. Nurse Gonzalez told us about you, but we didn't expect to see you. She thought you already made your rounds for today."

She answered him with, "Oh, I did, but this young man is very special, so I look in on him more often."

"How's he doing?" Niki asked.

"He's struggling. Besides, the surgery, he took a strong blow to the head. He has some inflammation around the brain that we're watching closely." The tone of her voice was optimistic, but the expression on her face was serious. "So far, there's no fluid buildup, but if there is, we're going to insert a cranial tube to relieve the pressure," she told them.

"Why won't he wake up?" Niki asked.

"I can give you all the medical terms in the world, but the bottom line is, he doesn't want to. He's not ready. As the swelling goes down, we'll be able to see more and know what's going on. He's gone through a huge trauma and his brain is tired. When a heart stops, we charge it with paddles. It's not that easy with the brain. We have to stimulate it in other ways. Talk to him, play music to him."

"That's pretty much what the nurse told us," Sal said.

"Well, she's right. Sometimes, I think the nurses know more than we do. They're with their patients more of the time and see the little things that we miss. Instead of reading a chart, they read the person. I'm going to give you my cell phone number. If there's any change in him at all, even an eye flutter, I want you to call me and tell the nurse on duty right away." All three of them nodded their heads, liking her right away.

Reaching out his hand, Sal took the phone number and said, "Thank you, Dr. Baker. Thank you."

"My pleasure, Mr. Fiore, let's keep our hopes up and in the meantime, keep looking for that kidney. Let's stay optimistic," she said removing her gloves and making her exit.

Theresa excused herself under the pretense of looking for a restroom and followed her out of the room. She found a small waiting room with no one in it and dialed her cell phone.

"Hey, Dad, it's me, Theresa," she announced when the raspy voice came to the other end of the phone.

"Yes, my Dear, and just what sort of emergency does your charity have today?" She hated it when her father mocked her.

"There's a problem and we need your help. I'm at Bellevue Hospital in New York City with Joey and his wife. Vinnie had a terrible accident and he's in a coma."

"What the hell are you doing there, Theresa? I know what he's doing there, but why you? Do you want to blow it all? What are his wife and son doing in New York? Has everyone gone mad?" Dominick could not hide his anger.

"Not now, Dad, you can lecture me later. Vinnie is in a coma and needs a kidney transplant. We need your help, your connections. They're going to screen Joey, Niki, and me, but if we're not a match, we need help finding him one." Theresa's voice was desperate and Dominick no longer had the strength to fight; he knew the end was near. He also knew that Theresa would not ask unless it was a last option and he envied the love she felt for her brother and his children, a love he never felt for anyone.

"What can I do, Theresa?" He asked knowing this pivotal point would change everything and repeated, "What do you want me to do?"

CHAPTER
38

The weather was beautiful as I left Watch Hill, but my racing thoughts kept me from noticing. I was already on I-95 heading south before I even looked at my cell phone to check any messages. I had three of them.

The first was from an agent in Atlanta asking if I was interested in a freelance assignment interviewing and photographing the Atlanta Braves. Not a bad assignment, I thought and smiled to myself.

Karyn was the next message. "Annie, I know you're pissed off at me, but just get over it and call me. It's about Mom."

The last was from Jackie. "Hey, Sis, it's me. Karyn's been trying to reach you. Mom's still in the hospital and not doing well. I know you're upset, but we really need to pull together on this one. I'm presuming you're still in town and can get to the hospital. I'm actually back home trying to get a couple of things sorted out. I'll explain later, but all hell broke loose here while I was in New York. Call me as soon as you get this."

I called Jackie right away and he answered on the first ring. "It's about time you called," he said. "I've been worried sick about you. Where the hell are you?"

"Well, little brother, I've got it! That's right, mission accomplished; I've got the old bastard's DNA," I announced excitedly.

"No kidding, that's awesome! I ordered the kit, but in the meantime, Bernie made a connection right there in Groton to get it done, so it'll be faster and it's legitimate. As soon as we hang up, I'll call him and let him know. He's back at work, but can meet us tomorrow night for the weekend."

"Are you coming back tomorrow night also?" I asked him.

"Actually, I'm on my way back now. Karyn is upset about Mom, not to mention your argument. I guess Mom just isn't coming out of it and they can't figure out why. According to Karyn, this has nothing to do with her having Alzheimer's. There must be something else going on."

"Okay, I'll go straight to the hospital when I get back. What's going on with you? You said in message that all hell broke loose when you were in New York. What happened?"

"Well, let's just say that my loving wife has filed for divorce and wants me to just hand the business over to her, along with the house, and everything else we own."

"Are you serious? I thought you said she understood and you had a great relationship going. What happened?" I asked.

"She fell in love, that's what happened," he said. "Evidently, her latest fling is more than a one night stand and she wants to start a new life, a normal life, she told me."

"What about Timothy? Does she want full custody? Does he know?" My heart broke for my brother.

"We both sat him down and told him we were splitting up. Actually, I don't think he was surprised because I'm gone most of the time now anyway. He's too young to understand the extent of it, but he does know that sometimes boys like boys and girls like girls. We're open with him, at least as much as we can be and keep it age appropriate. She agreed to joint custody as long as I promise to refrain from any flamboyance and not let any harm come to him by any of my sick companions, as she so deftly put it."

"You're not like that, Jackie, and from what I've seen of Bernie, neither is he."

"We're homosexual; we're not child molesters for God's sake! That's the problem with this ignorant society. We're just two people of the same gender who prefer to be with each other rather than someone of the opposite sex, that's all. We probably have a stronger bond and relationship than any man and woman that we know." He sounded angry and I let him vent. "I know it wasn't fair to MaryAnn and I never should have married her, but I didn't understand my feelings and I fought them. When she told me she understood and went about her own way, I guess I selfishly thought I could have the best of all worlds. What a fool I've been!"

"You're not a fool, Jackie; you've just been caught off guard. It'll all work out. Trust me, I'm experienced in the art of divorce," I said with a laugh and I thought I heard a chuckle from his end of the phone also. "Get a good lawyer and do your best to work it out amiably for Timmy's sake. Once the dust settles, you and MaryAnn will be the best of friends again."

"Are you the best of friends with John and Scott?" He asked sarcastically.

"Not hardly, but I married a couple of scumbags, you didn't. MaryAnn was a nice girl who thought she married her knight in shining armor, but it didn't work out. That's all."

"Go ahead and say it, Annie! I know you're thinking it. Instead of her prince, she got the princess!"

"Stop it, Jackie; you're being an asshole. I'm just saying that she thought she married one person and found out she married someone else. It happens to heterosexuals, too. You've told me many times over the years that you love her, so do what's right for you, for her, and for the son you have together and get on with life. Don't leave a bitter trail that you'll all regret." I was at a loss trying to console him.

"That's what I love about you, Annie. You always know what to say, unfortunately, you just don't follow it yourself."

I was angry now and snapped "Enough, Jackie; I don't need your cheap shots!"

"No, you don't and I'm sorry," he said. "I just need to vent and who better to vent to than my big sister, right?"

"Yes, you're right and I'm sorry for snapping at you. I've had quite a day of it, too."

"Now that you're apologizing, how about doing the same with Karyn?" He laughed, but I knew he was serious.

"Not likely," I answered and then changing the subject added, "Aren't you going to ask me how I got the DNA?"

"Of course, and just how did you get it?" He asked.

I went on to tell him every little detail about the visit and breaking the cup, adding the fact that I felt so sorry for Mrs. Foster and wondered how she could work for such a monster for so many years.

"So, where is it now?" He asked.

"It's in my camera bag," I told him.

"Just be careful because I heard Bernie mention that moisture and heat are the greatest enemies of DNA and after all this, we don't want it ruined, or contaminated in anyway. Have you told Karyn yet?"

"No, I got a message from her, but I haven't called her back. I'll see her at the hospital."

"Oh, I almost forgot," he said and continued, "And better warn you. Sara is beside herself also because she hasn't seen or heard from Mike since he left the hospital the other night. She's frantic because she thought she knew where he lived, but when she went there to find him, the landlord never heard of him. It looks like we're walking into a big mess when we get back."

"Great! How far out are you? I'm about 30 miles away from New London now," I told him.

"I'm about 50 miles out. I'll meet you there. Drive safely," he answered.

"You, too, and Jackie, it'll be alright, you'll see." I was worried about him.

"With you in my corner, how can it be any other way? See you soon...," and with that said, he hung up.

In less than an hour, I was back at the hospital in New London. I missed Karyn the night before when the ambulance rushed my mother to the hospital and I hoped I would see her this time. Jackie was right; we needed to pull together on this one. Facing my memories and my feelings in the cemetery did a great deal to ease some of my frustrations, but I still had the lingering recollection of my sister's smile when the doctor ripped my baby from my arms. After our argument and her comment about her feelings of jealousy, I knew how she felt, but I still could not understand how we got to the place where we were now. I wanted it to be right, yet I could not dispel my own feelings toward her, but for Jackie's sake, I decided to disguise them as best as possible.

The hospital was like any other and I went straight upstairs to my mother's room. She looked like a fragile flower lying there, so frail and vulnerable. For the first time since I came back, I felt a twinge of remorse for the days I missed with her, my thoughts flying everywhere. What did she really do to destroy my life? Was it possible I just blamed the messenger? Why did she harbor so much hatred toward Joey? What was her relationship with Gino? Who was Karyn's father? I had so many questions and now I would never get the answers from her. Even if she pulled through the injury, Alzheimer's stole her mind.

As I stood by her bedside, a nurse came in and cheerily announced, "There's good news today. She woke up once during the night and asked for some tea and we're showing much more brain activity. You just missed Dr. Hines, her neurologist, but he left instructions at the nurse's station for her daughter, Karyn to call him. Are you Karyn?"

"No, I'm her other daughter, Annie. I was hoping Karyn would be here, but I haven't seen her," I answered.

"Well, when she comes, please tell her to see someone at the desk and get the nurse to call him. In the meantime, I'm going to change her bandages and freshen her up a bit if you don't mind waiting outside in the hallway until I'm finished," she told me with the distinct tone that I needed to leave her alone with my mother whether I liked it or not.

"Not a problem," I lied. "Actually, I'm waiting for my brother, so I'll go downstairs to the coffee shop until he gets here."

"Good idea, by the time you get back up here, she'll be all clean and ready for visitors." Her tone was a little lighter and I wondered if I was just overly sensitive.

Just as I was about to enter the coffee shop, I saw Jackie walk through the front doors, so I waited for him.

"Have you been upstairs yet? How's she doing?" He hugged me and asked.

"The nurse said she woke up once last night, so that's a good sign. I'm starving so I came downstairs to grab something while the nurse is cleaning her up. Karyn must be her Medical Power of Attorney because the neurologist will only talk to her. I haven't seen her though. Do you know where she is?"

"I'm right here," the voice behind us announced. "I was running a little late because Mike usually brings Tommy to work and he's nowhere around."

"What's up with that?" I asked.

"We don't know. Sara never went to his apartment, but she knew where he lived and when she went to find him, the landlord didn't know him. The whole thing is so strange because he really became part of the family and no one ever questioned him," Karyn told us.

"How is Sara doing?" I asked with concern.

"She's beside herself. One minute, she's sure he was in an accident and the next minute she's cursing him out like a trooper. She filed a missing person's report and so far, it's like he never existed." I wasn't sure if Karyn was more upset because he went missing, or because Sara was so distraught.

"What about his parents, has anyone tried to contact them?" Jackie asked her while we walked through the cafeteria line picking out a late lunch.

"Well," Karyn said, "Mike spoke a great deal about his parents to Sara so she thought she knew about them. He told her they were an old established Portuguese family who owned commercial fishing boats in Rhode Island, but there's no record of them either. She's been all over the internet and they don't exist! There are no public records of any kind, any business advertisements, licenses, etc. She even checked property records and there's nothing. The whole thing is strange. Bob, in the meantime, is being a typical father and is furious because he thinks Mike was just using his daughter for sex, but according to Sara, if she's telling the truth, they weren't at the point yet."

"Actually, that's what she told me also, I think she's telling the truth. At her age, she has no reason to lie; she's certainly not a kid anymore. If anything, I got the impression she wanted to bring it to the next level and he wasn't ready. They just seemed so much in love and the way he doted over Mom was unreal. I hope nothing happened to him, but I almost think that's better than him running out on her," I told them.

"On another subject, while we're all together, we have to talk about Mom. What are we going to do with her if she pulls through this?" Karyn asked while sipping her coffee.

Without realizing it, I found myself coming to the defense of my mother, "What are you talking about? She'll pull out of this and she can go back home and live as she was living before this happened."

Karyn immediately took up the offensive and countered, "No way, she is not going home. You can't expect Sara to babysit for her the rest of her life, Annie. It's not fair. How can you even say something like that? We have to find a facility for her."

Jackie, sensing the beginning of another war, interrupted both of us and said, "Hey, let's take one step at a time and see what happens. There's no point getting into a heated discussion when it may turn out to be a moot point anyway. Even if she comes out of it, she might have a major setback with some physical problems, or advanced confusion. Karyn, I'm sure that Annie understands as I do that Sara cannot care for her forever, but we have to all agree that it was great to have the arrangement while it lasted. We have alternatives here. If Sara can't do it, we can bring in a nurse."

"Just how will we bring in a fulltime nurse, Jack? Maybe the two of you have money growing on trees in your backyard, but I don't and we all know now that Mom is broke! She doesn't have a dime. What now, Jack? What do we do now? Maybe you can call MaryAnn and ask if she can live with you, how does that sound?" Karyn's voice was tight on the verge of escalating. I glanced around to see if anyone was staring, but no one was, at least not yet. I avoided looking at Jackie after the reference to MaryAnn and wondered what he would say about her, if anything.

"Karyn, look," I interjected, "I'm really sorry about the other night. I never should have allowed our argument to escalate to the point it did, especially in front of other people. We're all adults and we can work this out, whatever it is. I just want what's right for Mom."

"Yeah, right," she scoffed. "You want what's right for Mom! That's why you left for twenty years."

"Enough, ladies, that's enough!" Jackie was clearly at the end of a short fuse. "Let's finish eating and go upstairs to see her. Karyn, you call the neurologist and find out what's going on. Annie, you need to calm down and show a little more love toward Mom and a lot more patience to Karyn. Somehow, we'll get through this. Do we all understand? Well, do we?"

Karyn and I both stared at Jackie and I sensed we shared the same thought. When did our little brother become so wise? In unison, we nodded our agreement without looking at each other.

Once we got upstairs, Karyn went straight to the desk for the phone number and called Dr. Hines. Jackie and I walked into the room and to our surprise saw our mother sitting up in bed holding her baby doll. A different nurse attended to her and smiled when she saw us.

"What a difference, don't you think? We've had a major breakthrough," the nurse said to us. "She's still a little groggy and I'm sure she has a terrible headache, but she's back with us. I'm waiting to hear from the doctor now to see if I can give her something. She seems to be a little agitated. It's probably from the headache."

I walked to the side of the bed where she cradled the doll and gently stroked my mother's forehead first and then the doll's cheek. She looked up at me with transparent eyes, lucid and clear, while my own welled with tears that I allowed to roll freely. "I love you, Mom, and I'm so sorry for blaming you. I still don't understand, but I know it wasn't your fault. Please forgive me, please forgive me," I cried with my head buried on the side of her bed.

She lifted her free hand to my hair and gently ran her frail fingers through it, then raised my chin to look at me. She smiled the sweetest smile and softly whispered something, but I couldn't hear her.

"What? What did you say?" I murmured quietly back to her.

I don't know what I expected to hear, maybe what I wanted to hear, but what she did say took me by complete surprise. She simply looked at me and with the blankness back in her eyes, she said, "Chocolate cake!"

I just smiled and answered back, "Yes, Mom, chocolate cake! I love chocolate cake!"

Jackie, standing behind me, pressed his hand down on my shoulder, and said, "We'll get through this, Annie. Somehow, we'll get through it," and I believed him.

CHAPTER
39

Dominick was still sitting in the library an hour later when Mrs. Foster entered to check on him.

"Is everything alright, Mr. Fontinelli? Do you need anything?" She asked him.

"Nothing is what it used to be, Mrs. Foster, nothing at all." She watched him fondly as he spoke laying out his pills and handing him a glass of water.

"I know, Sir," she responded thinking he was speaking of his illness. "God has a plan for all of us and sometimes it just doesn't seem fair."

"Bullshit, if it's not fair! He gave us the power to make it fair. What kind of pansy sits around waiting for God's plan? That's ridiculous! Besides, if there was a God and He was so tough, there wouldn't be any mealy mouse little wimps in this world waiting for their freebie handouts. They'd all be real men going after what they want. It's all bullshit!"

Mrs. Foster hated it when he cursed and went into his foul moods. They slacked off somewhat since the illness began, but something set him off tonight and she didn't know what. She only knew it was best to stay away from him and changed the subject, "The kitchen made some nice chicken soup for you tonight with a fresh salad. Do you want to eat early?"

"At five o'clock, exactly five o'clock, I want a porterhouse steak with fettuccine soaking in Alfredo sauce and green beans sautéed in fresh garlic oil," he bellowed back at her and then added, "Make sure the garlic bread is hot and crispy, not soggy like the last time!"

"But the doctor said...," she started to say.

"Fuck the doctor! I want what I want and I want it when I want it! If that's a problem, I can fix the problem if you get my meaning!" His face was bright red and his eyes pierced right through her.

"No, Sir, that's not a problem. I'll give the kitchen your request right now," she answered defiantly. "It's just going to upset your stomach, but I'll do it anyway!" She refused to quiver for him.

"One more thing, Mrs. Foster, I'd like some cappuccino cheesecake for dessert, a large piece, very large with whipped cream." He directed his defiance right back to her.

"Of course you would, Sir, and would you like some brandy and a cigar with that?" She asked with sarcasm.

"Not with it, after I'm finished," he retorted and spun around in his chair turning his back to her. As she stormed out, he yelled after her, "Double everything, Tony is joining me for dinner tonight!"

"Okay," she yelled back.

Tony answered his phone on the first ring when he saw the caller ID. "Hey, Uncle Dom, what's up?"

"Join me for dinner tonight," Dominick told him.

"Sorry, I can't do it tonight. I've got a date," Tony answered. He rarely denied his uncle, but this date was special.

"Break it, this is important," Dominick demanded.

"But, Uncle Dom, this one is...," Tony protested.

"You heard me, I said break it. This is big, Tony, and we need to talk."

The firmness in his raspy voice was all he needed to understand his uncle wasn't going to budge, so Tony complied as usual and said, "Of course, I'll be there at six o'clock."

"No, dinner is at five o'clock, so be here no later than four. I have a lot to go over with you."

"Sure thing, and by the way, do you remember asking me to check out that reporter dame when she first called you?" Tony asked him.

"Yeah, I remember and you told me she was legitimate. Is there a problem?"

"Oh, she's legitimate, alright, but my source told me there's a little more to her than we think. He's on to something and said if he's right, this will blow us away. Maybe he'll call before I get there."

"Nah, she's okay, I think, a little feisty maybe, but I enjoy her company. I'm sure it's not anything, or you would know by now," Dominick countered. "I'll see you at four o'clock and don't be late," then he hung up and sat in deep thought wondering how to handle the recent events until he dozed off.

Tony arrived promptly at four o'clock just as he promised and found his uncle still asleep in the library slumped uncomfortably over the desk. For an instant, Tony feared he passed, but his shallow breathing told him otherwise. Not wanting to startle him, he gently tapped his arm and said, "Uncle Dom, it's me, Tony. Wake up!"

Dominick woke up right away and looked with horror at the front of his pants, dampened with urine. "Oh my God, Tony, now I'm pissing myself! Give me a minute to clean up and don't tell Mrs. Foster! I'll be right back."

As Dominick left the room, Tony watched with sadness as the toughest man he knew shuffled weakly away to clean himself. He sighed deeply wishing he did not have to tell him about the reporter, questioning if he should, or not, but he knew the answer. Tony had the soul of the devil himself, but the one thing he always did was tell the truth to his uncle and not out of fear, out of respect.

Mrs. Foster broke his train of thought with, "Tony, it's good to see you. Did he go upstairs to clean up?"

"Yes, he wanted to wash his face and freshen up before dinner," Tony lied.

"Hopefully, he'll change his pants also," she stated in a matter of fact.

"So you saw it, then?" Tony asked. "Has it happened before?"

"He does it frequently now and, of course, I let him keep his dignity and don't let on that I notice, like I don't see the dirty laundry around here. It's getting worse and he's getting weaker all the time, not to mention, more ornery. I hope you're not going to keep him up late tonight; he's exhausted today. He doesn't tell me what's going on, but it's been a trying day for him," she said with concern.

Before Tony could answer, Dominick came back into the room wearing a clean set of clothes and a smile on his face. "Well, Mrs. Foster, I see you're out of the kitchen and bothering my nephew. Tony will have his usual beer, but tonight I'll have a single malt scotch on the rocks, in fact, make it a double and don't let our glasses run dry."

With a sour glance to Tony, she responded, "Yes, Sir", and left the room to get the drinks.

"Good help is impossible to get these days. I can't believe I've tolerated her insolence all these years," Dominick muttered, but Tony ignored him.

"Uncle Dom, I have something to tell you about the reporter," Tony said.

"Save it for later. We have more important business," he stopped talking to Tony when Mrs. Foster entered with the drinks and said to her, "Shut the door on your way out. I'll ring when our glasses our empty." She left without an answer.

"What's up?" Tony asked.

"It's about Joey; he never died, he's alive," Dominick blurted out the words and then remained silent giving his nephew time to absorb them.

Tony just stared back at him thinking his uncle's faculties were slowly dissolving from the cancer. He didn't know what to say and it was apparent that he didn't believe him, so Dominick spoke again.

"He didn't die in the accident, Tony. It's been a cover-up all these years to protect him and his son."

Still in disbelief and not wanting to mock his uncle, Tony said, "Uncle Dom, I know all this is difficult for you, but sometimes the medication can..."

"Don't patronize me, Tony! It's not the medication, you idiot! Joey is alive. He lives in Italy with his three sons, a daughter and a wife! He handles my overseas operations, like you handle my affairs here."

"What the hell?" Tony was aghast. "What about that guy Sal you always talk about? I thought he handled everything over there."

"I know this comes as a shock to you, but Sal is Joey and Joey is Sal! It's as simple as that." Dominick was never one to mince words and he certainly didn't this time. Then he continued, "After the accident, Gino and I decided that the baby needed to be protected, so we used our resources to fake Joey's death and the baby's death, then we got them out of the country and set them up nicely in Italy. Joey met a nice Italian girl, married her, and had three more kids. Everything was perfect, until now!"

"Uncle Dom, why would you send your son away? Why did he need protection?" Tony now believed what he was hearing and was full of questions.

"Well, there was that little matter in the cemetery many years ago that I told you about already. Your father and I got into a little trouble with the cute filly one night and your grandfather saved our asses by paying off her family. After the old man died, my brother and I kept up the payments as we promised him and everything was fine until Joey fell in love and eloped with her daughter."

"I'm confused. Did the woman have a daughter later on?"

"Not exactly, later on…I didn't tell you everything. The little tramp got pregnant and claimed it was ours," Dominick told him reluctantly. "We didn't believe it, but the old man thought it was true and we didn't argue."

"If that was the case, wouldn't she be a lot older than Joey?" Tony was not only in shock, but thoroughly confused.

"Not that daughter, the younger one she had by her husband later on. He was a real loser from what I hear, nothing but a drunken bum. I heard he died falling off a scaffold at Electric Boat, probably drunk," Dominick spoke bitterly.

"Are you talking about Annie? I remember her. She and Joey were inseparable growing up and Theresa was a good friend of hers."

"Yeah, yeah, I know…well, I never dreamed Joey would elope and marry the little slut, but he did. They ran off and when they returned, she was pregnant, very pregnant, about to pop! I tried to scare her off, but it didn't work. Your father found out they were running off again, so I chased them down to stop them. The details aren't important, but the weather was bad and there was an accident. Joey was hurt, but not as much as we made out. The girl on the other hand fell unconscious and went into labor. I wanted her to lose the baby, but she didn't, so I had to take steps to get it away from her."

Tony could not believe what he was hearing and asked, "Why? Why would you want to take her baby? It doesn't make sense!"

"Of course it does, Tony, just think about it! Her mother was the one your father and I had our way with, mutual consent, of course, but she ended up knocked up and had a kid. We did the right thing and paid for everything, but now my son had a kid with the woman's other daughter! What a mess! Gino and I couldn't let that happen! We each had wives and families by then who knew nothing about any of it. The last thing we needed was a merger of bloodlines with some Irish skank, not to mention adding more heirs."

Still confused, Tony asked, "So, which one of you fathered the kid? Was it you, or my father?"

"Who knows...we both had her. We shared everything, including that bitch," Dominick scorned.

"So, I might have a sister?" Tony found all this hard to believe, "And now you're telling me my cousin is alive?"

Mrs. Foster buzzed to tell them dinner was ready in the dinette off the kitchen. Dominick immediately scoffed back at her with, "Screw the dinette; I want to eat in the dining room tonight. We'll be there in five minutes."

Tony asked, "Why the dining room for just the two of us?" Dominick ignored him and Tony continued, "Now what, Uncle Dom? What happens now? At the very least, I have a new cousin, but then she might be my sister and not to mention, the cousin I grieved for is alive and well. This is all bullshit. How could you keep these things from me? What were you and my father thinking?"

Dominick never saw his nephew in this state of mind before; he knew the facts would upset him, but he underestimated just how much. In a much calmer voice, he said to him, "Look, Tony, I know this is all a surprise to you. There's no new cousin, or sister, so just forget about her. She's doesn't exist to this family. We were only sperm donors and as for Joey's situation, there was no choice. We did what we had to do. It took him a while to understand, but when your father and I explained it to him, he did the right thing. Of course, the death of his wife during childbirth saddened all of us, but that's life and eventually he got over it. It took quite a few years and mentoring from some of my loyal sources, but he is trained well and ensures the business runs well. His wife knows nothing of the business and life is good all the way around."

Tony watched his uncle with disdain, listening to the lack of compassion as he spoke. For the first time in his life, he knew for sure Dominick was lying to him. "Well, Uncle Dom, I've got a real surprise for you now. His wife did not die during childbirth. She's alive and well, not only that, but you've been entertaining her right here in your very own home. Your reporter, Ms. Anne Daley, is none other than Annie Mahoney herself in her very own flesh and blood!" Tony actually enjoyed giving his uncle the news after what he just heard.

Dominick, on the other hand, went stone cold. He knew Annie was alive, but he had no idea where she was, or what she was doing. "What could she possibly want with me?" He asked Tony, not bothering to explain his lie about her being dead. "Money, that's what she wants just like all the rest of the greedy little bastards in that pathetic clan," he answered his own question.

The buzzer on Dominick's desk went off again and they heard Mrs. Foster's voice, "Dinner is now being served in the dining room. It's waiting for you and getting cold."

"Fuck, dinner!" Dominick shouted into the intercom. "Eat it yourself, we're not hungry anymore...and don't bother us!" He slammed his fist on the desk, looking at Tony wildly. "Take care of this matter, Tony! Take care of it right away! I want her gone; do you understand me? I want her gone! Tony just stared at him as if he was looking at a stranger for the very first time. "I need her gone, I should have done it myself when I had the chance back then!" Dominick yelled. "Joey's son is in New York City and needs a kidney. Theresa called and wants me to find a kidney! Can you believe that shit? I need a new body and she wants me to find some kid a kidney! What does she want me to do, pull it out of my ass?" Dominick was out of control. "Don't' just sit there, say something!"

"What would you like me to say, Uncle Dom? Should I say I'm happy about this news? You promised me the whole operation someday and now my long lost cousin, your son, I might add, is back on the scene and you're telling me he heads the overseas operation. What else does he handle? Does he take care of your dirty work like I do, or is he just your handsome little figurehead?" Tony was shouting now.

"Look at you, afraid of what's coming! Yes, he handles everything he needs to and he has more balls than you ever did! You didn't fear him as Sal Fiore, but now you shake in your shoes because he is Joseph Fontinelli! You're a pathetic wimp! Get out of here and go take care of that little whore for me! If you don't, I'll get her back here and do it myself! Show me you have your balls back!"

"Not this time, Uncle Dom, not this time...do your own dirty work!" Tony rose and walked out of the library, slamming the door behind him, ignoring his uncle's screaming demands for him to return.

"I'll do it myself," Dominick muttered. "I don't need that little punk!" He waited a few minutes, finished the remainder of his single malt scotch and dialed Annie's phone number.

I immediately recognized Dominick's phone number and against my better judgment answered it on the second ring, "Hello?"

"Ms. Daley, this is Dominick Fontinelli. I'm so sorry to hear about your illness today. I was disappointed that we were unable to complete our meeting. I hope you're feeling better."

"Yes, I am. I'm not sure what happened, but I think I have enough...," I started to say, but he cut me off.

"Ms. Daley, I have something very important that I want to share with you. I've never told anyone before, but I want to tell you for the record. Is it possible for you to come back tomorrow morning? I know you're not feeling well, but I think you'll find this information very interesting and I will feel better getting it off my chest."

He caught me totally off guard and I didn't know what to say to him. Without thinking, I simply said, "Yes, yes I think I can do that. I'll be there around two o'clock in the afternoon if that's okay with you." The curiosity overwhelmed me. Could it be that he wanted to confess about Karyn? What else could it be?

"That's perfect," he told me. "It's just perfect."

Dominick went upstairs to retire for the night. He needed a good night's sleep to take care of business in the morning, business he looked forward to doing himself. He couldn't remember the last time he felt this alive.

Next to his bed were a steak sandwich and a glass of milk. He devoured them.

CHAPTER
40

S leep was scarce that night with everything on my mind. I stared at the prism on my dresser, thinking of it as my guiding light, wondering what was next. I asked myself repeatedly; why I told Dominick I would be there tomorrow. I had what I went for and I was done with him. Why did I feel a need to return? What did he want to tell me?

I thought about my mother, my feelings for her and my regret for missing so much while she was healthy, now it was too late. Her mind was gone and she was lost to me forever.

Then there was the situation with Karyn, could we ever mend our fences? I doubted it strongly. My recollection of her smile when they took my dead baby out of my arms was too vivid, too harsh to forgive and I knew I would not forget it. Why, did she hate me so? Am I so evil and uncaring that I appall my own sister?

Poor Sara, poor sweet Sara, heartbroken over her loss of Mike, wondering what happened to him. Why did he leave her, or did he? Was he in an accident? I'll help in the search for him tomorrow, I told myself.

What's next for me? Where do I go from here? These questions finally put me into a deep sleep, one without the horrors of the past. My demons were gone and I had only the future ahead of me.

My phone rang sharply at seven o'clock waking me suddenly. "Hello," I answered.

"Get up Sleepy Head and meet Bernie and me for breakfast. We'll meet you at the diner on Thames Street at eight o'clock. Don't be late!" It took me a few seconds to wake up and realize it was my brother.

"What's Bernie doing there? I thought he was coming this weekend," I said sleepily.

"You really do need some coffee, Kiddo. This is Saturday and he got in late last night. Meet us there and bring the broken teacup, okay?" I listened, asking myself how he could be so cheerful in the morning.

"Okay, I'll be there, but you're buying and I'm starving!" I told him.

"You're always hungry, it's a miracle you're not an elephant! See you there and don't be late!" I smiled as I hung up the phone, my brother knew me well. To coin an old cliché, I would be late for my own funeral, but maybe that's not so bad.

As I jumped out of bed, the phone rang again and being more awake this time, I looked at the Caller ID at an unfamiliar number. I was about to leave it unanswered and let it go to voicemail, but something inside me said to take the call, maybe it was my mother's doctor.

"Is this Annie Mahoney?" the man on the other end inquired.

"Yes, this is Annie, who is this?" I asked, not recognizing the voice.

"Don't go to Watch Hill today, do you understand? Don't go there today or any other day," he said in a firm and cold tone.

"What are you talking about? Who is this?" Something didn't feel right about this call and it make my blood curdle.

"Who I am is not important; I'm just someone with your best interest at heart. Don't go there today!" He hung up, leaving me staring at the phone in disbelief.

Aloud I asked, "Who was that? What was that all about?" I just shook my head and headed to the shower hoping the rest of the day would make more sense.

I really was starving when I got to the diner. Jackie and Bernie were already there and my brother could not resist announcing to the world as I walked in, "Well, here she is and she's only five minutes late, not bad!"

"You're such a smartass," I laughed. "Good morning, Bernie! It's good to see you anyway," and to Jackie I added, "I really am starving! I hope you brought your wallet!"

After a lot of small talk and a fabulous omelet with a side of greasy bacon, Jackie announced, "This place never changes! It's awesome!"

I could only nod as I chewed the last morsel of hash browns and swallowed it down with the last of my coffee. Bernie was still nibbling his muffin as the waitress filled our cups. "Give him the check," he told the server and pointed to Jackie. I liked Bernie; his quiet sense of humor was comforting.

Just as I was about to tell them about Dominick's call last night and the strange call this morning warning me not to go to Watch Hill, Bernie placed a small packet on the table. "This is the kit, all we have to do is complete the paperwork and package it up along with the DNA sample Jack got from Karyn and I'll take care of it this morning. Did you bring it, Annie?"

"I sure did, here it is," I said taking the broken piece of porcelain from my purse carefully.

"Was it exposed to any heat or moisture?" Bernie asked.

"No, just the coffee he was drinking," I said. "Will it be okay?"

"It should be, but if not, I'm sure they'll let us know. I'm actually not going to send it out. I have a colleague who works here in town at Pfizer and he is willing to do this for us," Bernie said.

"Will he get in trouble for doing it?" Jackie asked.

"No, he's one of the decision makers, or head honcho, as you might say. I don't think he would offer if it meant putting his job on the line. If I get it to him today, he promised to have it back to us next week sometime. Is that okay with the two of you?"

Jackie nodded and I said, "She's waited this long, I think another week won't kill her." Jackie threw me a disapproving look, so I added, "I'm not being facetious, and really I'm not. Have you heard from her today?"

"No, not this morning, but late last night she said that Mom seems to be doing much better. The neurologist is pleased with the progress. They're waiting on some kind of blood work to come back and they want to discuss the next step when they release her from the hospital. Like it, or not, we have to have the conversation."

"I know we do, Jackie, but talking to Karyn is impossible. Whatever her mindset is the way it will be. She won't listen to anyone else," I said.

"Annie, you're headstrong yourself and the two of us have to admit that she has been here with Mom when neither of us was around. That says a great deal and I think we need to respect that." Jackie was firm with his opinion and I knew this was a battle to be lost. "Please try to be reasonable. Unless you are willing to stay here and take care of her yourself, we need to make other arrangements and let Sara off the hook."

"You're right; I'll give it more thought. Speaking of Sara, is there anything new going on with the Mike situation?" I asked.

"No, Karyn said the police called Sara yesterday and they still have no leads." Sara is beside herself," Jackie said.

As we spoke, there was a commotion among some of the patrons in the diner. A few of them were hovered around the television overhead and listening to a Breaking News report.

An aerial view of a large estate was on the screen and the news commentator was saying, "We're not sure what's going on yet, but our sources are telling us that there's some unusual activity taking place at the famous Fontinelli compound in Watch Hill. Hold on...hold on...we're getting more information. Our News Team is reporting that there was an apparent murder-suicide at the estate, but we are unable to confirm the identity of the victims at this time. We do know that the famous real estate mogul, Dominick Fontinelli has been seriously ill for quite some time. We cannot, I repeat, we cannot confirm at this time if he is one of the victims. What you're seeing on your screen is our Channel News Helicopter flying over the grounds giving us an aerial view. We will continue our coverage of this event, so stay tuned and as soon as we have more information, we will get back to you."

"Oh my God," I said. "Oh my God, this can't be true." I was stunned and unable to say anything else.

Bernie spoke first. "Wow, did you expect this? I wonder what happened. Annie, do you think he shot someone and then himself. I wonder who the other victim was."

"Did he seem wacky? Was he depressed when you met him?" Jackie asked.

Again, all I could say was, "Oh my God...there must be a mistake."

"I didn't give a rat's ass about him before, Annie, but now I'm curious. What was he like? Did he seem like the type of person who would shoot someone and then himself?" Bernie asked.

"No, no he didn't. He was feisty and I always felt he wanted to live, not die. The reporter didn't say he shot someone and then himself, did he?" I asked not really sure what I heard.

"No, I'm just resuming that, or maybe he shot a lover and then himself," Bernie speculated.

"I don't think it was any of that, but listen to this," I said commanding their full attention. "He called me last night and said he needed to tell me something. He asked me to come back today at two o'clock to see him and I don't know why I agreed, but I did. I was planning to head there after we finished breakfast."

"No, shit," said Jackie.

"What's even stranger was the phone call I got this morning right after I hung up with you, Jackie," I continued.

"What phone call?" Bernie wanted to know.

"I didn't recognize the phone number from my Caller ID, but I answered it anyway. It was a man with a deep, almost eerie voice and he told me not to go to Watch Hill today. I asked who he was and what this was about, but he would not tell me and just repeated his warning not to go there."

Jackie looked around to make sure no one was listening to our conversation, but everyone was too busy staring at the news, or talking to each other. Then he said softly, "What if that was the killer who called you? Maybe we should go to the police and tell them."

"Why? I don't know who called me. You just heard the same news I did; we have no idea if he killed someone, or if he was killed himself." I was feeling very uneasy with all of this, but one thing I knew for sure, I would not being going to Watch Hill that afternoon.

CHAPTER
41

New York City

Theresa didn't tell Sal that she called their father. She thought she would keep that to herself until her father made the next move. Secretly she hoped he would be the superhero, find a kidney for Vinnie, come to New York City and convince his son that he was the father they should be proud of, not the coldhearted man Sal thought him to be. She knew the vision was just a product of her imagination, yet since a child, she wanted him to be like every other father. Unlike her twin, she held tightly to that dream, refusing to believe what she heard about him from those closest, accepting instead to only listen to the those talking about his generosity and acts of kindness, most of which she initiated. Money meant nothing to her; family meant everything. She would unselfishly forego everything she owned for the chance of a life with the unity and love of a normal family. Without realizing it, she did just that when she devoted all her time and energies to the worry of her brother's existence and her father's demands. Just as she didn't know her father, she knew less of the metamorphosis of her brother during his absent years. To her, Joey was the same.

Niki and Sal were in a serious conversation with Dr. Hartmann when she entered the room. Niki was crying and Sal had his arm around her shoulders comforting her. He looked at Theresa and said, "He's improving, there's some normal brain activity and he's coming out of it, but none of us are a match, Theresa. He's on a list, but we're running out of time."

Theresa gasped, holding back her own tears, as Dr. Hartmann said, "We need to go to the next step. You mentioned his birth mother was dead, but what about her family? Is there any way you can contact them and ask?"

Niki looked directly at Theresa and asked, "What can we do, Theresa? Please, help us if you know a way." She then looked at her husband who remained silent and said, "Whatever it takes, we need to do it."

Sal pulled Niki's chin up to look her directly in the eyes and said, "There's a way, Niki, but it will change our lives forever. Are you ready for that?"

"What could possibly change more than it has already?" She had no idea.

"Call him, Theresa and tell him to pull every connection he has," said Sal in full command. "Tell him he doesn't have to come here, we know he's sick, but he needs to do whatever it takes."

"I already did," Theresa told him softly. Sal just shook his head not at all surprised.

"What about his mother's family?" Niki choked on the word mother.

"For now, we'll leave them out of it," Sal said to her while giving his sister a look that told her not to think about that option.

Right at that moment, Theresa's cell phone rang and she said, "Oh good, it's him now." She answered the phone by saying, "Hey Dad, what did you find out?" Then she went pale and quiet.

Knowing something was wrong, Sal asked, "What's going on?"

Theresa kept repeating, "Mrs. Foster, slow down, I can't understand you. Please calm down. What are you saying?" She listened a few seconds and then started crying, "No, that can't be! That can't be! Why, why would he do that? Why would he do that?" Theresa pointed to the television in the room indicating to turn it on which they did. A much younger likeness of Dominick Fontinelli filled the screen.

The commentator was saying, "It is now confirmed, Dominick Fontinelli, was shot and killed in an apparent murder-suicide at his mansion in Watch Hill. According to a note found by police, his nephew Antonio Fontinelli shot his uncle who was suffering with cancer and then took his own life. We have little information about the nephew except that he was in his mid-forties and the only son of Dominick's identical twin brother, Angelo Fontinelli, who passed away four years ago. According to our sources, Antonio worked for Fontinelli Enterprises, which is one of the largest real estate holding companies in our nation and abroad and he was very close to his uncle. The contents of the note are not open to the public, but officials do confirm that it is legitimate and we can only assume that this was a final and compassionate act of love to end his uncle's suffering. As one of the greatest real estate moguls and philanthropists of all time, we will remember Dominick Fontinelli for his generous donations to charity. He contributed an estimated amount of more than eighty million dollars per year to various organizations. He leaves behind a daughter, Theresa Fontinelli, also known for her philanthropies and a son Peter, often photographed as one of the most eligible bachelors in America, neither of whom is married. His youngest son, Joseph, died in his early twenties in an automobile accident more than twenty years ago. For more information and photos about the Fontinelli family, please go to our online website."

Dr. Hartmann remained in the room during the phone call and television broadcast. Still lacking a bedside manner or any type of compassion, he looked at Sal and Niki and said, "This boy is your top priority. He's running out of time. We need a match and we need it soon!" With that said, he walked out of the room.

Joey's face was solemn and stone while Theresa cried and Niki stood there confused. "Do you know him?" Niki asked.

"Yes, he's my father. I haven't seen him for years and only spoke to him when I had to. Most of my communication was through the family attorney, who was the liaison between Tony, my cousin, who handled everything in the states and me. Tony thought I died in the accident, so he knew me as Sal Fiore, not Joseph. We didn't meet in person, so he was unaware."

Still confused, Niki said, "I thought you said you are Sal, not Joseph. This is so confusing to me."

"I am legally Salvatore Fiore and that's the name that will remain with me for the rest of my life, but I was born Joseph Fontinelli and once a Fontinelli, always a Fontinelli. I can't change who I am inside, Niki. I'm not going back to that life and I'm not going to reveal my identity, but I am a Fontinelli. With Tony gone, I will be running both continents. I'm asking you to stay with me, support me and I will give you a good life, but I am whom I am; that will never change. I am my father's son."

Theresa watched and heard her brother's comments knowing that Niki's only knowledge of their father was the brief commentary she just heard by an unknown reporter. To Niki, Sal would be a great man if he followed his father's footsteps, but to Theresa, the man before her no longer had a soul to mirror hers. He had changed forever. Her tears rolled for the death of her father and her heart broke for the passing of her twin's soul.

"I'll stay, Sal," Niki whispered. "I love you and I'll stay." Sal gently kissed her on the cheek and then turned to Theresa with all gentleness gone.

"Call her," he demanded. "Call her and tell her she needs to be screened for a match."

"Call who?" Niki asked, but they ignored her.

"What if she refuses? What if she tells someone?" Theresa objected.

"She won't refuse and she won't tell. Call her right away," Sal demanded.

"Call who?" Niki asked again.

"His mother," Sal answered coldly. "We need to call his mother."

"But I thought she was dead? You said she died in childbirth," Niki protested.

"I lied, but all that is over now. We need to do what is right for our son, your son, Niki. He is yours, not hers."

"Sal, I have to ask, are you divorced from her? Does this mean we're not married? You have another wife out there!" Theresa felt so sorry for Niki, but she felt it best not to interrupt.

"She was married to Joseph Fontinelli who is legally dead and shall not rise again. You and I are married, nothing has changed, Niki...nothing has changed," but she knew it had.

"I'll call her tonight, Joey," Theresa interjected.

"No, call her now and don't ever call me Joey again!" Theresa just nodded her head and walked out of the room with her cell phone in hand wondering what she would say to her childhood friend, Annie.

CHAPTER
42

K aryn called Jackie when she heard the news on the television and we decided to go over to her house, including Bernie. It was less than two minutes away.

In typical Karyn fashion, she met us at the door with tears as if she just lost her father, but then maybe she really did. I just had such a tough time dealing with her emotions one minute and her lack of them the next. I decided, however, that I would be a good little sister, or at least make an effort at it, and console her, so I said, "I'm so sorry, Karyn. This is terrible."

As always, it didn't work and she snapped right back at me. "What do you care? Now I'll never know the truth!"

"That's not true, Karyn," interjected Bernie who ignored her look intended to incinerate him. "Your sister gave me the DNA from Mr. Fontinelli and Jack gave me the swatch of yours, so I'm going to deliver them today to a colleague of mine who will determine if they're a match in any way."

She continued to ignore him and said, "Well, there's something else going on here today, too. I'm going to get Tommy and let him tell you." She yelled to the other room, "Tommy, your aunt and uncle are here. Come on out and bring that box with you."

Tommy came into the living room and greeted us with the smile that was always present, the one that never failed to warm my heart. "Hi, Aunt Annie...Hi, Uncle Jack...Hi, Mister..."

"Tommy, tell your aunt and uncle what you told me about the box," Karyn told him pointing to the wooden chest that I instantly recognized as the one I purchased at the Mystic Seaport Museum store for Mike.

"Mike says Nana likes sugar...Mike gives Nana lots of sugar," Tommy said.

"I don't understand, Tommy," said Jackie. "She likes cookies and sweet things, so Mike brought her dessert all the time."

"Mike gives Nana more sugar in the pudding. He puts it in the cookies to make her happy," Tommy said looking a little nervous with all of us staring at him. "I'm sorry...I took the box with the sugar...Mike's box. I'm in trouble, Tommy's in big trouble, big trouble." He was rocking side-to-side and clearly upset. I stood up and put my arm around his shoulders hugging him closely.

"No, Tommy," I told him. "You're not in trouble for taking the box. When he comes back, you can give it back to him. It is okay; really, it is, but Tommy, where did you find the box? Do you know where Mike is?"

"Mike doesn't come to work anymore. He doesn't take me in his car. Mike is my friend. I miss Mike." He looked as if he was ready to cry.

"It is okay, Tommy, it is. Where did you get the box?" Jackie asked him.

"Under his locker in a black bag...I watched him keep it there. There's sugar in it and he gives it to Nana to make her happy. Now, I make her happy. See? I put it in a cookie for Nana, just like Mike. Nana will be happy. Tommy will make Nana happy just like Mike," Tommy held up a chocolate chip cookie with a little pill pushed into it.

"Tommy, my name is Bernie and I am Uncle Jack's friend. May I see the sugar? Would that be alright with you?" Karyn scowled at him, but Bernie continued, "I know a lot about sugar, maybe there's a better kind for her." He reached out to take the cookie from Tommy who gave it up willingly.

Bernie popped the pill out of the cookie and held it gently in between his fingers reading the inscription stamped into it, then said to all of us, "This is a 150 mg. tablet of Bupropion. Let me ask you, Karyn, what drug does your mother take for her Alzheimer's?"

"Aricept, she takes Aricept, but not anything else. Other than the Alzheimer's she's in great health. We have to watch her sugar level because she has a terrible sweet tooth, but we control that with diet. Her one sugar treat a day was the dessert Mike brought home for her and most of those were sugar free. As long as they were sweet, she didn't know the difference. Is there a problem?" She actually answered decently, I thought.

"Actually, there's a big problem," Bernie told us. "I don't know this Mike, other than what I've heard about him, but if by chance, he was slipping Bupropion to her, it was potentially deadly."

"I don't understand," I said.

"Well, Bupropion is usually prescribed for patients who want, or need to quit smoking. The side effects are minimal, but it has a deadly drug interaction with Aricept. It can cause muscle spasms and even seizures. When someone like your mother is unable to tell you what she's feeling, it's even more dangerous because you have no indication that anything is wrong until it's too late," Bernie said.

"Oh my God," I said. "Her arm was twitching terribly the other day. I questioned Sara about it and she was going to run it by her doctor, but the accident happened before the appointment.

"None of this makes sense to me," Jackie said. "Why would Mike give her something like that? Maybe we're just overreacting because we're looking for things," then to Tommy he asked, "Tommy, do you have any more of this sugar?"

"I have lots of sugar," Tommy announced happily now that he was not in trouble.

"Can we see it, Tommy?" Karyn asked him.

Tommy opened the box and took out a small plastic sandwich bag with several pills in it. He handed them to Karyn who in turn gave them to Bernie.

"Hmmm," Bernie muttered aloud. "Why wouldn't these be in a pill bottle? If the young man took them himself, he would surely keep them in the prescription bottle unless, of course, his motives were not entirely on the up and up. What do you know about him?"

"Not much at all," Karyn said. "We only know what he told Sara and none of it has turned out to be true. It's as if he didn't exist except in our imaginations. If I didn't meet him myself, I would think he was a fantasy of Sara's. I never liked him myself, but Bob did. He was Portuguese, you know."

"Maybe he wasn't even Portuguese if everything else was a lie," Jackie said. "I wonder if that's where her money was going."

"Oh, my God," Karyn muttered. "He had access to everything because he was always around, even when Sara wasn't."

"Well, what matters the most here is that we find out if your mother really was taking this drug along with the Aricept. Karyn, you need to call her doctor right away and tell them what we found. They can run some blood tests to check. You said she's improving, so maybe it's leaving her system now that he's no longer in contact with her. If I were all of you, I would make sure he doesn't get near her if he shows up again until you get to the bottom of it all," Bernie said.

"When Bob gets home from work, we're going to the hospital to see her. I'll call her doctor now and drop off the pills to him on our way," Karyn said to Bernie as he handed her the small bag.

Tommy became agitated when Karyn refused to return the pills to him, protesting, "Nana likes sugar...give me the sugar!"

Karyn was about to raise her voice to him, but I interrupted, "I've got something better for Nana, Tommy. There's a better sugar for her, maybe we can go shopping later and get her some of her favorite cookies with the sugar already in them. Would you like that?"

"Yes, Tommy goes shopping," he said grinning from ear to ear.

"Okay, I'll pick you up later and we'll go," I said just as my cell phone rang. It was Sara.

"Hey, Aunt Annie...I hope I didn't catch you at a bad time," she said without her usual cheerful tone.

"Not at all, I'm at your mother's house. What's up?" I asked.

"Some lady called and said it was really important for you to call her as soon as possible. I wouldn't bother you, but it was a little weird," Sara told me.

"How was that?" I asked her curiously.

"Well, she asked if this was the Mahoney residence, then asked if Annie

193

still lived here. I told her you didn't live here anymore, but you were visiting and she asked to speak to you. When I said you weren't here right now, she said it was urgent for you to call her right away. I just thought it was strange because she didn't know you lived here, but she said it was urgent. She just sounded a little weird to me and I heard a man's voice in the background telling her what to say. I was going to give her your cell phone number, but I didn't know if you wanted me to, or not."

Great, I thought wondering which one of my ex-husbands wanted to destroy my day. "Did she leave her name and number?" I asked Sara.

"Yes, she said her name was Theresa and she was an old friend of yours. She left a number, but I don't recognize the area code."

She gave me the phone number and I knew right away that it was Rhode Island. "Are you sure, she said her name was Theresa?"

"I'm sure, but I have to run. I have a job interview in an hour. I'll see you when I get home later," she told me and hung up.

Why would Theresa call me after all these years except to tell me about her father's passing? Why would she even bother to call and tell me that? I was puzzled and decided to call her later on. His death meant nothing to me. I would call when I was ready to call, not a minute earlier. After all, she showed her true colors when she didn't call back after Joey's death. I owed her nothing.

CHAPTER
43

As promised, I took Tommy grocery shopping and we bought several different kinds of pastries, most of them sugar free and fancy. Of course, I bought extra for us and we indulged heavily while sitting in the parking lot at Eastern Point Beach watching the boats in the river. It was overcast and drizzling, so the interior of the Lexus got an initiation of sprinkles and frosting. I didn't care; life was finally good.

Sara broke the spell of our special moment, however, when she called to tell me that the lady named Theresa called again. This time she insisted on getting my cell phone number, but Sara still refused to give it to her. She said the woman was adamant that it was urgent for me to call her right away, the same man was in the background, and this time Sara heard him yell, "Whatever it takes, get her here right away! We're losing him."

Now my curiosity was overtaking me, so I dialed the number, not knowing what to expect. "Hello," I announced coldly, "This is Ann Mahoney. I received a message to call you."

DonnaMarie

"Thank God, Annie...I've been on pins and needles waiting for you to call," said the voice I clearly remembered to be Theresa Fontinelli.

"What's this about, Theresa?" I remained cold wanting her to know I was annoyed that she called after all these years.

"Annie, we've got to talk...I don't know where to begin, but..."she said, but I cut her off.

"Theresa, if you're calling me after all this time just to tell me about your father passing away...," but this time she interrupted me.

"No, no, it has nothing to do with him. Yes, he passed away, but that's not why I'm calling you. We have a situation here and we need you desperately." I wasn't sure, but thought she was crying.

"Who are we?" I asked, not having a clue what she was trying to say.

In the background, a man's voice shouted, "Just tell her! Spit it out and get it over with!"

The blood in my veins froze, sending tiny pricks of energy throughout my entire body as I heard the voice that brought back his memory. The voice came from someone who was definitely a relative of Joey's, someone with shared genes and I wondered what he looked like, but I quickly pushed the thought from my mind.

"Annie, I really don't know where to begin, so I'm just going to come out and tell you. It's about the baby, Annie, your baby." I froze in silence and just listened. "He didn't die, Annie, he lived and now he's in trouble. There's been a terrible accident..."

"You cruel bitch, how can you tell me a lie like this? Who the hell are you to call me after all this time and tell me this bullshit?" Tommy's eyes were saucers as he stared at me while I screamed in the phone.

"Listen to me, Annie, please listen to me! It's true! I wouldn't lie about something like this!" She pleaded.

"Theresa, I held my dead baby...I held him in my arms until he was pulled from me! Why are you lying to me? How can you be so cruel?" I cried out.

"The baby you held wasn't yours, Annie. It was all a cruel plot designed by my father and uncle to get the baby away from you. I'll explain every detail to you when I see you, I promise, but you need to come quickly, Annie. He's going to die; our Vinnie is going to die if he doesn't get a kidney and none of us is a match.

Please...," she begged. "Come quickly, he's your son."

I couldn't speak; the words wouldn't form. Vinnie, she said the name Vinnie! Was she telling the truth? Why would she lie? Was it a cruel hoax? No, I refused to believe her, yet I could not justify her lie with a reason.

"Where is he?" I choked on my sobs.

"We're all here at Bellevue Hospital in New York City," she answered.

"What do you mean by we're all here? Who else is there?" I asked not wanting to see any of her relatives, especially her brother Peter.

She ignored my question and said, "I'm sending a helicopter to pick you up at the airport in Groton. I'll be on it to meet you, we'll be there by four o'clock and he'll take us directly to the hospital...and Annie? I promise to tell you everything...I will."

I stared in disbelief at the cell phone clutched in my hand. What just happened? Is it true? Is my son alive? Is he going to die? Who had him? Who raised him? Oh, God, is this true? I wept aloud.

Tommy reached over and gently touched my arm and said, "Don't cry, Aunt Annie. Do you want some more sugar?" I assured him I was crying out of happiness and I was telling the truth.

Somehow, I managed to get through the next couple of hours, arriving at the small airport a half hour early. When I called to tell Jackie what happened, he insisted on joining me and, of course, he included Bernie. I was glad to have to the company; I didn't want to do this alone. When they met me in the terminal, Karyn was also with them. She was company I didn't want, but was drained and unable to argue.

At exactly, four o'clock, the helicopter arrived and Theresa descended to meet us. She changed little over the years, still the dark beauty I remembered, resembling her brother with her chiseled features, dark eyes and olive skin. She reached out to hug me, but I stood rigid and she pulled away.

"I hope you don't mind, but I'm bringing my brother, sister and a friend," I told her without giving her the opportunity to desist.

"Of course not," she said, but I felt she disapproved. "We have some personal things to discuss however and I wanted to go over them on the flight."

"It's not a problem, they know everything I know, which is obviously not much," I sneered. My feelings were outside my realm of understanding. I wanted to cry, laugh, and shout in anger all at once.

"Okay, then, follow me," she said and we did.

As promised, she started from the beginning, telling me how Dominick and his brother, Angelo thought up and executed the plan to steal the baby. She told me about substituting the dead baby of another grieving mother, so I would never question the death of my child. It was trickery and deceit from the night of the accident on. I let her speak, asking minimal questions.

She showed me photos that chronicled his life from birth to the present and in some of them, there was a beautiful dark woman who appeared to be a mother. I inquired about the other children in the photographs and she told me he had two younger brothers that bore his resemblance and a much younger sister who looked like her mother. He grew up in Italy and his primary language was Italian, although he also speaks French and English. He wants to attend college in the United States. It was as if she was telling me about a character in a novel, not my son. I listened; I wept and clung to her every word. Karyn, Jackie and Bernie just sat in silence, taking in the bizarre tale.

The helicopter landed gently on the helipad at the hospital and Jackie, Bernie and Karyn disembarked first. Before I rose from my seat, Theresa reached over squeezed my arm and I saw the tears in her eyes as she said, "Annie, there's something else you need to know..."

CHAPTER
44

I hate hospitals and this week dealt me more than my share of them. This visit, however, was as if I was giving birth and watching a loved one die, all at the same time. I was sick to my stomach with fear and anger, a deadly combination and each step forward intensified my tangled emotions. My mind raced like never before with everything Theresa revealed to me. Joey was alive! He was alive and when I heard it, I felt the rush of elation warm my body with happiness, relief, ecstasy, but if he was alive, then he betrayed me. How could that be? "Why would he do that to me?" I asked Theresa over, and over, but she was so vague and just kept saying it was part of her father's and her uncle's plan to protect Vinnie. She said Joey thought I was dead. None of it made sense to me.

The hospital spokesperson, Ms. Wright, took me to Vinnie's room. I desperately begged her to allow my brother to come upstairs with me, but she was adamant in her refusal, saying Vinnie was too critical and already exposed to outside elements more than he should be. I could hardly walk on my own, my entire body was shaking and my legs were jelly.

Bleeps from the monitor sounded softly as I entered the room where a nurse was standing over her patient adjusting his breathing apparatus. I walked slowly up to the bed and the shock of the sight of the tubes and drains hit me like a bolt of lightning, but it was nothing compared to the jolt when I looked at the person lying there. More than two decades later and I was seeing my son for the first time, a young man who was a stranger to me, but a clone to my memory of Joey. I had no doubt this was my son, my baby boy.

"Are you alright?" the nurse asked me and when I didn't answer, she walked around the bed and put her arm around my shoulder. "Maybe you should sit down," and she tried to lead me to the chair next to the bed, but I waited too long for this moment and I couldn't budge if I wanted to.

"I'm okay," I said through my tears, but I wasn't okay. I found my son and I was losing him again. I just stared down at him, afraid to touch him, afraid to wake up if this was a dream. "My baby," I whispered softly, "my baby..." What would I say to him if he woke up? He is my son, but I am not his mother. The cruelty of it all was beyond my comprehension.

"Annie?" I knew the voice without looking up. He said it again, "Annie?" I lifted my eyes and turned to see him, a stranger. The man standing there was foreign to me.

"It's me, Annie. It's Joey," he whispered, but I couldn't answer. "It's really me, Annie," he repeated, but I didn't recognize him. He had Joey's voice, but this was not Joey. What kind of cruel joke was he playing on me?

Again, he said, "It's really me, Annie. I know you don't recognize me. The plastic surgeons performed their skill well." I just continued to stare at him in silence.

Anger finally gave me the strength to speak and I sneered bitterly, "What a cruel, sick joke! Who, the fuck, are you? What, the fuck, is going on here? Where's Theresa? Where's that bitch?" I wanted to tear out the eyes of the alien standing there telling me he was Joey.

"Let's take a walk," he said softly, but I just stared at him with all the hatred I could muster. "Please, Annie, I will explain everything to you."

"Explain what? Who are you? Is this really my son lying here in this bed? Why am I here?" My voice was escalating, but I didn't care. I wanted to strike out at the monster that stood there.

"Look at me, Annie! Look into my eyes and you'll see! I am Joey! I'm telling you the truth and this is our son. Look at him! Stare at his face. Look at his hands; they're yours. You know he is our son! Please, Annie, please let me explain."

"Stop the bullshit and let me out of here," I screamed at him and turned to leave.

"Annie, I kissed you the first time at Fort Griswold. Do you remember? We were thirteen years old and I asked you to marry me. You promised to love me forever." I froze with his words and stopped to listen. "We were together every minute. It was always the three of us, Theresa, you, and me. Do you remember sneaking out at night to go to the fort? We all smoked our first cigarette behind the monument. Theresa vomited all over the place and you laughed when I got mad at her."

"You sick bastard! Who told you this stuff? Was it Theresa?" Without a glance to Vinnie, I turned to leave, but pushing past him, he grabbed my arm roughly and pulled me toward him.

"Let go of...," I protested, but he pulled me tighter, hurting me and I winced.

"Theresa didn't know about that night on the beach, did she? Remember? Remember the first time? Remember the tears? Remember what you said to me... that you gave me the most precious gift you had and now you belonged to me forever?"

I stopped fighting him and felt the tears well in my eyes. How could he know these things? Why was he being so cruel?

He continued, "We stayed naked and held each other under that nasty old tarp we found until the sun betrayed us with dawn. You wanted to take the canvas home and I wouldn't let you. We pledged our love to each other and vowed to be one until death tore us apart. How old were we, sixteen? Don't you remember, Annie? I know you do. You made me promise not to tell Theresa about that night and I didn't."

"But you don't...," I mumbled with my tears flowing freely now.

"Look like Joey?" He asked. "No, I don't look like him because I'm not him anymore. Look into my eyes, Annie. I'm there. When I left, I had plastic surgery."

"Why? Why are you doing this to me? I don't understand," I cried out. He loosened his grip and that's when I saw the familiar scar on his knuckles.

"I got that trying to pull you off the rocks at Eastern Point Beach when you slipped. You scraped your knee and you bet me I would have the bigger scar and you were right. You said it made me look like a fighter. It's all that identifies me now, but I couldn't...no, I wouldn't have it removed."

"Your voice, your eyes, your hands, but it can't be true. It can't be!" My body slumped and I fell into him, burying my face in his shoulder and beat his chest with my fists. "Why? Why, did you leave me?" I cried.

"I had to do it, Annie. I had to do it to protect you and protect our son. There was no other way. How can I tell you how sorry I am?" His arms felt like home.

"My husband died in the accident. I saw him die! I went into labor and gave birth too early. I heard my baby cry, I know I heard him, but they told me he died. I held his sweet lifeless body in my arms, giving him my breath, my love, trying so hard to rock him back to life. Karyn, my sister, was with my mother when she took him away from me! I remember it, every second of it. Why would anyone do this? Why?"

"I'm so sorry, Annie...so sorry. If I could only take it all back, I would, but I can't," he said softly and held me tighter.

"We were leaving town! I saw you die! Your head hit the windshield and I saw you die!" I pulled away from him and stared deeply into his eyes and all doubt left me. I was looking into the eyes of the man I loved for so long.

"All I remember is the bad weather and you were sleeping. We hit something slippery, but the brakes wouldn't work. I kept pumping the pedals, but there was nothing. The crash happened quickly and the impact knocked me out cold, so I don't know what caused it. When I awoke in the hospital, my father and Uncle Gino were both there and told me that the accident put you into labor. They said you died in childbirth, but the baby was going to be okay. I fell apart hearing that you died. The baby meant nothing to me without you. Then they told me there was another problem, a bigger problem with the baby and I had to snap out of it and take care of my son, our son."

"What problem? Was he sick?" I asked him.

"No, they said a good source told them that he was going to be kidnapped," he told me.

"Kidnapped? Who would kidnap our baby? That makes no sense, no sense at all!"

"Well, it didn't to me either, but they said it was time for me to know the truth. They said that your family, specifically your father, was going to make sure the baby went to some relative of his living in Ireland. They said your father didn't want him to grow up as a Fontinelli, he would do whatever it took to make sure of it, and I would never see him again. I believed them."

"They hated me! Your whole family hated me!" I said bitterly. "Why did they hate me so much? I never did anything to them...for God's sake; I never even met your father and uncle!"

"They insisted that the only reason they refused to accept you as my wife was your father's strong ties to the Irish mob. His connections ran deep. They feared for the baby's life and said the only way I could save him was to move away with him."

"My father had ties to the Irish mob? Are you crazy? You can't be serious! I loved my father, but if you remember him, and if you are really Joey, as you say, you will remember that he was a drunk and his only connections were to a whiskey bottle! He died falling off a scaffold while working on a submarine at Electric Boat because he was dead drunk. Everyone tried to cover it up, but we all knew the truth. I know your family hated me, but this is a little absurd!"

"I had no reason not to believe them, Annie. The doctor told me my wife died and my family told me I needed to save our son. Of course, I did everything I could to protect him. Do you think I would take a chance on something like that? I couldn't lose both of you. Everything happened so fast, it was a blur. They already had arrangements for me to leave right away. I met with my grandfather's attorney who took care of everything and before I knew it; I had a place to stay in Rome, a job with an international corporation and they enrolled me in the university. They even had daycare set up and medical insurance in place and ready to go, not to mention a complete new identity for Vinnie and me. Oh, I almost forgot the plastic surgeries. The first one happened immediately and the second one was a year later."

"Did you find out I was alive?" I asked him.

"Yes," he said and I felt my heart rip.

"When did you find out?" I had to know the truth.

"Several years ago, Annie..."

"Voi suina, voi americani maiale! Tu sei una vita bassa, un marito barare e ora si sono catturati!" I jumped away from him at the sound of the woman's voice. I didn't speak Italian, but it was obvious that she was directing her anger to Joey and I immediately recognized her as the woman in the photographs Theresa showed me.

"This is not what we need right now, Niki," he snapped at her. "Please keep your voice down! We've got to get through this."

"You must be the whore," she barked to me while I just stood there in shock.

"Everyone, please, let's take this elsewhere. Please, Niki, calm down," said Theresa who until now was silently waiting in the hallway, but Niki turned on her, outraged at the interruption.

"Don't tell me what to do, you filthy bitch! You walk into my life and turn it to shambles and you tell me to calm down. Get out of my life! That's what I want...I want you out of my life! Get out and leave us alone, both of you!" Her gaze left Theresa and buried deeply into me.

At that moment, the Intensive Care nurse who was tending to Vinnie, stormed in the room shouting, "Everyone out...he's coding...everyone out!" Three more people came rushing into the room, followed quickly by a doctor. Caught up in our own emotions, none of us noticed Vinnie convulsing.

"I said, leave the room!" She shouted again.

Quietly, I followed the others into the hallway.

When the crisis was over, the doctor came out asking to speak to Joey, but he called him another name. "Mr. Fiore, we need a kidney match, or he isn't going to make it. He's on every list, but there's nothing. You told me about his birth mother. Have you been able to reach her?"

"That would be me," I interrupted. "I am his mother." To my surprise, the words came easily.

"Then come with me," he said and I followed him.

"I'm Dr. Hartmann, your son's surgeon. Have you been informed of the seriousness of his condition?"

"Yes," I answered, "but this is the first time I've seen him since..."

He abruptly interrupted me before I could finish my sentence, "Yes, I know, you gave him up at birth, but..."

"I did not give him up! He was taken from me," I snapped. It was my turn to interrupt him.

"Excuse me, but the details of your personal life are of no consequence to me. There's no time for drama, I'm...,"

"You think this is a drama, is that what you think?" I was furious.

"I'm taking you to the lab for a test and we are running out of time! That's the only thing I'm thinking right now and if you want to see this boy again, you might want to do the same!" I bit my tongue and followed him in silence because I knew he was right.

The test was quick and simple. I was not a match and the doctor dismissed me coldly, but I had another idea and decided to tell him about Karyn.

"Call her right away," he said. "How soon can she get here?"

"Actually, she's here already," I told him. "She came with me, but wasn't allowed to come upstairs. I'll go get her."

"Yes, do that right now and bring her up here to this room. If anyone questions you, just have them page me," and with that said he stormed off in a hurry.

I found Karyn, Jackie, and Bernie in the waiting room downstairs. All three jumped to their feet when they saw me. I'm sure I looked a ragged sight and I was weak from the emotional drain, but somehow I had the strength and stamina to move toward them.

"I saw him," I told them, "and there's no doubt he's my son. I'm not a match to give him a kidney though."

"What about Joey? Did you see Joey?" Karyn asked excitedly. "Was Theresa telling the truth? Is he really alive?" She sounded as if she was asking about the update of a soap opera, not my life.

"Karyn, can we go someplace privately and speak?" I asked her.

"Yes," Jackie said, "there's a quiet little room off the cafeteria where we can all go."

"No, I need to speak with Karyn alone," I said and saw the look of apprehension come across Jackie's face, so I added, "It's okay. It'll be fine. I just need to speak to her alone."

The coffee was complimentary in the cafeteria, so we each poured a cup and found the little area Jackie mentioned.

"Karyn, I don't know how to ask you this...really I don't," I started.

"Well, just say it as you always do and blurt it out," she said, but without her usual sarcasm.

"I'm not a match and he's going to die," I said and started to cry. "I found him, Karyn...I found my son and now he's going to die and I'll lose him again. I need your help. Please, Karyn, please help me! Help my son, please!"

"I don't understand," she said. "How can I help? Bob and I have a little money, but not much and maybe Jack could come up with some. How much do you need?"

"It's not about money, Karyn," I sobbed. "It's not about money at all."

"Then what's this about?" she asked.

"He needs a kidney and I think you're the best match," I prayed she wouldn't get up and leave. She didn't.

"You're not serious, are you? This is preposterous, Annie. Are you asking me to give up a body part for some kid that you don't even know? You can't even be sure he's yours to begin with...this is insane!"

"I am sure he's mine. He's Joey's clone and he has my hands. The nail on my left pinkie is half the size as the right one. He has the same thing, Karyn. It's a duplicate of mine. His hands are my hands. He is my son and the lab just verified it. He's my baby, my baby! I'm begging you to help him, Karyn...please!"

"No, Annie, I will not. You must be insane asking me something like that. I have three children, a husband and a grandchild on the way. I will not give up part of my body for a stranger! This discussion is over," she declared and started to get up to leave.

"Sit down, Karyn," I snapped at her. "Sit down because I'm not finished with this discussion. I know that you knew about the plot to take him away from me." She slid slowly back into her chair and I continued with my bluff. "You were there when they gave me a dead baby to hold and you knew it wasn't mine." She was squirming slightly and I kept going. "You knew what they were doing and you never said a word. Instead, you just stood there and smiled, gloating over my pain. I saw you, Karyn...I saw you!"

"I was young, Annie, I...," she stammered and then it hit me. She really did know. My sister knew about it!

"Why did you let it happen, Karyn? Why did you and Mom do it?"

"Mom didn't do it, Annie. She really didn't know. I was there when the doctor came in and told her Joey was dead and that you lost the baby. He said it would be best to give you some closure and let you hold him and say good-bye. She was devastated, but agreed with him. She really believed the baby you held was her grandson and it broke her heart to lose him and see you in such pain. You didn't see her fall apart when she left the room, but I did."

"How did you know?" I couldn't believe what I was hearing. "How did you know that wasn't my baby?"

"I didn't at first. After they took the baby from you, I needed to use the restroom before going home, so I went to look for one and I passed an office with the door cracked. I heard the doctor speaking to a man and he called him, Mr. Fontinelli. I was curious because I never met Joey's father and I wanted to see what he looked like. I thought the doctor was telling him that the baby died, but that's not what I heard."

"What were they saying?" I asked.

"I heard the doctor thank him for his generous donation. The man just sneered and told him to hurry up and get it done. He wanted the baby as soon as possible because the new parents were waiting for him. The doctor said something about the baby being too young to leave the hospital, but the man said he didn't give a damn. He wanted the baby now, or the deal was off. The doctor said okay."

"How did you know he was talking about my baby?"

"The man said something ugly, Annie. I really don't want to give you more pain," she said.

"Tell me, Karyn, I have a right to know. I need to know!"

"He said he didn't care what happened to the little Miss Annie and her Irish slut mother, he just wanted his grandson. I don't remember what the doctor replied. I got scared and left to go tell Mom."

"You didn't tell her though, did you? Why didn't you tell her, Karyn?"

"I hated you, Annie. I hated everything about you. When you eloped with Joey, I finally got some attention and then you showed up again!" Then she fell apart and cried out, "Oh, God, what have I done? I'm so sorry! What have I done?" Her head fell to the table and she sobbed in her arms as I never saw before. "I'll do it, Annie; I'll do it for you. Oh, God, please forgive me..."

All I could say to her was, 'We need to go upstairs; they're waiting for you."
I was sick to my stomach and my feelings were gone with my past.

CHAPTER
45

Karyn didn't follow me right away; I knew she was calling Bob to tell him about her decision. I wondered how the conversation would go, but I really didn't care. It was a bittersweet victory.

I found the sitting room where Joey, Theresa, and Niki were waiting to hear the results of the match and walked in to hear Joey speaking with Dr. Hartmann.

"His mother is in contact with a potential donor as we speak. If she agrees to be tested, she is already here, so we will proceed as soon as we confirm the match. This is a huge decision for someone, so I hope your son's mother can be convincing. Otherwise, we don't' stand a chance in hell unless there's a tragic accident someplace tonight."

"Thank you, Doctor, I'll stay right here until I hear from you," I heard Joey tell him.

"There is one more thing, Mr. Fiore. If you, or your family, make one more scene like the one you did in your son's room earlier, I will personally see to it that you are banned from this hospital altogether. Do you understand?"

"Yes, I understand…just save my son." Joey answered with cold and penetrating eyes, a strange, threatening expression on his face.

I walked into the room and made the announcement. "We have a donor. She's willing to do it and they have confirmed the match. Joey, I need to speak to you outside."

I avoided the daggers flying from Niki's eyes and went into the hallway. "Who is the donor?" He asked.

"My sister, Karyn, is going to do it."

"Are you kidding me? How is she a stronger donor probability than either of us? I don't get it."

"No, you wouldn't get it, would you? Your family is the scum of the earth, always was, and always will be, Joey." I had no idea where this was going, so I just kept speaking. "Recently, my sister found out that your uncle, Gino, was her biological father. It seems that he, and your father, raped my mother when she was young."

"Annie, that's preposterous! Believe me, I know everything about my family these days and there's not one shred of evidence that will convince me of that," he said, but I didn't believe him. He was so different from the man I remembered.

"Well, you obviously don't know everything, or you would know it's the truth. For all we know, your own father could be her father, because according to him, they both had their way with her. What would that make you, and my sister… siblings or cousins? It doesn't matter which way; you're related and she is related to Vinnie on two levels."

"I'm surprised she agreed to it. I remember that the two of you never got along."

"We still don't get along, believe me, but she has my blood in her, too, and she's doing what's best." I couldn't look at him when I spoke.

"What about us, Annie?" He asked. "I can't let you go again…I can't." He leaned forward to hold me and this time, I allowed my eyes to raise and look deeply into his and I saw the evil that lurked behind the hidden mirrors.

"Excuse me, Mr. Fiore, but I don't know what you mean by us. Go home to your wife, your family and your new life. I wish you well…"

"But, Annie, we can…," he started to protest.

"No, we can't! We share a son, that's all. I buried a good, decent man, my husband, years ago! What happened to you, Joey? You didn't grow up this way! What turned you into the man you are today?"

"That's just it, Annie...I didn't grow up; I was molded, protected. There was never a question that someday I would carry the torch, along with my cousin, Tony. Now that's he's gone, it's all mine."

"What about Vinnie? Is he being molded, Joey? What are you doing to him?" My eyes were locked to his gaze, his cold, uncaring stare.

"I have three sons, Annie, not just Vinnie, and each of them will follow the path of their choice. Only God knows what their future will be and I am not God," he said.

"No, you're not God, Joey, but you mock Him and you'll pay one day. You'll see...you will pay!"

"Annie? I have to know...," he started to ask, but he didn't have to finish the question. I already knew the answer.

"Don't worry, Mr. Fiore, I will keep your dirty little secret, but I will get to know my son and he will know me. I don't care what you tell him, but you will tell him I am his mother. I hope that's understood."

"Of course, it is and I'll tell him as soon as he is well and back on his feet," he said.

"No, you will tell him as soon as he wakes and is able to understand," I said staring into his eyes. "If you don't, I will."

"Yes, I will tell him, Annie. I promise. I'll have Theresa keep you informed." He looked tired, but not defeated as he challenged me with his stare.

"One more thing, Joey...it's true. The eyes really are the mirrors of the soul and when I look into yours; I see the devil and the fires of hell and you're burning in it."

I felt his eyes boring into me as I walked away, but I never turned around. I never looked back again.

EPILOGUE

Several years passed and here I am sitting in my bay window looking out over Narragansett Bay. Every time I gaze at it is like the first time, the power and immensity of it overwhelm me much like life itself.

Dominick Fontinelli would roll over in his grave if he knew the estate he left to his daughter is now a halfway house for young Down Syndrome adults learning the life skills needed to succeed in society. Tommy is a fulltime employee here, our Hospitality Representative, and greets all the newcomers. I finally have him around all the time because he lives in the dormitory rooms on the second floor. I reside on the third. That's right; Theresa donated the mansion and several million dollars to start its foundation. The neighbors weren't happy at first, but they're coming around and with Theresa's charm and fundraising abilities, several of them are now benefactors and volunteers. I called it Maggie's House after my mother. I know it would please her and it pleases me to walk by the giant oil painting of her that hangs over the fireplace in the lobby. She was truly beautiful, both inside and out.

My mother passed quietly in her sleep a few years ago. I do regret immensely that I failed her before the Alzheimer disease. I did my best, however, to help her to the end as hard as it was to watch her slip away. Alzheimer is a cruel disease, yet with it comes the peace of knowing that sometimes, a stolen memory is a blessing.

How did I take the news that the man I loved so deeply and unconditionally, without boundaries deceived me on so many levels? Not well, I didn't take it well at all. To this day, I get chills remembering the night I stood over my son's hospital bed and heard the voice behind me say one word, my name, "Annie..." At that point, my world stopped and everything I knew as truth became a fallacy. The boy I knew and loved became a man who grew into his dark side. Was it genetics? Was it environment or circumstance? Who knows? I can only pray the circle of life will be broken and his children won't slip into the shadows of immorality. I hope that his wife, Niki, and I choke on those words, will be the icon they follow. Legally, I remain his widow and she is his spouse, at least until the day he reveals the secret of his past; maybe that will be another story.

As desperate as I was to help my son, I was unable to save him. In an ironic twist of fate, Karyn, who held the secret of his existence from me, was the perfect match, and to her I owe his life. Speaking of Karyn, she began receiving monthly checks from an offshore bank account. Like clockwork, she receives a significant amount on the first of every month. We don't question it, but we know where they originate. She came to terms with her heritage a long time ago, although she will never know which twin was her father, Dominick or Angelo. Unfortunately, we never mended fences, but maybe in time, maybe...

His father held true to his promise, so Vinnie knows I am his birth mother. He fulfilled his dream of attending school in the United States and ultimately went on to complete his graduate studies in Europe. We're not close, but we're working on it. He will be here for Thanksgiving this year. It's one of his favorite American holidays, now it will be mine also. He's bringing his new wife and I can't wait to meet her. Maybe I'll be a grandmother someday. He doesn't speak much about his parents, or siblings. I think he's embarrassed and aware of my pain.

Poor Sara lives in my mother's old house. She never found Mike and still pines for him. I wish I could tell her my story and have her understand, but each person has to walk an individual path in life. No one else can do it for her. She would never listen, never understand that time changes things, but it can also heal old scars.

I doubt she will ever find Mike, but I pray she finds happiness someday.

Jackie and Bernie are still the best of whatever they are and I'm happy for them. Actually, Bernie and I are best of friends; I often threaten Jackie by saying I'm going to steal him. We both know it's not true, but I tease him anyway.

Theresa and I are also friends, good friends, but with one condition. Neither of us speaks about her twin. He is dead to me, still buried in Colonel Ledyard Cemetery along with my demons. When I need to remind myself about how far I've come, I visit there occasionally when I go home, that's right, I said home. Groton is my home; the place I look back to when I need to feel my roots.

What a beautiful day today is, I can't help thinking as I glance at the sun's beam sparkling through the prism that is still my guiding light. Then I look down at the handsome man on the veranda below teaching the basics of using a hammer and nails to a group of young students. He glances up and smiles while I look down at the simple gold circle on my left hand. His name is Martin and Bernie, of all people, introduced me to him. They're distant cousins and after a whirlwind courtship, I became his third wife, so he's not new to the game of marriage either. Who knows, maybe the fourth time will be the lucky charm for me...maybe.

How do you decipher between truth and fallacy when lies consume your very being? You look deeply into the eyes of the source to see the soul, that's how. Sadly, however, hidden mirrors can deceive and distort the truth, but life goes on and that's a good thing... a very good thing.

The End...or Not?

ABOUT THE AUTHOR

DonnaMarie grew up on the shoreline of Connecticut playing daily on the beaches overlooking the Long Island Sound. She attended college in Massachusetts and lived in several states prior to settling down in Florida several years ago with her husband of 40 plus years.

After more than three decades in the banking industry, she still works for a local community bank while also teaching as an Adjunct Professor in a Florida State College. She teaches Employment Skills to Special Needs Adults and believes this is the most rewarding experience in her lifetime.

Her first love is writing, but she also loves to read the works of others, play golf, and enjoy beautiful Florida days on the waterways of the Treasure Coast with family and friends. She has a passion for life and works with several organizations to give back to others less fortunate than herself.

When missing, you just might find her under a palm tree in the park reading a good novel and watching the waves dance in the Indian River...

COMING SOON!

TWISTED IMAGE
by DonnaMarie

Twisted Image takes the reader back in time to learn more about the characters in *Hidden Mirrors,* exploring how innocent hearts evolve into evil.

This new book delves deeper into the lives of the infamous Fontinelli family and the roots that entangle each of them in its smothering grip—making it impossible to break free. When does enough become enough...or does it?

A Preview from *Twisted Image*

PROLOGUE

Whose image does one see when looking in the mirror? Is it one's own? Truly, it is not real if reversed, the opposite of what we hold to be the truth.

He stared into the glass expecting to see the man he was, but the hollow, empty eyes of the stranger staring back offered no sign of familiarity. Slowly, carefully, he unfolded the green felt with his fingertips and with ritualistic movement, placed the beret firmly on his head. He stood rigid before himself; a soldier adorned in his finest uniform, and slowly raised his right hand in salute, allowing his left to gently stroke the silver wings pinned to his chest.

"For God and Country, I accept this duty with pride. I will not fail," he said to the twisted image before him and repeated, "I will not fail."

A single tear splashed on the cold metal as he reached down to lift it for the final mission. "I will not fail."